Forty Words for Love

ALSO BY AISHA SAEED

Written in the Stars
Yes, No, Maybe So (with Becky Albertalli)
Amal Unbound
Omar Rising
Grounded (co-author)

FORTY
WORDS
FOR
LOVE

Aisha Saeed

Kokila

KOKILA

An imprint of Penguin Random House LLC, New York

First published in the United States of America by Kokila,
an imprint of Penguin Random House LLC, 2023

Visit us online at PenguinRandomHouse.com.

Library of Congress Cataloging-in-Publication Data is available.

Printed in the United States of America

ISBN 9780593326466

1st Printing
LSCH

Design by Jasmin Rubero
Text set in Carrig Pro

For my editor and friend, Zareen

Before

one

RAF

The first clear moment Raf recalled from that night was the sound of laughter. Hers.

He'd heard her easy laughter a million times before. But that night it made his pulse quicken. Picking up his pace, his feet pressed into the packed sand beneath him. He needed to speak to her. Before he lost his nerve.

Faint music from the Moonlight Bay Festival carried over from a distance. He thought he'd glimpsed her slipping away from the celebration. She'd probably grown weary of the crowds. Maybe she'd gone looking for him. How would she react when he finally told her how he felt about her?

The golden leaf on his wrist pulsed against his skin. Raf frowned. This birthmark—the one physical difference between the Golub and the locals—only ever warmed in warning, when they'd strayed too far from home. *The leaf protects you—it does so at all costs.* How many times had Tolki Uncle said this? But right now, he stood mere steps from his forest home.

Raf slowed. All thoughts of his leaf vanished. There she was. Yas. Partially obscured by a grove of palmettos, with her back pressed against a tree. She wore a white sundress. The star-shaped necklace resting against her collarbone glinted in the moonlight. Her dark hair was loose around her shoulders.

Before he could take a step toward her, Raf realized she was not alone.

Her boarding-school-raised summer neighbor, Moses, heir to the Holler Candy fortune—came into view. Moses drew closer to her. Laughed. His arms encircled her waist. She looked up at him. Their foreheads touched.

Heat flooded Raf's face. His chest constricted as he stepped back. Why hadn't Yas told him? They had been best friends ever since his family fell, shivering, from the Golub tree over a decade ago. They shared everything with each other. Didn't they?

But this was a mercy, wasn't it? If nothing else, he had his answer. He didn't even have to ask.

A sudden jolt of pain burst from his wrist. Electric currents shot through his body. He doubled over. Tears pricked his eyes. The burning grew sharper by the second. White-hot. As if the sun itself had burrowed within his skin. He bit his lip until he tasted blood.

Panic bubbling, Raf staggered toward the shoreline. Only then did he see that the ordinarily sleepy pink-and-lavender sea had transformed. Enormous dark waves rose in the distance before crashing to shore. The color of charcoal. Howling winds whipped through his hair. The chaos around him mirrored the chaos within. What was happening?

Then came the scream. High-pitched. Wailing. Clenching his jaw, Raf ran until he found himself before the towering specter of Holler Mansion and saw the image that would never leave him for as long as he lived: five-year-old Sammy Holler lying by the shore. His nanny, Melinda, knelt over his frame, her body racked with sobs. Sammy lay facedown on the sand. He didn't move.

As though playing a part in a movie, Raf numbly grabbed his phone. Fingers fumbling, he dialed for an ambulance. He wasn't sure when Moses and Yas arrived. When the red and white ambulance lights at last flashed in the distance. A team of paramedics lifted Sammy's limp body onto the stretcher.

One thought ran in a loop in his mind: *This can't be real.* This couldn't happen here. Not in Moonlight Bay. They'd fix Sammy. That's what doctors did. That's how stories like these ended. Sammy couldn't die.

Raf couldn't be sure how he made it back to Willow Forest, to Tolki Uncle's door, practically falling into his arms. He only knew that Uncle would have the answers. He always did. Uncle wrapped Raf's wrist in a soothing compress. He brought him a warm cup of almond tea. A blanket. It was only when the teacup clattered against its saucer that Raf realized he was trembling.

Through ragged breaths, he managed to get the words out: Sammy on the damp beach. The sea churning dark and deadly.

Uncle's expression grew grim. He ran a hand through his hair—pure white, like the snowcapped mountains of Golub they'd left behind.

"What were you doing out there, son?"

"I . . . I was looking for Yas." Raf's shoulders slumped. Raf had to tell him. Of course he did. Uncle needed to know.

"Raf," Uncle said slowly. "Were you going to—"

"I didn't say anything," Raf said quickly. "I saw her and Moses, and . . ." He looked at his leaf. Gold and green as ever. "It's not like she feels the same."

Tolki Uncle was quiet, translating Raf's broken words into

meaning. Shame coursed through Raf. His father had died three years earlier, but Tolki was a father figure to all the Golub who ended up within the forest of Moonlight Bay.

"What happened when you saw her?" he finally asked.

"That's when it began to burn."

"Had anything been amiss with the water?" Uncle hesitated. "*Before* you saw Moses and Yas?"

"I don't think so." Raf's mouth grew dry. "D-do you think my leaf had something to do with this?"

A moment of tense silence passed.

"This is my fault," Uncle finally said. "I warned you away from Yas. I had hoped that would be enough."

"You said I could never be with her because we were returning to Golub soon," Raf said shakily. "But, Uncle . . . it's been ten years, and—"

"I didn't tell you the rest of it," Uncle interrupted. "Just as leaving the safety perimeter erases one's leaf, choosing to be with someone who is not of us—that too can have devastating consequences. Though, until now, I hadn't been certain what sort of consequences."

Raf thought of the waves. The darkness. What he had almost told her.

"My leaf . . . It couldn't have done all *that*." Seeing Uncle's ashen face, his voice grew smaller. "Could it?"

Uncle didn't reply, his silence its own answer. Raf sank his head into his hands. He felt light-headed. Had his birthmark disappeared, he'd have lost any ability to return to Golub or to remain with his own family within their forest home. Lost leaves were catching.

Before they could speak more, a fist pounded against the

front door, followed by a shout. "Come quick! The Golub tree is opening! Someone is here!"

Raf froze. New arrivals? The tree hadn't opened in years. Gripping his cane, Uncle rose. He placed a hand on Raf's shoulder and leaned close.

"We will speak more on this later, but not a word to anyone, Raf. Ever," he said gently but firmly. "Do you understand?"

Raf looked at his wrist. The leaf was calm now, a glittering etching on his skin once more.

The leaf protects you—it does so at all costs.

Raf Javan hadn't said a word to Yas. But a price had been exacted all the same.

After

two

YAS

Yas knew her father wasn't there. She didn't need to see it with her own eyes to know. Still, she stepped onto the salt-rubbed back porch and slipped on the flip-flops she'd left resting on the feathery welcome mat. The clouds looked thinner than they had in months, and wisps of sunlight streamed through their gray pockets, casting spotlights on the sand below.

Glancing at the driveway, she saw that, sure enough, there was nothing but gravel where her father's gray sedan should've been parked. The one with rusted spokes and a cracked leather interior he'd driven cross-country to college. The same car her mother refused to sit in because the seats sagged so much, you felt each unearthed pebble that bounced against the metal as it drove.

It was gone. He was gone—again.

She took the steps down to the near-empty stretch of sand. At first she'd shrugged off the lit-up VACANCY signs hanging in the hotel windows and the deserted bed-and-breakfasts dotting the beach. Summer was slow because of the forecasters predicting rain, spooking visitors who feared a repeat of the tropical storm that had raged through the year before. The one that battered the Ferris wheel, twisted the pier like a rag doll, and pummeled the welcome mural framing its entrance. But no storms came. It hadn't so much as rained since late May. Not a drop for the thirsty flower beds around town. Still, no umbrellas dotted the sand. No children raked seashells into buckets or dug sandcastles while parents with wide-brimmed hats looked on. It was the last week of June and no one was here.

Looking at the sea, could she really blame them?

Patty was here, though. At least there was that. She waved to Yas from her spot at the edge of the shore, flashing her bubble-gum smile. She'd been coming each summer and renting out a room at the Iguana Motor Lodge since before memories were a thing Yas could grasp. Patty wore a floral slip and reclined on the same green chair under the same canvas umbrella Iguana provided free of charge every year.

Yas had taken a step toward the shore, when something sharp and familiar poked at the bottom of her sandal. Kneeling, she picked up a seashell the size of her palm. It was white like dusted sugar and smooth as polished granite. Blowing off the sand grains, she turned it over, checking for cracks and bruises. There were none to be found. It was perfect. Yas hesitated before slipping it into her pocket.

The murky, swirling gray sea in the distance looked the same as it had every day these past ten months. Yas studied the choppy waves for glimmers of color to surface, a pop of pink or lavender, a promise that the pastel waters lingered beneath the surface somewhere. It was a habit, nothing more. As expected, there were no hints of what once was.

The Weepers huddled in the distance, the ocean lapping at their ankles. Every day they came. Their heads bowed. Their tears dripping into the sea, willing the ocean to feel their pain. To bring back what was.

How they'd decided *this* was the solution remained unclear. Yes, there were legends passed down from previous generations that tears could brighten the sea, but there was just as much lore advising complete stoicism. *All* of it was ridiculous, though. The sea was the *sea*—an inanimate body of water. What did it care for their tears? No one understood why the pink-and-lavender waters had appeared and no one knew why they'd left. Couldn't these Weepers see, nearly one year later, that nothing had changed?

There *were* far fewer of them now. Only Kendall, Mateo, Melinda, and Olive remained. Yas had known them all before. In a town like Moonlight, it was hard to not know everyone. But like everything else, they'd changed. Kendall, who once presided over city council; Mateo, once a renowned artist; Olive, the owner of the now-shuttered bookstore; Melinda, Sammy's nanny—all of them were Weepers now. When would they too stop hoping?

Practically everyone in the high school's graduating class scooted out of town last month, their diplomas still warm in their hands. Some started summer sessions as far away as they could get, and—like her friend Hisae, who was now a waitress in a nearby town—left for work. Soon Raf would leave too. Surrey University was only fifty miles from Moonlight but far enough for him to no longer be an ever-present presence in her life.

Her fingers instinctively trailed her collarbone for the star necklace she'd once worn each day without fail. She and her mother crafted it together when she was fifteen. Of course, now she grazed only skin.

s stole a glance
work they did
he sea could be
rts. Every day,
. They settled
onto carefully
nd shaped into
uffering. There
s that her fam-
had been her
s mother. Eight
way down to—

one day—Yas.

She'd once eagerly painted each star before it left their home. Delicate birds. Flowers. Yas had loved the work. The art of catching and cutting and sanding and smoothing. It was meant to be her legacy, but now all Yas could think when she saw a customer clasp on a necklace was: Didn't they notice they still ached? Their work was not a religion. She did not worship the sea. But she'd lost her faith all the same.

Yas knew she should toss this shell—her mother claimed to have premonitions about such things—which shells would heal and which wouldn't—but it was perfect for star making: nearly flat, with just a hint of curve, thick and sturdy. The size of her palm. The sort that had been plentiful once. Lately the seafloor was littered with brittle shards, crushed shells that crunched painfully beneath her feet. This one only needed a once-over sanding to smooth it out. How could she *not* hold on to it? *Besides*, Yas looked at the sea and thought, *even if I had found this within the sea's depths, it wouldn't have made a difference.* There were no such thing as premonitions, and certainly no healing properties were within the water's depths anymore, if there ever had been in the first place.

The sound of hammering pierced the morning air. Two workers in cargo pants and plastic helmets laid out blue tarps alongside Holler Mansion next door. Another perched atop the roof, yanking off weathered salmon-colored shingles and flinging them to the ground below. A noisy jackhammer tore into concrete on the back patio.

Since the Holler family left last year, Yas had not seen so much as a cat slink past the property. Raf had dared Yas to slip through the crumbled brick gate with him just last month. They'd dangled their legs at the edge of the abyss of the once aqua-blue pool. The bell lights strung overhead on cracking lattices gathered dust on their bulbs. The exterior, once buttercream yellow, faded more and more each month, battered by the salty wind that didn't care if the owners had packed up and moved away.

"Figured out what they're up to yet?" a voice said over the din.

Raf. He walked along the shoreline toward her. Her shoulders unclenched. His stonewashed jeans were rolled just above his ankles. Sand clung to his bare feet. His favorite hoodie covered his head, but his brown curls framed his forehead like they did when they'd first met in first grade, after his family arrived through the enormous ice-cold Golub tree in Willow Forest. Everyone had gawked at his mop of brown curls and scraped and bruised arms when he stepped into their class. They'd edged away when he approached the circle for morning meeting. Their eyes fixed on the one thing that differentiated him from the others in the room—the beautiful shimmering leaf etched on his inner wrist—delicate and green along the edges. She'd been so mesmerized, she'd immediately pulled out a marker and tried to make her own. Ms. Stein asked Yas to be his buddy. Eleven years later, the assignment had stuck. Raf got Yas the way only someone who knew you before you learned long division could.

"What's the Golub word for 'annoying' again?" She nodded toward the house.

"Lesan." His dimple deepened. "That constant hammering is a lot."

"Any more ideas what they're up to?"

"Someone must've bought it. Fix it up, and who wouldn't want it?"

"Raf. I'm serious."

"Me too," he said. "It'll come back, the water. When it does, they'll have gotten a house with one of the best views in the world for pennies on the dollar. Rich people love getting a good deal."

She fixed her eyes on the sea. *Not this again.* Yes, in the past, the colors of the ocean had shifted from time to time from the brilliant pink and purple to dimmer versions for seconds or moments at a time. In the weeks leading up to the tragedy, there'd been a few mornings of gray that'd lasted several hours, but the colors always returned by the afternoon. Never in the two centuries of recorded history of their town was there *any* evidence of their sleepy, warm-watered bay shifting to colder temperatures with dangerous riptides swirling within. In the early days, she'd combed the town's archives in the damp library on the edge of town. Praying that history would provide hope. A cure. But she'd only found contradictory legends and lore. Nothing grounded in science. Nothing that could truly help. In the end, her question was one without an answer.

Have faith, Raf always said. Droughts could last for years, why not the ocean losing its spark? This was life. Things ebbed and flowed. The Golub held on to hope like no one else. It was their North Star.

When they first became friends, Yas listened with rapt attention to his tales of Golub. Trees with gold-flecked leaves. Playscapes with slides and climbing structures carved entirely of ice. *We're only here for a little while,* Raf used to tell her. *Until things get safer and we can go home.* But with each passing year, their Golub tree only grew frostier, and Raf didn't talk about leaving as much anymore. By now, he'd lived on this side longer than in Golub. He was headed to university soon.

Yas didn't blame the Golub for hoping, but she had lost her own hope for Moonlight. Yas knew. It was a knowing she felt in her bones. It was why she'd long abandoned the star necklace she once swore by: Hoping for the waters to return was futile.

When she met his gaze, he shrugged.

"The workers are good for business, at least there's that," he said. "We sold out of waffles already. Bura just went on a run to restock the flour."

"You didn't see my father around town, did you?"

"He's gone?"

"He left before I woke up."

Her father used to stick notes on the fridge to let her and her mother know he'd dashed to Jake's to grab milk and eggs for a pancake breakfast. Now he disappeared for hours at a time, casting his job-hunting net farther and farther.

"I'm sorry, Yas. I'm sure he'll find something soon." His hand grazed her bare arm for the briefest of seconds before pulling away. But not before a jolt of electricity passed through her.

She ignored it, of course, as she always did, but she couldn't help but wonder: Did he feel it too? She studied the brown of his eyes, the set of his jaw. If he did, his face showed no trace of it.

She cleared her throat. "Any word on Kot?"

"Not yet." His expression fell.

A layer of heaviness had settled over Raf since Kot left without explanation. He and his sister, Nara, had the misfortune of arriving to Moonlight Bay through the Golub tree the same night Sammy died and the ocean grayed.

Gray like their eyes, the townspeople would whisper. Just the thought of it made Yas's blood boil.

This remained the hardest change for Yas to witness. The Golubs had been trading partners with Moonlight Bay for centuries—they once traversed regularly through their enormous tree in the center of Willow Forest. Their spices, minerals, gems, and prized fabrics were coveted in Moonlight and beyond, and they'd always been received as revered guests. Yas thought their town was special to receive visitors from lands beyond their own. Jasmine Cove to the north had portals through carved glaciers for the Dilcut. To the west were the sand dunes and caves for the Minas and the Smus. Moonlight Bay had the Golub tree.

When the weather in Golub turned, eighteen years earlier—homes buckling beneath sheets of ice, frozen freshwater refusing to warm for drink, their gardens unable to grow—the people of Moonlight didn't blink. They offered up the six acres of Willow Forest and promised the Golub they would always be welcome.

Yas now knew not all promises lasted forever.

When Raf left, Yas looked at Holler Mansion. The blue tarp lay dusty on the grassy ground; cracked shingles were tossed into a comfortable-sized heap. Spanish tiles peeked out of brown boxes, waiting patiently in neat rows. Whoever was fixing it up was trying to restore the home to what it'd once been. But *she* couldn't go back in time. Yas was no longer the carefree girl who wore a star necklace. Who kissed a pretty boy home from boarding school on a whim. *That* Yas believed things always worked out. *This* Yas understood sometimes there was no fixing what was broken.

Yas rolled up her sleeves. She pulled out the shell from her pocket and went to the sea. Kneeling, she coated it with salt and brine. She looked at the Weepers at the ocean's edge, their hands cupped in supplication. Something tough and solid lodged in her throat. Why couldn't they face facts? The water of before was gone. Sammy was gone. The sweet boy she'd spent hours babysitting on nights his nanny was off had drowned while Yas had stood mere yards away. The Hollers had fled, leaving Moonlight Bay to sink in their wake. *It's over,* thought Yas. *Neither stars nor tears change any of these truths.* She tucked the shell into her pocket and rose. *Accepting this is the only way to survive.*

three

RAF

"Keep up the good work," Ernie said, clapping Raf on the back as he locked up the diner.

"Thank you, sir."

"I mean it." The mayor's drawl elongated each word as though he had all the time in the word to say what he wanted to say—which, Raf supposed, he did. "This diner is one of the shining examples of what works in this town. Don't think I don't remind everyone any chance I get."

Ernie was the best mayor anyone could ask for. He'd made it his personal mission to get a cup of coffee from the diner every day, without fail. *An act of solidarity,* he told Raf. Raf knew he meant well, and in the early days, when the seas first grayed, they'd *needed* his support. But once upon a time, they hadn't needed the mayor ordering coffee to drum up business from the townspeople. Once upon a time, deep in summer as they were, there'd be a line of tourists clamoring for a seat at a stool.

Once upon a time.

Raf's mouth twitched. That was how fairy tales began, didn't they?

It felt like a fairy tale now, but it *had* been real. Soon after his family arrived through the Golub tree with teeth chattering, toes white and blue from near frostbite, the locals had welcomed them with baskets of treats and thermoses filled with honey flower tea. Later, they'd parked their trucks packed with lumber, brick, and shingles at the edge of the forest and helped haul the housing materials down their dirt path, wheelbarrow by wheelbarrow. When the Golub pooled their dwindling reserves of gems and minerals to purchase Seaside Diner from Aluna Otieno, who was retiring, the locals were among those celebrating the grand opening.

In the early days, his family's sudden move to Moonlight had been dizzying for Raf. Gone were his family's acres of farmland. Their snow-capped mountains. The frozen waterfalls. It was the kindness of the locals that had made the adjustment easier. As time pressed on, he realized that despite the differences between Golub and Moonlight Bay, there was much that was the same. The lively square—this one located far closer to his house—filled with cafés, theaters, and bookshops. Festivals and playscapes. And Raf was certainly grateful that in all the years in Moonlight Bay, he'd never needed to slip on woolen gloves three layers deep.

"Feelings can turn like the tide," Uncle had warned, even in the early days. "We are grateful for their generosity. For this land they have lent us. However, we must be mindful. We are not of them and they are not of us. We must take care until we can return home."

But with each passing year, Golub faded more and more into memory. Moonlight Bay with its shimmering pink-and-lavender sea, the gleaming Ferris wheel at the edge of Main Street Park, and Yas—this was what *felt* like home.

Now Raf understood: Uncle had worried with good reason.

"Taking over full-time now that you've graduated?" Ernie asked Raf, pulling him to the present.

"That's the plan." The unopened financial aid application for Surrey stuffed under his mattress poked out uncomfortably in his mind.

"Glad to hear it." Ernie thumped his back. "You keep the place running like clockwork."

Raf watched Ernie's retreating figure and tucked his keys into his pocket. He walked past a row of boarded-up stores that had once been art galleries, cafés, and boutiques. Oscar's gas station, which doubled as the post office, and Moonlight Bay Pharmacy, two stores over and with peeling shutters, both still had neon OPEN signs blinking above their entrances—the few hanging on. For now.

Raf tried pushing away the thoughts that Ernie's question dislodged. He'd applied to eight colleges, but Surrey had always been the hope. Professor Sandeep Singh, who summered in town and ate pancakes with coffee in their diner every Tuesday without fail since Raf was ten, taught architecture there. Raf would pepper him with questions about designing houses and creating floor plans. The professor's eyes always lit up whenever Raf shared stories of Golub—their homes with domed roofs and thermally heated and cooled floors. He was eleven when the professor gave him an architecture textbook. Raf was hooked. This—he'd once thought—was his destiny. He knew a thing or two about constructing homes, having helped his family and others build their dwellings within the forest and then, in recent years, reinforcing and fortifying spaces not created to house them for quite so long. He had notebooks filled with sketches. Blueprints of buildings. Cities. Combining Golub designs and Moonlight architecture. Now those plans were just papers gathering dust in the back corner of his bedroom closet.

Stop, he told himself. Fixating didn't change things. College had always been a dream—and dreams were never one's birthright.

Raf's phone vibrated in his back pocket. He knew without looking who it would be. It was mostly ever her. Yas.

Dropped some pretzel
brownies off with your
mom!

> Yas! You're the best.

No arguments there!
Movie night?

> What's playing?

Does it matter?

Raf's mood brightened. She was right, it didn't matter. Gil and Finn, who ran the theater, played the same movie for months, but Raf and Yas showed up each week all the same. The buttered popcorn and caramel pretzels were too good to pass up. Raf promised to meet up after dinner.

He stepped onto the beach and trudged through the loose

grains of sand until he reached the shoreline, where the ground beneath lay compact and firm. Even after all this time, the grayness stung. Once upon a time, pink dolphins swam not far from shore. He and Yas would wade out to see the newest calves and swim alongside Mira and Hira—the names they'd given the sweetest two with matching crooked fins.

Once upon a time. There it was again. And the next thought, never far behind: The Golub had fled unimaginable circumstances that slowly—then all at once—became all too imaginable. Here in Moonlight, in just under a year, the waters had gone dark, as had the local sentiment toward his people. What would come next?

If his father were still alive, Raf knew what he'd say: There was no use trying to look around corners, for while there could be darkness, there could also be light. It was healthier to hope. Hope that whatever came next would be better.

Turning toward the grassy edge of Willow Forest, Raf saw a wooden rowboat floating in the ocean a short distance away. The man inside held a reed-thin fishing pole; a straw hat obscured his face. When he looked up, his eyes locked onto Raf's. Then narrowed. Jake.

Tolki Uncle regularly reminded the Golub to make an effort with Jake and others like him. Especially these days. Raf knew he should wave to Jake. Smile. But did these efforts really soften the hearts of those whose feelings had seemingly hardened into concrete against him and the 103 people of Willow Forest? Tall, shaggy-blond-haired Kot had been full of smiles—unfailingly friendly—but something happened to him all the same. Something that made him flee without so much as a farewell to his own sister.

Raf picked up his pace. Slipping into the thicket of trees by the edge of the beach, he winced as his hoodie caught against a thorny branch.

"Why didn't you make a path to our home from the ocean?" Raf had asked Uncle when he was younger and came home with thorns pierced into his jeans. Pinching at his elbows. There was a longer, mulched path cleared through the forest to the main town square. Tolki Uncle created it himself when he arrived with his daughter eighteen years earlier—the foot traffic kept it maintained.

"It's safest to have one way in and out," he replied.

Raf once found these precautions over the top, but today he was grateful for the barrier.

Stepping into the clearing, he shivered. The Golub tree, measuring two hundred feet tall, stood steps away. It was as wide as a redwood, with a thin layer of frost burrowed within its creases. Its plentiful dewdrop leaves created a crown the color of the inside of a cracked papaya, with the branches toward the bottom bare and icy. The limbs of the simple eastern pines surrounding it were coated with tendrils of orange frost. This tree was their compass. The day it warmed like the others surrounding it was the day they could return home. *Would* they, though? Raf had his doubts. Uncle said hope was like a flame, it needed regular tending, but each new arrival painted a bleaker picture than the last.

Using the drawstring to pull the hoodie tighter, he stepped around the decorated stone pit set beneath the shade of the Golub tree's branches. The annual Hamra gathering was fast approaching. Each year they lit a fire in that very cauldron with the precious pebble-shaped minerals they'd brought from the other side. This year, there were already inscribed Golub leaves—filled with people's longings and grief—strung together by thread, dancing in the wind from the branches of nearby trees. Soon these leaves would be placed in gold-tendrilled flames to cleanse their hearts and bring peace. Raf looked forward to it this year. Between college and Yas, he had his own matters to let go of.

Earlier today, his leaf had flared its warning when their arms accidentally brushed against each other. After what happened last year, Raf *was* careful around Yas. But he couldn't *not* see her. She was his person. He was hers.

Pressing a hand to the trunk, he watched the golden leaf etched on his inner wrist glow. Before things turned, a touch like this against a warm trunk would have made the trunk glow, ready for egress or ingress. But times were different now. Lately it glowed haphazardly, without rhyme or reason. The tree was cool to the touch, but not numbingly so today. He thought of Kot on the other side, navigating his way through the tundra-like lands. *Why* did he go back? Where was he right now? Raf prayed his friend was safe.

Stepping into his home, Raf heard the familiar Golub folk melodies his mother played while cooking. They sounded a bit tinny lately on the portable stereo she'd squeezed in with her belongings when they'd left Golub. She sewed custom curtains for customers around the continent, but she was home early today. Slipping off his shoes, he placed them on the built-in shelf by the door. He'd been so young when they left, but hearing the music in the air—he could close his eyes and be back in Golub. Each of the forty-five identical homes scattered through the six-acre forest also hearkened back to the simple houses of his birthplace. Three bedrooms, a bathroom off the main room. A kitchen with a wooden table that seated six.

Raf couldn't imagine what it was like for people who lived in houses like Yas's. To inhabit a place that had existed long before you had. Was it strange to know how many other lives came and went, wept and laughed in the walls you inhabited now? All Raf knew was starting fresh.

Tolki Uncle sat at the kitchen table, chatting with Raf's mother. Raf inhaled the scent of cardamom-infused chicken, pickled beef, eggplant, and steaming saffron rice simmering on the stove. They tried to approximate the spices in Moonlight Bay to their tastes of home, but it was difficult to replicate some—like lak, which turned meals into savory *and* sweet, or min, which gave food an extra thickening. Supplies were scarce nowadays, so their precious herbs and minerals were stored away for special occasions.

Thimba, his cat, nuzzled her head against his leg. He kneeled down to pet her. Before Raf could greet anybody else, his younger brothers lunged for him, nearly tackling him to the ground.

"Raf!" they shouted in unison. Mac was six; Louk, five. Though small in size, they could take down a linebacker without blinking.

"Uncle said my drawing looks just like a lupta." Mac thrust his lined notebook toward Raf. "I copied it from that show we watched!"

"It looks like a toilet," Louk countered.

"Stop," Raf chided. "It *does* look like a lupta."

"Do you remember them from back home, Raf?" Tolki Uncle asked.

"I do," he said. "We had our own. Their fuzzy ears and black snouts made them look like overgrown rabbits."

"They loved Raf," his mother said. "Always wanted to eat from his hands." She gazed out the window. He knew from her faraway expression that she was looking at a memory.

What had happened to their farm animals? Raf wondered. He hoped they were okay. He remembered his parents leading the lupta to their neighbors. The howling winds had whipped against him, straight through his bones, despite the layers his mother had bundled him in. The neighbors promised to look after them. But everyone who came through the tree over the years shared only that things were worsening. What became of the neighbors?

"*I* want to feed a lupta!" Louk exclaimed. "Can't we go to the farm to see them?"

"One day, child," Uncle said. "One day you'll see the lupta, the plains and fields, and the mountains for yourself. When the winds calm and the ice thaws, we will return home."

Mac gasped. "*Return?* I don't want to *live* there!"

Louk pointed to the floor. "*This* is my home."

"Louk. Mac." Raf's mother looked at Uncle, her expression reddening. "I don't know what's gotten into them lately."

But how could anyone blame them? Only Raf and his mother remembered the scent and feel of a world beyond this. His brothers were born here, and Raf's own memories grew dimmer each day. He remembered the cold, though. Iced-over lakes and frozen ponds. Limbless trees and roofs collapsing under sheets of ice that clung like plastic wrap.

"It wasn't always this way," his mother had told him as they'd hurriedly packed their belongings. "The air once warmed just enough in the summers that I'd swim in lakes and sun myself on the shore. Things will return to normal soon enough. We'll be back."

Eleven years later, they continued to wait. When was the last time she'd mentioned going back? Raf couldn't recall. His father would never return. He was buried on the edge of Willow Forest. If they left, they left him too.

"Can we open the door and take a peek? Just a tiny one?" Louk asked. "Maybe a lupta's wandering around just outside?"

"You can't just open the door—*it* decides when to let you in or out!" Mac poked Louk's shoulder. "Remember?"

"Even if we had a measure of control over this, we can't know the conditions on the other side," their mother said. "If there was a wind gust or a hailstorm . . . Even a touch could damage Willow Forest irreversibly."

"If it's that dangerous to go through the door . . ." Mac's expression grew solemn. "Is Kot okay?"

Uncle's smile faltered.

"Dena said Kot might not've gone back at all!" Louk told Raf. "He could've wandered too far on this side. But if he strays too far, won't he lose his leaf? And then he can't be with us ever again."

"It would warn him!" Mac smacked his little brother's arm. "He'd know if he went too far, right, Uncle?"

"Boys," his mother said sternly. "Repeating idle gossip helps no one."

Uncle sighed heavily. "It's difficult, but we must hope for the best. Wherever Kot may be, let's pray he's safe."

Uncle had tested the safety limits himself when he first arrived. Raf knew the rules by heart. If they went beyond the forty-mile perimeter, the leaf warmed in warning. It took two hours before it flashed in earnest. Three for the etching to dim. Four before the loss became irreversible.

He'd pored over those details when he'd applied to college. He was among the first raised within the forest. One of the first, it felt like, to wonder about a future set outside of Golub. Surrey University was ten miles outside the radius. He risked his leaf with this dream, but there had to be options. Living on the outskirts close to the perimeter. Commuting. But even then, he didn't have an answer for *how* he could leave when Uncle relied on him to carry on his father's work running the diner.

When Kot and Nara arrived ten months ago, Raf glimpsed an opportunity. Kot with his infectious smile. His easy demeanor. He'd paid the whisperers no mind. He was twenty years old, but Kot's self-assured style made him seem a decade older to Raf. "They can think what they like," he'd said to Raf with a shrug. "Not my concern." His family had owned a café in Golub, and he needed to work to keep his mind from running in circles. Uncle had worried, of course, but Raf promised Kot would stay in the back. Out of sight. Safe. At the diner, Kot's hands were like magic. His salted caramel cakes were so delicious, the locals ordered extras to take home. Maybe, Raf had hoped at the time, college could eventually be a possibility.

When Kot showed up at the diner last month looking somber and troubled, but dismissed it as a headache, Raf had believed him. He hadn't pushed. Hadn't pried. The next morning, they found leaves and branches scattered beneath the Golub tree. The telltale signs of an opening. Kot had vanished. His sister was heartbroken, and Raf's dreams for college—a life beyond the forest—were gone.

His mother shooed the boys out of the kitchen. She turned to Raf.

"How was work today?" she asked.

"Packed," Raf told her. "I told Bura to pick up extra produce."

"Another busy day. A good sign." His mother kissed his cheek.

But workers didn't replace the tourists who had still not arrived. Raf was beginning to understand they weren't going to come at all. They'd need to dip into their pooled reserves at the rate they were going. He needed to consult with Uncle soon. Raf wasn't going to bring this up now, though. He liked seeing his mother smile.

"Did the plumbing patch fix the leak last night?" Raf asked Uncle.

"There was not so much as a drop. Thank you, Raf. You're a lifesaver."

A crash sounded from the other room. His mother grimaced. "Mind shooing them to the clearing while I finish up?" She tossed him a rag. "Wipe down the table while you're there."

"First one out gets tossed in the air," Raf called to Mac and Louk.

"I'm too big for that," Mac said, scowling, but he slipped on his shoes and raced outside with his brother.

Raf grabbed the broom resting on the back wall and the spray bottle from the cabinet beneath the sink. He followed them into the clearing. *This* was also why college had never been practical, Raf reminded himself. His father was gone; his mother needed him more than ever.

The fifteen-foot table with matching benches flanking each side was made of sanded-down oak. There were several such tables scattered throughout the forest for each hamlet to eat communally, as they did back home. Raf swept away the strewn pinecones and sprayed the table as his brothers piled up fallen leaves before leaping in, their laughter ringing through the forest. A neighbor's daughter joined them as daylight waned between the trees. He lit the first of the kerosene lights. The gas flickered. Raf lit each one until all the lamps strung around the table were aglow. Stepping back, he took in the scene. He had to admit it was a beautiful evening. Even in the midst of so much uncertainty and sadness all around, there were reasons to feel grateful.

Looking at the house across from him, he saw Nara. She sat on the front stoop. Her white-blond hair was swept up in a knot. She wore jeans and a gray top that matched the gray of her eyes; the crescents beneath them deepened each day. Ever since her brother disappeared, she barely slept. She barely ate.

Seeing Raf, she rose.

"Did you talk to Yas about the stars?" she asked. "Would her mother consider coming here to make me one?"

"Let's go get one made. You know, Kot was thinking about getting one for himself."

"That? He wasn't serious. Kot was only teasing Uncle." Nara smiled a little. "You know how Uncle doesn't believe in any of that."

"You don't have to believe in it. They're pretty necklaces. And you'll get out of here for some fresh air."

"I can't leave the forest," she said. "Look what happened to Kot."

What could he say to this? He thought of Jake's steely expression earlier today. Did *he* accost Kot? Raf tried to remember if he'd noticed a welt on Kot that last morning. Bruises. Despite the growing tensions, no one had ever laid a hand on them. Not even after Jake, Crissy, and others bought a full-page advertisement in the *Moonlight Gazette* days after Sammy's death, outlining why the Golub were not to be trusted. Someone had pasted a copy of it on their diner window the morning it ran. Yas ripped it off as soon as she laid eyes on it, her face flushed pink with anger.

But removing it from a window didn't remove the sentiments from people's hearts. For Kot to have chosen to do this, what other explanation could there be? Uncle had noticed Kot lingering by the tree in the days before his vanishing, but no one could have imagined why. That he had been waiting for an opening to leave.

"He'll come back," Raf said. "We have to believe he will."

"We barely made it the first time," she said softly. "Our parents died of frost two hours into our journey. To go back?" Her eyes brimmed with tears. "I touched the tree today."

"Nara . . ."

"It's cold, Raf." Her lower lip quivered.

"It's warmer than in days past."

"It's no different. Not really."

After Kot vanished, Raf and his mother had to pry Nara from the tree. Even now, the once-soft skin of her hands was cracked and scabbed from trying to tear open the door. There was no point. The door opened when it wished—and lately, hardly at all.

He patted her arm. "I'm sorry," he told her.

"Yeah, me too." She wiped her eyes. "Need help setting the table?" She nodded toward it. "I'll wipe the seats down while you grab the plates?"

"Thanks, Nara."

Yas often told Raf how bewildering it was that everyone here slipped back and forth from matters that were life-and-death to everyday matters, but what else were they to do? If they sat and cradled their pain, the enormity of it would destroy them. They had to keep doing and going. Hoping. There was no other way.

"I believe dinner is nearly ready." Tolki Uncle walked over. He picked up a fallen twig and tapped the copper bell dangling from a tree branch. Just as in Golub, the chime echoed through the trees; in the distance, other bells chimed.

Dena and her five-year-old son stepped out of their home alongside her sister, Dar, as the table filled with food. Som and Meed were next; their ten-year-old daughter, Ruh, hopped over to join Raf's brothers in the leaves. Then the Samli family and the Jugnus. Soon everyone in their little enclave was gathered.

Tolki Uncle bowed his head. "Thank you to the Sustainer for this meal. Let us pray for Moonlight Bay. For the waters to return. For succor from those who mean us harm. For Dena's mother. Bura's father. And let us pray for the missing. For my own daughter, Shar. For Jib and Mah—"

"Let my boys stay gone," Som said, his expression dark. Uncle moved to speak, but he cut him off. "I mean it—they made their choices."

Unlike Kot, Som's twin boys didn't return to Golub. Five years ago, they'd simply left. Choosing this world over their leaf and thereby cutting off any connections to the people within the forest. Their parents refused to speak of them, but their expressions belied their sorrow.

"I would like for us to pray for Kot as well," Nara said. "May he return to us."

Tears slipped down Nara's face. Raf looked at Uncle's drawn expression. He knew more than most what she was going through.

After a moment of silence, Uncle asked, "Would anyone else like to say a prayer?"

"For the locals to stop with the glares," said Dena.

"Did something happen at the diner?" Uncle asked quickly.

"Same as every day." Her green eyes flashed. "Wears on you to serve people who think you're beneath them. Put on a long-sleeve shirt and I dare anyone to tell us apart, but they act as though they're inherently better."

Others murmured in agreement.

"They are not better than us. We are not better than them," said Uncle. "However, we *are* different. The leaf is a small distinction, but one that matters deeply. Our names, our prayers, our way of life—all of these set us apart. And this leaf? One day it will lead us home."

"But it's been years. The tree's still not warm enough for us to return," Raf blurted out. All eyes turned to him. His face blazed. Why had he shouted that out? Maybe it was just that Uncle said it so calmly each time such matters came up. As though their return was imminent.

"You touched it, didn't you?" his mother scolded. "As if Nara's hands aren't scarred enough? We don't have unlimited healing herbs."

"I just . . ." Raf thought of Kot. "I wanted to know."

"What good is there in that? Doesn't change what is."

"The cold means warm will follow," Tolki Uncle said. "The Sustainer tests us for reasons They know best. We must trust in Their wisdom."

Uncle was the first to come to Moonlight. His daughter left early on, and he'd lived in solitude for two years before the door opened again, bringing newcomers. He knew better than most how painfully long a test like this was. Raf had been young when he blithely asked him why he hadn't gone in search of his daughter when she'd left the perimeter.

"Lost leaves are catching," Uncle had explained. "I have obligations to my community. As much as my heart breaks, I cannot take that chance. I pray every day for her well-being."

Raf longed for Uncle's steadfast patience, but looking at Nara, he also wondered: Why did some lessons have to be this difficult?

His phone buzzed in his pocket. Pulling it out, he saw a message from Yas. Just seeing her name on the screen lightened his mood.

> The Golub word for cat is
> nafriz, right?

She'd sent a photo of a coffee shop with a gaggle of cats. Raf smiled. Before he could respond, she texted again.

> Check out this nafriz café
> walkable to the College of

Architecture. I might need
to apply now.

Nafriz was one of the dozens of Golub words Yas had inte-
grated into her everyday speech over the course of their
friendship. His smile didn't last too long, though. He needed
to tell her he wasn't going to Surrey. She'd be disappointed,
but he couldn't put off telling her for much longer.

He attached a picture of Thimba from this morning, her
head poking out from between the folded towels as though
sleuthing for a top-secret mission. He clicked send and
watched the three dots as Yas began her reply.

Raf wasn't sure the exact moment this dream of becoming
an architect had seeped into his mind. That maybe he could
graduate and find work in a nearby town like Mill Creek or
Ridgeview, safely within the perimeter of the tree. He could
build a home for his mother and brothers. Maybe work at a
firm. Open his own. Or teach, like Professor Singh. He'd be
close enough to the forest. And close enough to Yas so they
could see each other as much as they'd like. As he'd gotten
older, another dream seeped in—maybe he and Yas could be
together.

But it had been asking for too much, hadn't it? College
wasn't in the cards for him. He had responsibilities to his people and to his family. He owed them his presence after what
happened. What *he* had accidentally done. And his family had
already survived a brutal journey out of Golub. Had made a
makeshift home for themselves and managed to stay together.
These were such huge miracles. He had his family. He had Yas's
friendship. What business did he have wanting more?

four
YAS

Her parents' bedroom door was wide open when Yas stepped out of her room. The lights were off. The bed perfectly made. She heard the distant sound of hammering. The tinkling of shells from the guest room down the hall. She felt her father's absence. He'd been gone since yesterday.

Her phone buzzed. Yas grabbed it, but it wasn't her father. She clicked on the social media notification from her friend Hisae. A selfie in front of a four-story whitewashed building with blue shutters.

Jessi's moving out September 13th ☹, **Hisae's caption read.** Anyone need a roommate? Lowman's Collective is a DREAM!

Lowman's Collective. She knew that name. A quick search revealed why. She scrolled through murals painted on red brick. Goats and chicks wandered about on a grassy lawn. Back when shells were abundant, she and her mother had traveled to the town of Edgewood for Lowman's annual market to sell their star necklaces. She remembered the smell of butter and sugar wafting over from the on-site bakery and the sculptures of marooned spaceships and metallic trees spread throughout the thirty-acre property. Hisae wasn't an artist. Was she?

I didn't know you were at Lowman's, **Yas messaged her.**

Hisae's reply was swift. I work at their café! It's a ten-minute drive from Surrey. Does Raf need housing this fall?

He's at the dorms, **Yas replied. Though, come to think of it—** Yas frowned—had he said he was dorming, or did she assume he was? It'd been some time since they'd spoken about Surrey.

The collective's a great place to live, **Hisae texted.** Even if you're not super artsy.

That's awesome, **Yas replied. But Yas didn't feel very awesome. Scrolling through Hisae's posts, a strange feeling passed through her. A twisty sensation in the pit of her stomach. Almost like nausea.**

Or envy?

Her phone buzzed again.

You want in? **Hisae asked.** You'd LOVE this place. It's a painter's dream. I could probably get you a job with me too!

Yas reread the message. Living in an artists' collective? *Of course* **she wanted in. She'd pack her belongings and head there now if she could. But her work was here. This was the year she was meant to begin her apprenticeship with her mother. Even if she no longer believed in the sea's powers, even if her own necklace still lay tucked in a drawer untouched since last year, the work was hers to carry on. She wasn't the kind of person who'd walk out on her family.**

Besides, thought Yas, could she even call herself a painter if she hadn't touched a paintbrush in nearly a year?

Not for me, **Yas managed to reply,** but I'll keep an eye out.

Checking her calendar, she blinked. September 13 was exactly one month after the Moonlight Bay Festival, which they celebrated the second Thursday of August every year. It

was marked automatically in perpetuity in her online calendar, even though the festival definitely wasn't happening this year. What was once a yearly celebration was now a death anniversary. No one had called it off—not officially—it was more like they'd all decided to pretend it never existed. Which was just as well.

"Yas?" her mother called from the hallway. "Can you grab your scissors? Mine are going dull."

Yas opened the top drawer of her dresser and pulled out the handmade red scissors gifted to her on her thirteenth birthday. They cut through shells like paper.

Her paintbrushes were also tucked away in there, untouched since last year. Her old sketchbooks were stacked in a row next to them. She pulled one out. This one was from grade school. She flipped through the crude charcoal sketches of dolphins. A water-colored sunset. Yas trailed a hand over her first—and last—attempt at portraiture. Raf. Who else would've given in to a nine-year-old demanding they sit motionless on her bed for hours while she stood at her easel attempting to bring his likeness to paper?

"It's weird being painted," he'd complained.

"I'm *sketching* you, not painting you."

"Still weird."

"You won't be alone. I'm adding myself in later."

"Yeah?" He grinned.

"I'm going to call it . . ." She pursed her lips. "*Together Forever*."

"But we can't be together forever," he'd blurted out. "Uncle told me I can't marry you. It's not allowed because we're going back to Golub soon."

She wrinkled her nose. "Raf, why are you so weird?" She tossed a pillow at him, and that had been the end of that. They'd never spoken of it again, but she still cringed at the memory.

Yas stepped into the hallway. The floorboards creaked beneath her. Cracking open the door of the guest room, where dime-size stars glittered from the ceiling, she handed her mother the scissors and set a basket of newly collected shells on the side table. The shell from yesterday was in there too, the perfect one with rounded edges, plucked from the sand. It was the only promising one among the bunch.

"Don't turn on the light," her mother said quickly. She wore a blue skirt and peasant top, her long hair wrapped in a floral bandana. "Outlet's acting up."

"We need to get an electrician over," Yas groaned. "The oven was finicky again this morning."

"I'll tell your dad to call Jamal."

"Dad didn't come home last night," Yas said. "He promised he'd give me an update after his interview, and he didn't call either."

"He's driving up tomorrow," her mother said.

"Where is he?" she asked. "It's got to be farther out if he's gone this long. And if he gets this job, then what? Not like we can move. Our work is here."

"We'll cross that bridge when we get there." Her mother's eyes remained fixed on the work before her. "No sense worrying now."

Her father loved Moonlight Bay—but he was a transplant. When the Hollers left without so much as a two weeks' notice to their longtime loyal employees, her father changed. Gone was the person who kicked the soccer ball with her on the beach. Strategized with her over chess every Sunday. That man was replaced by a stranger with a cloudy expression. Who was eager to abandon Moonlight as soon as possible. "It's time to cut our losses," he urged a few months into their gray new world. He didn't understand why this was impossible. His DNA didn't link him forever to this soil like Yas's and her mother's did.

Just then, the windows vibrated. The stars strung overhead trembled.

"Jackhammer again." Her mother grimaced.

"They're redoing the pool. When will they wrap it up? It's been forever now."

"Wish I knew." She nodded to the cracked stars strewn on the guest bed. "I have to rethread each one twice to make sure more don't break. Not sure if it's tied to the vibrations or if this batch of shells is just weaker, but Olive won't be happy."

Yas cringed. Olive was once perpetually happy. They'd owned Tilted Tales and never shooed Raf and Yas away, even when the pair parked themselves on the oversize ottoman for half the day, working their way through the comics. Sure, they'd lost some of their spark after their messy divorce two months before the sea turned gray. But never could Yas have imagined this. Olive, a Weeper. Lately, they were either shivering ankle-deep in the sea or here in Yas's home awaiting a star. Each newly created necklace soothed a different pain. Some customers came yearly. Others monthly. Olive came every week, their attention fixed on their phone while waiting to be called back. Yas stole a peek over Olive's shoulder last time and instantly regretted it. It was a four-second clip from last year's Moonlight Bay Festival. Twinkle lights strung around lampposts. The ocean glimmering pink and lavender in the background. The happy cries of children. Again. And again. An endless loop.

Yas's mother tossed her a spool of silk. "Double-knot them so they don't sway so much. I'll dust out the guest sheets after."

They still called this a guest bedroom. Pretending her mother hadn't slept here every night for nearly three months. *For whose benefit do we do this?* Yas wondered. She got to work double-knotting and hanging up the stars.

"Can you check my phone for any new appointments?" her mother asked once Yas was finished.

Three messages glowed on-screen.

"Lisa wants to come in tomorrow morning. Marie needs to reschedule, and—" Yas winced. "Olive wants to know if they can come by in a little bit."

"Text everyone else yes, but don't reply to Olive. I'll call them."

The jackhammer pulsed again. Dust rose in plumes outside the window.

"Is Ernie making Holler Mansion a tourist stop?" she asked her mother.

"Don't think he got the yes from the council to take it to a public vote."

Not like anyone even shows up to vote on anything these days.

"Those town halls are less and less well attended. Crissy barely attends any herself, and she's *on* the council."

"She is? Since when?"

"She took over Kendall's position," her mother replied.

"Can't blame Ernie for his nostalgia. Holler Candy *was* a big deal at one time. The biggest candy manufacturer in the region. Each piece coated with our waters. The Hollers used to lead guided factory tours when I was a kid. A tourist stop isn't going to happen, though. You'd need money to create something like that. Whoever's fixing it up, they have plenty of it. How was your collecting?" she asked. "Any luck?"

A year ago, her mother never asked this. She didn't need to. Sturdy shells were as ordinary as leaves strewn in a forest. One year earlier, they could stand calf-deep in the ocean and scoop out perfect shells ready for a quick cut, snip, and smoothing. They had so many shells back then, they set aside extras to sell as trinkets for tourists. It was hard to believe, except it *had* been real. So real she thought it could never change. Now only shards of shells, too fragmented to be of any use, littered the seafloor.

"Gray ones are aplenty." Yas handed her mother the basket. "Raf said they're no better on the other side of the forest."

"That's a shame. They used to be most plentiful out by their beaches." Her mother sifted through the basket. "How *is* Raf? Can't believe he's leaving soon."

"Me neither."

She tried not to dwell on this. She was happy for him—she was! She'd pored over websites with him and read through his application essays. Now, instead of sketching in notebooks or building intricate sandcastles so complex that tourists regularly mistook him for a performer and dropped coins at his feet, he'd be one step closer to what he'd always dreamed of doing. What he was meant to do.

But that doesn't mean I won't miss his smile when I step into the diner most mornings. The milkshakes he spins just for me because he knows how I like them. Yas wasn't ready to process what it would be like to live in Moonlight without him.

"I heard the recent diner boycott plan was a bust," her mother said. "I don't know what Jake and Crissy were thinking. It's the only restaurant left standing."

"Ernie shut that idea down quick," Yas said.

"Good on Ernie." She raked through the basket. "The sooner people can get over blaming the Golub, the better. It's just—" She paused. Her eyes widened. She pulled out the shell. "Yas, am I seeing things?"

Yas fidgeted. She knew her mother took the rules of shell gathering seriously, but it was superstition and nothing more that required their shells be found in the sea. Seeing her mother so happy, smiling like the before times—it made her ache.

"It's very smooth," Yas said. "We'll hardly need to sand it."

"Want to paint this one?" She looked hopefully at Yas. "Too pretty not to, don't you think?"

"Oh." Yas faltered.

"It's like the ones we had before." She examined the underside. "Makes you hope . . ." Her voice trailed off. She ran her fingers over the surface. She looked at Yas, searching her face.

"Is this from the ocean?" she finally asked.

"What do you mean? What's wrong with it?"

"Yasmine. Did you gather this from the waters?"

"All shells are from the ocean."

"That wasn't my question."

Her smile was gone. Had Yas waited a beat too long before she answered? What gave it away? *There are no such things as premonitions. There aren't.* Yas met her mother's steely gaze.

"I found it on the beach," Yas said, exhaling. "You said yourself this is like the ones we used to collect. It's perfect."

"But it isn't," her mother said. "Honestly, Yas. Did you think I wouldn't be able to tell?"

"It looks—"

"It's not how it looks! It's how it feels. It's how I sense which shells will heal and which won't . . ." Her mother sighed. "This isn't a game, Yas. This is our lifeblood. It's what keeps a roof over our heads."

"We need *stars* to keep a roof over our heads." Yas's voice rose. "The water's not the way it used to be."

"That means we're *more* careful. Not less."

"I dipped it in the sea. What's the difference?"

"The difference is, one works and the other doesn't." Her mother placed the shell on the nightstand and closed her eyes. "The difference is, I believe in what we do. My daughter doesn't."

Yas hated the look of disappointment on her mother's face. She *wanted* to believe. Nearly a year ago, she did. When her father still played football with his factory friends on weekends. When Main Street was packed with tourists filtering in and out of Cake Story, Tilted Tales, and Sampson's Deli, which sold sauerkraut sandwiches. She'd watched them shutter like collapsing dominoes, one after the other. Boarded-up windows. Tangled vines snaking through the abandoned mini-golf on the edge of town. The Ferris wheel tilting more and more toward the sea. The candy factory a dusty relic up a hillside in the distance. She'd seen Sammy Holler's body lying limp on the sandy shore. Drowned by those *healing* waters.

She'd watched the ocean dim—like a light bulb flickering off.

And she watched her mother press star after star into the palms of their neighbors. But they still wept. The ocean still churned gray. A million shells dipped in all the tears in the world couldn't do a thing to ease the pain of any of it. It was people like her mother, like Olive, the ones waiting and looking over their shoulder at what was, who were going to be left behind.

"What's the Golub word for 'this is the best milkshake known to man'?"

"Frimos."

"Is there really a word for 'this is the best milkshake known to man'?" Yas laughed.

"*Frimos* means 'delicious.'"

"*Frimos,*" Yas said with dramatic conviction.

"You like?" Raf leaned on the counter and grinned.

"Always." She pressed her mouth to the straw and took another sip. "The heat's intense out there. This feels extra refreshing."

"Any luck collecting?"

"There were a handful near your forest. Otherwise, the usual shards."

"Those things are *sharp*. Ernie ought to get city council to put up warnings."

"Good thing no one goes swimming anymore. They poke through my boots." She tucked a strand of hair behind her ear. "I might scale back to collecting once a week. Not like I'm having much luck lately anyhow."

"You could use that freed-up time to paint again."

"Or maybe I'll just become a barfly here."

"We sell milkshakes and orange juice." He laughed.

"You know what I mean!" Her phone buzzed. She looked at the screen and grimaced. "Mom needs me to pick up more thread."

"I thought you weren't speaking?"

"Does texting count?" She rose from her stool and slung her bag across her body. "Movie tonight?"

"Yes, please," he replied.

The wind chimes above the door sounded when the door closed behind her. Raf picked up the wall phone and pressed his ear to it. No luck. The line was still down. They'd tried to switch to online ordering, but the website crashed so often it became more of a hindrance than help. Uncle was trying to get the phone company to come sooner, but they kept rescheduling their service visit. They were now at three weeks without phone service. A diner on razor-thin margins without the ability to receive phone orders made tricky times even trickier.

He flipped on the coffee maker and surveyed the diner. Ernie had staked out a booth since they'd opened two hours ago. He sat across from Bea, Gil, and Ayo, some of the members of city council. Bea doubled as the town plumber, Gil ran the one and only movie theater in town with his husband, Finn, and Ayo managed the Iguana Motor Lodge. They were all in a heated conversation. Ernie punctuated his words with swift jabs in the air every so often, as though conducting a silent orchestra.

A handful of locals milled about, finishing up their breakfasts. Kendall—a Weeper—sat at his usual spot in the corner overlooking Main Street Park, nursing the same cup of coffee since morning. Workers from Holler Mansion in paint-splattered smocks finished up their omelets. The diner wasn't empty, but this wasn't how things were supposed to be this deep into summer. Tourist season accounted for half their yearly income, and this was going to be the first year without the crowds the Moonlight Bay Festival drew in. How bad would the shortfall be this year? He'd talk to Uncle tonight. He hoped their reserves would be enough to see them through.

Grabbing the coffee carafe, he walked through the diner and refilled empty mugs.

"Thanks, kid." Kendall gave him a weak smile once Raf topped him off.

Dena swung past Raf. She had on her white diner apron, her ginger hair tied up in a bun. When he returned to the counter, she looked Raf square in the eyes. "We need to discuss Nara."

"Dena—"

"The diner needs the help. She needs the distraction. Staying in the forest day and night this long is bad for her."

"She won't leave. She won't even step foot on the sand."

"We must give her a *reason* to leave," Dena replied. "Speak with Tolki? He listens to you."

"I'll . . . I'll think about it, Dena."

Her eyes flashed with frustration. She brushed past him through the swinging doors into the kitchen. Raf hated upsetting Dena, but he had to protect Nara. He'd already let down Kot.

As difficult as things had been this past year, Kot and Nara's presence had been a balm. They'd packed precious herbs and minerals from Golub with them, replenishing the dwindling stores in Willow Forest. But it was their stories that'd meant the most to Raf. Kot was a natural storyteller. His tales of hiking icicle-laden waterfalls and attending local festivals held in the hollowed-out mountains made Raf's own hazy memories come into focus. The stories also underscored the reality of the cold. It was deepening.

"Time flows in one direction," Kot would say. "We must follow its current. Pushing back, hoping for what might never come back to us, will only sharpen the pain."

Why, then, did Kot return to Golub?

Raf was stacking menus on the counter when the front door chimed. A man wearing cargo shorts and a pink polo shirt entered, his dark hair neatly parted.

"Professor Singh!" Raf exclaimed.

"Raf! Was hoping you'd be working today." He slid onto the barstool across from him. "You know you can call me Sandeep."

"You'll always be Professor Singh to me."

Raf smiled. Professor Singh had arrived! Summer was far from over. Perhaps more tourists would also come.

"The usual?" Raf asked.

"You can't possibly remember!"

"Pancakes. Side of decaf. Inch of cream?"

"Impressive. Hash browns too, please. Deciding to live dangerously."

"Is the family sleeping in?" Raf handed him coffee. "I can pack the girls some food to go. Rainbow sprinkles on the whipped cream, right?"

"Oh." Professor Singh studied his mug. "We picked a different beach this year. On account of . . ." His voice trailed off.

Ah. Of course. Travelers still stopped by to grab a meal

before traversing to more northern beachside destinations. He couldn't blame the professor. Who wanted to look out at those choppy charcoal shores? But it was official now: Tourist season was toast.

"I got roped into extracurricular duties, so Monica and the girls went up a week earlier." Sandeep smiled guiltily. "I couldn't miss stopping here on my way up. Best diner on the east coast. Best service too, I might add."

"Thanks, Professor."

"Before I forget." He reached into his canvas bag and pulled out a gold-rimmed text. "I found this at a library sale—it's about nature-based architecture practices. Made me think of you."

Raf eyed the raised lettering and braced for the question that was surely coming next.

"Where'd you end up settling on for college?" The professor took a sip of coffee.

There it was. Raf traced a finger against the counter. "Well—"

"Blankman was a good one, but I hope Surrey was at least a contender. If you wanted a campus job, I'll be in the market for a research assistant for my next textbook. You'd be a perfect fit."

"I got into Surrey," Raf said. "But I decided against college."

He lowered his coffee. "You were so excited."

"College isn't for everyone. Lots of people say it's overrated."

"It can be," he conceded. "But you'd seemed certain it was for *you*. The sketches of nature-inspired homes you shared last summer were incredible."

"Everything's been complicated since . . ." Raf gestured out the window. "I can't leave while we're figuring it all out."

"Surrey's only an hour away," Professor Singh said. "Less if you drive like I do."

"It's too late anyhow. I missed the financial aid window."

Professor Singh studied Raf for a moment. He smiled. "Well, how's this for fortuitous timing? I said I needed a research assistant, didn't I? Job comes with a stipend and tuition waiver."

"Oh." Raf blinked.

"Haven't posted it yet. Say the word, it's yours."

"That— That's so generous."

"I assure you, this is a very self-serving proposition," he replied. "I know your work ethic."

When the professor finished his meal, he grabbed the receipt and flipped it over.

"I don't mean to pressure you, Raf." He jotted down his number. "I was planning to post it by August first, but school's not starting until September, so I can probably push it a bit if you need more time to mull it over." He pushed the scrap of paper toward him. "Think about it? If you're in, we'll make it work."

Professor Singh took Raf's number. The bell above the door chimed as the door shut behind him. Raf looked at the receipt.

How many hours had he spent in this diner, dreaming about Surrey? The professor's offer resurfaced every crushed hope he'd buried. They splintered inside him once again. But this offer changed nothing. What would his father think of him right now? Wanting a future that required leaving his family behind? Crumpling the receipt, Raf tossed it in the trash. He was tired of wanting what he couldn't have. It made the not-having hurt even more. Professor Singh didn't understand his limitations. He didn't know why the ocean turned gray. No one except himself and Tolki Uncle knew why Raf couldn't afford to take any more risks.

six

YAS

Yas made her bed for the first time in months, a stalling tactic while she waited for her mother to leave the kitchen. How long could she stay angry with her? Her mother wasn't out there twice a week pulling in seaweed and jagged shards of shells. Their stockpile was dwindling. Yas had been *trying* to help. Why did her mother only look at her and find her wanting?

Grabbing her phone, she clicked on Hisae's profile, scrolling through photos of Edgewood. The café. A tastefully appointed bookshelf. Flowers on the windowsill.

When everyone from high school scurried off—who stayed? Yas. Sure, she had plans to travel here and there. To visit the famed art museum in Brink Valley. Mini-trips to the mountains up north. But *she* always planned to return. Moonlight was home. Her family's work was here. Her happiness was here.

What was here for her now?

Did you find a roommate? Yas messaged Hisae.

Three dots immediately appeared on-screen.

No! Wait. Seriously, do you know someone?! Hisae replied.

Seriously? Yas felt light-headed. *I'm not serious at all.* Except . . . why *was* she intent on staying? She looked down on the people in town who kept waiting and hoping for the waters to return. But what was worse: Staying and hoping? Or staying while knowing nothing would be the same again?

What about me? Yas replied.

Hisae replied immediately. If. You. Could. See. My. Face. I could tackle-hug you!

And then—

It's a $1,000 security deposit plus half of last month's rent, wrote Hisae. Then just five hundred a month for each of us!

One thousand dollars. And *just* five hundred a month after that. Yas flopped backward on her bed. She wanted to laugh. Had she really thought it would be so easy to leave? *Of course* she couldn't pick up and walk away. Leaving required money. That's how the Hollers packed up and disappeared within the week, wasn't it? They had endless resources and homes on every continent. Hisae's father had moved his dental practice to Ridgeview six months earlier—she probably didn't even *need* to work to pay her way. Yas? She had less than two hundred dollars to her name. So that was that.

Her phone buzzed. A video call from Raf.

"Raf," she groaned as she sat up, running her hand over her matted-up hair. "You can't just video call without warning! I'm a hot mess."

"Impossible."

"Uh-huh." Yas rolled her eyes.

"Everything okay?" he asked.

He knew something was up. He always did.

"Long story. I'll fill you in when I see you next time."

"Fill me in now? Bura just dropped off a crate of strawberries, and the diner's dead." Raf turned the camera and panned it over the empty restaurant. "Come by while supplies last?"

And just like that, the day felt a little brighter.

Putting her phone away, Yas heard the rusty hinge to the patio door creak in its familiar way. Her father. It had to be. She rushed into the hallway, and sure enough, there he was. He wore khakis and a button-down shirt, a gym bag slung over his shoulder. His golden hair parted to the side. His shoes dark and polished. And new. Her mother stood by the kitchen counter watching him as he brushed his feet on the welcome mat and closed the door behind him. Her cup of coffee frozen in her hands.

"Dad!" Yas hugged him.

"Hey, you." He squeezed her tight. He smelled of sandalwood and lemons—safe and familiar. *He's back. He didn't just run off.* Of course he hadn't! Why had she ever thought he would?

"Seems like you had some luck." She nodded to his clothing.

He looked hesitantly at her mother, but she had opened up her laptop, her expression impassive.

"I found a promising opportunity," he told her. "It's in sales."

"That's great." Yas brightened. Her father had worked in the sales and marketing division for Holler Candy since before she was born. "Where?"

"Jacoby's."

"Jacoby's?" She frowned. "The electronics store?"

He nodded. "Going back to my roots, the good old sales floor." He saw her expression and added, "Job market's tight these days. I'm lucky to have found this one."

"But the Jacoby's in Ridgeview closed down. The next closest one's in Yaksta."

"That's the one."

"It's over three hundred miles away!" She turned to her mother. "Aren't you going to say *anything*?"

"Your father told me the news on his way here," she said. "I told him he ought to be the one to tell you he's leaving."

"Leena"—he exhaled loudly—"I'm not leaving."

"You're *not* taking the job? In Yaksta?" Her mother closed the laptop. "That's called leaving, Chris."

Her words were measured and careful, her posture still, as though she was balancing on a tightrope only she could see. Her mother had dismissed her worries each time Yas said anything, but now Yas saw the pain her mom had kept carefully locked away.

"If there was something in town, something even *remotely* close to here, anything, I'd have grabbed it in a second," her father said, and then turned to Yas. "I'll *still* keep searching, but this is the first offer I've gotten. Just because I have to physically leave to take this job doesn't mean I'm leaving the family. I'll be back whenever I can."

He told her he'd let her know as soon as he was situated. How much he hoped she'd visit him. His words landed with a dull thud around her.

"I'm sorry," he said. "I wish there was another way. I really do."

He took the steps to the converted loft upstairs. The one with the messy office and foldout futon. Yas's mother stared hard at her coffee mug before setting it on the counter and walking to the guest room. The door shut with a click.

This time last year, her parents were happy. Could things fall apart *that* fast? The sea had turned practically overnight. Why not their home? Photographic evidence of happier times still graced the mantel: her mother in her wedding dress, her father's arm around her waist. The framed one of them as brand-new parents curled around a swaddled Yas.

They were the saccharine-sweet couple who insisted on holding hands over dinner. Yas had told Raf she wished they would quit it already with the hugs and stolen kisses.

Then the ocean dimmed and her wish came true. Her father was moving to Yaksta. Her mother didn't even put up a fight. Yas blinked back tears. *No crying,* she chided herself. *Tears don't fix things.* She needed to slip on her water boots, grab the catcher from the wicker basket by the back door, and get to work. Maybe today was the day she found the perfect cluster waiting to be scooped from the sea. Maybe today she would make her mother smile.

The doorbell sounded—the screeching sound made Yas wince each time. They needed to get that fixed soon.

She opened the door; it was Marie. Her face looked more gaunt than it had months earlier, but as usual, in her matching gold necklace and earrings, her cardigan and high-waisted pants, she was perfectly put together. Marie managed the art gallery that belonged to her husband, Mateo, the one that once featured blazing portraits of the sea. When Yas was younger, he'd let her wander into his back studio. She'd watch him work for hours. Mateo didn't paint anymore. He was a Weeper now.

"Was heading to the gallery to clean up," she said. "Is my necklace ready, by any chance?"

Yas gestured for her to come in. Marie's forehead seemed permanently creased with worry; their stars did nothing to ease her pain. Yet here she was.

"Are you planning to reopen?" Yas asked.

"More like getting ready to shut it down," Marie said. "Mateo still refuses to set foot inside."

"Oh, Marie. I'm so sorry."

Mateo had been known to close his gallery for weeks at a time without warning. When his mother had passed away two years ago, he'd shut it down for the entire summer. But now the gallery had been shuttered for over ten months. How much longer could they possibly hold on?

"Even if he *was* up for painting—who's buying?" Marie said. "Kept digging into our savings, hoping to hold on until things improved, but sometimes you have to know when to call it. Only wish he hadn't left the studio looking like a hurricane tore through it."

"He could post his art from the gallery online?" Yas suggested. "That way you're not limited to foot traffic."

"Online?" Marie chuckled. "I'm afraid Mateo's not in a place to be proactive about any of this, and I wouldn't know the first thing about that."

"There are lots of virtual galleries," Yas told her. "I can help you set up his work. We could make a landing site for him, and I can see how to cross-post them to other places. His work is powerful—I'm sure people will love it. And don't worry about the mess back there, I can help you clean it up."

Marie bit her lip, considering the offer.

"The rent's all paid up through next month," she said slowly. "It can't hurt, I suppose. I'd pay you, of course, for your assistance with picking up his studio. It's a complete disaster back there."

"That's not necessary. I'd love to help," Yas said. "Mateo was a mentor to me."

"Work is work," Marie said firmly. "And if anything *actually* sells, you'll get a commission."

Money. Out of nothing—something. Yas's heart jolted. Just like that. Here it was—a way to Lowman's. A way out.

Her mother emerged from the guest room as Yas pulled on her water boots.

"Things are shaping up nicely next door." Marie nodded toward the window.

"And it's quieter now." Her mother motioned to her temples.

"I heard the new neighbors move in this weekend."

"Not sure I'd call them neighbors," her mother replied. "It's a summer house, from what I hear."

"Someone wanting to buy it at all is *something*," Marie said. "Rumor is they're the Naismith family."

"You really think they'd come *here*?" her mother asked.

"The sea is here—and they *are* a pharmaceutical business," Marie said. "Maybe they'll revive the old factory. Ernie's beside himself. Hoping they'll settle down. Plant roots."

"Poor Ernie. Every plan he's come up with to revitalize has landed flat on its back."

"Pretty soon *he'll* be flat on his back, running in circles like he does. Poor thing."

Yas pressed the door handle and stepped onto the back porch—she'd heard a version of this a million times by now; it was all anyone who came by wanted to talk about.

The weather outside was cool. Patches of gray clouds hovered overhead. Yas rolled up her pants mid-calf before walking toward the ocean. Inky water pooled around her boots. She eased the shell catcher into the water, swiping from left to right. Her gaze shifted to the faded mural framing the pier in the distance. Mateo had painted it over a decade ago. She'd sat cross-legged and watched him for hours that summer. He even let her paint a bit of pink into the sea. It'd grown faded after last year's storm, but she remembered the curled letters of *Moonlight* splashed along the center—the illustrations of the sea and surf.

Her thoughts drifted to Marie's offer. Could she *really* earn enough to leave? And if so—would she do it? She looked at the catcher. This was her family's work. It fed them. Kept a roof over their heads for generations. Was this her father's influence seeping through? When the going got tough, she got going?

Glancing at Holler Mansion, she saw it was back to its original buttercream yellow. Unblemished Spanish tiles shone beneath the summer sun. The windows gleamed. Her chest constricted. Nearly one year ago, a boy named Moses peered out from the corner window on the second floor. Their eyes met, and everything fell apart.

They'd played as children, but he'd been in boarding school since sixth grade, and with the Hollers usually summering elsewhere during the crush of tourist season, she hadn't seen him in years. He'd looked almost unfamiliar when he stepped out to greet her, tall and muscled, with dark hair and clear blue eyes, but when his face broke into a smile, there he was.

They'd sat by the shore that afternoon, catching up. Wandered to the festival that evening. Danced near the bandstand. He tried—and hilariously failed—to win her a stuffed bear at the ringtoss booth.

Melinda was meant to watch after Sammy that evening. To

make sure he slept after she tucked him in and not sneak off in search of two teenagers who'd slipped off to the thicket of palmettos in the distance.

How had they ended up there? Yas still wasn't sure. But she remembered the moon sliced like a crescent in the sky. Her back pressed against the curved trunk of a palm tree. He'd leaned in, their foreheads touching, his lips grazing hers. She'd never done this before—kissed a boy within hours of meeting. She had no illusions of love. It wasn't love that led her to him. It's just that Moses was beautiful. Magnetic. And only here for the summer. She couldn't help herself.

Yas wished she could forget what followed: The tiny figure on the beach. The nanny's wails. Raf's stunned face—he'd been among the first to arrive. She couldn't bear to think of Moses. His frenzy. Unwilling to accept what was in front of him at first. Then the way he'd dropped to his knees. His cries filling the air. An anguished howl unlike anything she'd heard before.

No. No. Tears filled Yas's eyes. She clenched her metal pole so tight, her knuckles grew white. How long could this go on? Everywhere she turned was a memory. The screams from that night lived inside her still.

I have to leave. Yas wiped her eyes. *Maybe not forever—but for a while.* She needed a break. No one was meant to live this way every day.

Suddenly, she paused.

Something was in the distance. In the ocean.

Someone.

His hair dark and closely cropped. He wore a blue rash guard. The rough waters rose past his waist.

He held a mason jar in his hands, which he dipped into the ocean, then lifted toward the sun to examine before screwing it shut.

He looked over.

Their eyes met.

He cocked his head to the side. Then lifted a hand in greeting.

She wanted to wave back, but something inside her twisted. Her mother was the one who claimed to have premonitions. Why, then, did *she* feel a shiver, hard like the color red, run through her for no reason at all?

seven

RAF

"Out with it," Raf said once he'd locked up the diner.

"Out with *what*?" Yas put a hand on her hip and smiled.

He knew that particular smile—her eyes crinkled, her lips pressed together as if the words might spill out of their own volition.

"Hmm." He took in her faded T-shirt. Scuffed-up jeans that hugged her hips. His eyebrows shot up. "You're painting again!"

"Oh." Her smile faltered. "Not exactly."

They walked past the mostly boarded-up storefronts. As they passed the grocery store, Jake stepped out, pulling an unlit cigarette from his breast pocket. Yas visibly stiffened, her attention resolutely ahead. Thinking of Uncle, Raf tried to make eye contact with Jake, but he looked through Raf as though he wasn't there.

Why are we slowing down? Raf wondered as Yas pulled out a key and turned the lock to Mateo's gallery. Before he could ask, they were inside. Glancing around, Raf was momentarily speechless. Recessed lighting shone from above. Framed canvases hung on the walls, with images of purple surf. Sleepy sloping waves. From the outside, the shuttered buildings appeared uniformly abandoned and desolate. Inside, Mateo's gallery was a mausoleum of the past.

"I know," she said. "Felt spooked when I first stepped inside."

Her bare arm brushed against his. Raf edged away, toward the painting in front of him. Pretending her touch did nothing. That it hadn't seized his leaf.

"This style of his was always my favorite." Raf pointed to the surreal seascape. He looked back at Yas. "What's wrong?" he asked.

"Is everything okay?" She regarded him curiously.

"Yeah. Why?"

She shrugged. "It's nothing."

It was something. Of course Yas noticed how he'd moved so quickly, but he couldn't tell her why his wrist etching flickered at her touch.

"Marie hired me to clean up Mateo's studio and create a website to sell these pieces," Yas said. "Hisae said Lowman's will signal boost his work once it's online."

"Mateo's okay going digital?"

"Mateo doesn't have a say anymore."

When they stepped into the back studio, Raf let out a low whistle.

As cool, calm, and pristine as the gallery was, the back space was in shambles. Wooden shavings littered the floor. A half-painted canvas in pink and gold was perched on an easel to his left, with strewn paint cans and brushes beneath it. A paint-splattered smock hung from the wall as though Mateo had simply stepped out for a moment.

"You've got your work cut out for you," he said. "This is . . . a lot."

"As the Golub would say, it's a complete biyan." She winked at him. "On the bright side, Marie said I could take whatever I wanted, so I grabbed a few nice brushes. Paints. An unused canvas."

"So you *are* thinking of painting again!"

"I don't know about that," she said quickly. "But paint supplies are expensive. I couldn't turn her down."

"What would you paint first?"

"I just said I don't know if I will." She swatted him playfully.

"Hypothetically," he said, *"if* you were to paint, what comes to mind?"

"Hypothetically, I have no idea."

"I know!" He grinned. "What about me?"

"You?" Yas blinked.

"You never finished the portrait of me, remember? The one from when we were—"

"Nine." She raised her eyebrows. "Seriously, Raf?"

"I didn't want to make a thing out of it, but I've been waiting." He shrugged.

"Wow—you've been keeping a lot in all these years." She bit back a smile. "If I ask you to sit for me again, there better not be as much complaining as last time."

"Deal." Raf nodded solemnly.

Yas placed her hands on her hips as she eyed the mess. Here in Mateo's studio, Yas looked happy. Really and truly happy. When was the last time he'd seen her like this?

"This is the perfect gig for you," Raf said.

"Bonus, I can crash here when things get rough at home. Maybe use the sleeping bag I bought for the senior-year camping trip."

"That bad at home?"

"My parents are sniping at each other constantly, and I'm *over* it. It's getting harder and harder to be there lately. And actually . . . Raf." She stuck her hands in her pockets. "I need to tell you something."

"Uh-oh." He tensed. He knew this look too.

"Remember Hisae? Her roommate's moving out. She needs a roommate this fall."

Raf tilted his head. Understanding dawned on him. "Wait. Yas, are you . . . are you leaving?"

"No. I mean yes. Maybe?" She wiped her brow. "It's an idea right now. I haven't told anyone. Even if I actually decided to, I can't afford to go if I don't sell enough paintings."

Raf nodded. He tried to pretend this news wasn't an ice pick straight to his foundation. Yas was thinking of leaving. No. She *was* leaving. She had a plan. She was saving money. Soon, she'd be gone.

"I'm not abandoning my mom or our work or anything." Her voice wavered. "Edgewood's not a million miles away. I'll still help my mother like I always do, though it's not like she wants me around lately anyway."

"It's got to be really bad at home for leaving to even cross your mind."

"Between my parents and the endless chatter about the creepy family at Holler Mansion, I just need a break."

"Creepy? Did you meet them?"

"Sort of. It's not fair to call them creepy. I saw one of them—a boy our age, I think— in the water. The way he looked at me . . . I got a bad vibe, I guess. Anyway." She crossed her arms. "The one major perk about Edgewood is it's one exit from Surrey.

I'm not going to say it was a big part of my decision, but"—she grinned—"it was a big part of my decision."

Raf studied the wood-paneled floor. It was his turn to tell her the truth. He'd put it off long enough. "About Surrey."

"What about it?" She drew a sharp intake of breath when she saw his expression. "Raf. No."

Like a bandage.

"I decided not to go to college."

"What do you *mean*, you decided not to go?"

"It was never realistic. For starters, it's too expensive," he said. Pretending it didn't matter. Pretending she wouldn't see through him.

"That's what financial aid's for—they didn't give you any?"

"I didn't send the paperwork in."

"Let's call the admissions office. We'll tell them you changed your mind." She pulled out her phone. "There's got to be *some* way to fix this. What about Professor Singh? He's your biggest fan. I bet he could pull some strings for you."

"He came through a little while ago," Raf said, studying his feet. "He had some ideas, but, Yas, I've made my decision."

Yas's eyes brimmed with tears.

"You knew I wasn't sure."

"I hoped you'd change your mind." She touched his arm, searching his eyes. "You *need* to go."

"I *need* to work at the diner." She stood so close. He could smell the lavender scent of her hair. Gently, he disengaged.

"And the notebooks? The rolled-up blueprints?" she asked. "The sandcastles? What was all that?"

"A hobby."

"Yep." Her voice cracked. "Lots of ten-year-olds save up to

69

buy copies of *Architecture Daily*. After everything that's happened, you *deserve* to get away from here."

"They've eased off," Raf said.

"Easing off isn't good enough. You think I didn't notice how Jake looked at you? Don't you want to get away from it?"

Of course he did. College was the pathway to a dream. To what he'd once believed was his destiny. He'd also thought it was a way out for himself and his family. But Dena's hands were full with her son. Kot was gone. Staring at closed doors did not make them open.

Raf remembered a summer day when he was nine. Knee-deep in sand, creating kingdoms with Yas. Uncle had beckoned him. Over a cup of almond tea, he scooted close.

"You and Yas are close," he said.

"She's my best friend," Raf replied.

"That is wonderful. But I want you to understand something about Yas and yourself. While I'm glad you have each other, there are limits to your friendship."

"Limits?"

"Golub do not fall in love with those who are not."

Fall in love? Raf had frowned. What did that even mean?

"There are many different Golub words for love," he explained. "Our love for our children. Our parents. Our community. But the kind of love that binds two people forever, that can lead to marriage, that is the love I speak of. That cannot be. We are here in Moonlight Bay temporarily. Once Golub warms enough to safely make the journey, we'll return home. It is not our destiny to be with those who are not of our world."

Nearly a year ago, Raf decided to defy this destiny. He hadn't known what the price would be.

"Raf. Where'd you go just now?" Yas watched him expectantly.

"Nowhere." Raf affixed a smile. He said the words he needed to. He'd thought this over carefully. It was the right decision. It was fine. Really.

And he told her he was happy for her—because he was—a break sounded like exactly what she needed. Tolki Uncle would say this separation was the best thing for Raf as well. The universe sorting itself out. But after all those years planning, hoping, and dreaming about what their futures would look like, it was Raf who would stay. It was Yas who would leave.

eight
YAS

Ankle-deep in the water, Yas tossed her catcher into the sea. Cold water lapped against her boots, but she'd take this in a heartbeat over the iciness of home.

Just a few moments earlier, she had been in her kitchen while her mother sat at the counter silently scrolling her laptop.

"I'm sorry," Yas had said into the stillness.

Her mother's fingers tapped on the keyboard.

"Are you never going to talk to me again?" Yas tried to keep her voice from cracking.

"Yas." Her mother looked up. Dark circles framed her eyes. "Do you believe the slightest bit in what we do?"

Yas had studied her chipped nail polish. Seashells were her earliest memories. Star making was part of her DNA. She'd loved snipping them into shape, sanding down the edges. Looping and knotting the cords. Seeing the relief on people's faces when they clasped them around their necks. There was a time she'd believed in it as firmly as she knew the sun rose in the east and set in the west. At first, after the seas grayed, she'd worn her necklace constantly, praying for ease. Ease never came.

"Mom. Does it seem like anyone's troubles are at bay here?"

"The stars *soothe* bruised hearts. They can't erase one's troubles. They can't wash away all grief. They never could."

Except Yas's memories told her otherwise. She'd seen how Lisa had walked through the door two years earlier, her face streaked with mascara after her husband announced he had fallen in love with someone else. Days later, the star woven with golden thread and strung around her neck, Lisa had smiled. A true smile that reached her eyes.

Now Yas wondered: Had it always been a trick of the mind? Was her family business a sleight of hand which, in the face of the tragedy that slammed Moonlight Bay, had been revealed for the chicanery it was?

When Yas met her mother's eyes, they were moist.

"It's all right, Yas. I'm processing." She returned her attention to the laptop. The conversation was over.

Yas looked at the faded mural in the distance. She'd been helping out at the gallery for three days, with twenty-five dollars to show for it. At this rate she'd be thirty before she could afford to move out. With one hand on the catcher, Yas pulled out her phone with the other. She swiped to the proto-website. White with black font. Mateo's name in a swirl across the top center. She'd photograph the art this afternoon.

Yas texted Raf the link. Feedback? she asked, hitting send.

There was so much more to say to him. His revelation still reverberated within her. How could he not go to college? How could he blow it off like she didn't know better than anyone how much this mattered to him?

I'll head to the diner before I go to the gallery, she decided. *I'll talk to him.* There had to be a way to change his mind.

Yas clicked to Moses's social media feed. It was as frozen as it had been yesterday, the day before that, and the one before. It'd been frozen for nearly a year. A photo with his cross-country team. A selfie with Sammy. Then, the final one. A snapshot of blue skies and leafy palms from the morning of the festival. He'd never updated his feed again. She longed to reach out. A simple click. A comment. To see how he was. To apologize. But what would that do? Nothing she said would change what happened.

Their porch door creaked behind her. Her father stepped onto the deck. An overstuffed gym bag hoisted over his shoulder.

"Yas," he called out. "Was looking for you."

She walked toward him. "You're leaving already?"

"Training starts tomorrow," he said. "I have to figure out my lodging situation too. Figured I'd get up and at 'em earlier than later."

"Dad. You don't have to do this."

"Yas—"

"I know things are tight," Yas interrupted. "But we're hanging in there, aren't we? Our work is getting us by."

"This is hard for all of us," he said. "I'm sorry. I wish there was another way. I do." He kissed her forehead. "I'll call as soon as I reach Yaksta."

A few moments later, the engine grumbled to life. The car disappeared from view. He was gone. *How can I be mad at him for leaving,* she thought, *when I'm trying to do the same?*

But she *was* mad. He was her father. And he was washing his hands of Moonlight Bay.

She turned to look at the mural again. Tilting her head, an idea began to form. Mateo created that mural, but *she* could touch it up, couldn't she? His paints could restore it. Before she left Moonlight, this could be a tangible way to fix this broken town just the littlest bit.

"What're you doing?"

The boy she'd seen the other day with the mason jar. He stood steps away. His pants dark and damp, folded to his calves. Up close, he looked taller—so tall he towered over her. How long had he been standing there?

"Fishing?" He nodded to the catcher. "Saw you earlier by the shore. You'd have to go way deeper to catch anything, and the current's sneaky. Knocked me down when I waded in the other day."

"Not fishing," she said. "Collecting shells."

"Shells? Gearing up for arts and crafts?"

His lips curled the slightest bit. Amusement danced in his eyes.

Yas tightened her jaw. "I'd say it's none of your business what I'm doing."

"Whoa. No need to be so sensitive." He raised his palms. "I wouldn't blame you. Choices are limited in this cesspool."

"Cesspool," she repeated. "Got it."

"Hey, wait. I'm sorry," he said as Yas slipped past him. "I was only joking."

It's always a joke when the words don't land the way people want them to, she thought.

"I didn't mean to get off on a bad note." He jogged until he was next to her. "Sorry. That *was* rude."

They walked quietly side by side, and then he tried again. "I'm Warren."

"Yas," she said in a clipped voice.

"I saw you the other day. In the water."

Yas didn't want to have small talk. She wanted to go home and lock the door behind her. But he kept walking alongside her. Yas gritted her teeth. *He apologized, didn't he? He's only trying to make conversation.*

"I collect shells for my family's business."

"There's a market for dredged-out seashells?"

Her eyes narrowed, but his expression was neutral, curious even.

"The shells collected from this stretch of sea had . . . *have* certain properties, and . . ." She hesitated. "We work with them."

"Heard about the water. Supposed to have something to it, right?" He looked doubtfully at the gray expanding into the horizon. "Not trying to offend you, I promise. It doesn't look too magical if you ask me."

"If wielded properly," she said, repeating the words she'd said and heard so many times before, "it's believed the shells can soothe anxious hearts."

"Those people must be *super* anxious." He pointed toward the Weepers. "They're *always* out there."

Anxious was a good way to describe them, thought Yas. Even before everything changed.

"Why are you in Moonlight?" she asked him.

"Why does any seventeen-year-old get dragged where they'd rather not be?" He shrugged.

"Are you a Naismith?"

"I guess word gets around in small towns."

So it's true. Yas tried not to look surprised.

"Listen, sorry again. I think lack of contact with the outside world for days got my brain all mixed up, and I'm not good at small talk even on a good day."

"I get it," she managed to reply.

She watched him leave. His hands in his pockets.

Pulling out her phone, she texted Raf again.

> Met neighbor. They really are the pharma folks.

His response was immediate.

> Is he cool?

> Remains to be seen.

It was entirely possible Warren's apology was genuine, but as she watched him vanish behind the wrought-iron gate, her shoulders softened. She was grateful to be out of his presence.

nine
RAF

"Sama," Raf said—the greeting for the departed—as he approached his father's gravestone. It was still early morning, the grass beneath his feet wet with dew.

He knelt before the headstone and wiped away the thin sheen of pollen. He removed the wilting roses and laid down new ones. Yellow—his father's favorite. Settling next to him, Raf pulled his knees to his chest. Birdsong sounded through the forest. Red flowers bloomed wild across from him. Yas's favorite. He'd clip some and take them to her in apology after. A *sorry for not going to Surrey* offering. She'd looked as crushed as he'd felt. Everything settled and done felt untangled and raw once more. He needed to speak with his father.

"Professor Singh texted me last night," Raf told him. "He wanted to know if I had given any more thought to Surrey."

He shook his head. Had he given it more thought? Raf was *full* of thoughts. Thoughts that slammed against one another, refusing to quiet. What good were second chances if you couldn't take them in the first place?

"Part of me feels like this is a sign," Raf continued. "Except I know that our family, Tolki Uncle, and the diner, they all need me here. Yesterday, I caulked Dena's leaking windows.

Everyone needs me. So how do I go? Sometimes I think you'd be proud of me. That you'd tell me to follow my dreams. Other times I'm pretty sure you'd wonder what was wrong with me for wanting any of it in the first place." He pressed a palm against the gray stone. "Why can't you be here?" His voice caught. "Why can't you tell me what the right answer is?"

He sat quietly beneath the tree canopy for a moment longer. There were no answers his father could give, but as always, telling him eased his heart.

The smell of coffee and saffron tea wafted over from the windows as Raf walked home. He saw Tolki Uncle in the forest, by the stone encirclement, speaking with Mac and Louk. They listened with rapt attention, no doubt hearing stories of Golub, just as Raf had at their age. He smiled at them. He missed his father so much—but he was grateful Tolki Uncle was here. Looking out for them all.

"Raf?" his mother called through the open window.

She slipped on her shoes as he stepped into the foyer.

"Work *today*? It's Sunday," he said.

"Took an extra drape order," she replied. "Can you watch the kids for a few until Dar's back from the doctor?"

"Of course. Dena can open."

"Almost forgot." She pulled her note inscribed on a Golub leaf from the table and handed it to him. "Don't forget yours. Nara didn't put hers up yet either. How is she? I haven't had a chance to swing by to check on her."

"All right as can be."

"Takes time. Even then, look at Tolki and his own daughter. You don't ever truly move on."

She was right. Nara's pain was the most recent, the one he

was bearing witness to firsthand, but she wasn't alone in her grief. And if Raf felt burdened, Uncle carried the weight of the entire community while also nursing his own sorrow.

"I keep telling Nara not to lose hope," said Raf. "But it's been over a month. Maybe everyone can add an additional prayer leaf for Kot. We can devote a few branches to him. Might help Nara see we're all behind her."

"That is a wonderful idea." His mother hugged him. "She's lucky she has you watching out for her. *We* are lucky. You've been running the diner since high school, helping Uncle keep track of Golub finances. Working with the boys on their homework, keeping me from losing my mind. I don't know what we'd do without you."

I don't know what we'd do without you.

Raf shivered. He'd been by his father's side moments earlier. He'd asked for an answer. This was it, wasn't it? There was nothing Raf could say to counter this. She was right.

Reaching the diner later that morning, for a fraction of a second Raf wondered if he'd conjured up the image before him, because it was one he so desperately wanted to see: The diner was full.

Ernie was parked at his usual booth overlooking the main drag. His elbows rested on the table as he conferred with his fellow council members. Kendall was in the corner, nursing his coffee. Fanned at tables around them were people who never frequented the diner anymore. Today they drank coffee and ate waffles.

"But if we come across too strong, we'll seem desperate!"

Bea, one of the councilpeople, shouted. The chatter in the diner grew quiet.

"But we *are* desperate!" Ernie protested. He glanced around and lowered his voice.

Ah, Raf realized. These townspeople were here not for honey-drenched waffles and raspberry jam toast. They wanted front-row seats to Ernie and the council members to glean information on the newest residents in town. But if gossip filled up the seats, he'd take it.

Grabbing a pot of coffee, he refilled empty mugs. Outside the window, a group of children raced toward Main Street Park. He winced as the youngest ones scrambled into one of the rickety Ferris wheel buckets. In summers past, the lines to ride the golden wheel stretched around the block, with tourists clamoring to reach its full height and glimpse the full expanse of the sea, where the shimmering colors met the deep blue in the distance.

In the off-season, Jerry let the kids ride for a dollar. Raf and Yas spent countless afternoons going for a spin with the other kids in town. They'd make up elaborate games of catch, dropping a ball from bucket to bucket, waiting to see who broke the chain.

These kids would never have such memories. These rusty buckets, this tilted wheel—this was their reality.

A car engine's loud hum sounded outside. A Jeep pulled into view. It parked by the curb next to Willow Forest. A woman hopped out of the driver's side. She was waif thin, with steel-colored stripes streaked through her waist-length hair. A dark messenger bag was slung across her shoulders. With swiftness of purpose, she marched straight toward the forest. His forest.

Raf tensed. In the before times, tourists often wandered in: children playing hide-and-seek, couples seeking a quiet respite on days the beach was uncomfortably crammed. But this woman—Raf could sense it—wasn't a tourist.

He moved toward the door to offer his help. Before he could open it, a figure rushed out of the forest. Straight toward the woman. Tolki Uncle. Raf had never seen him move so fast. His face was blotchy.

Opening the door, he heard Uncle shout, "Go! Now!"

The woman stopped walking. She crossed her arms and tilted her head. She was speaking angrily. Raf strained to hear but could not make out her words. Raf saw how Uncle looked at her. His face was pale. *He needs help.* Raf moved toward them, but then he paused. The woman's profile. The curve of her nose, her arched eyebrows forming a perfectly rounded letter *m*. Was this woman Uncle's daughter, Shar? What was she doing here? Why would she show up now? And—

His heart hammered in his chest. She'd left the safety perimeter. She'd lost her leaf. Uncle couldn't be within speaking distance. Right now they stood only a few feet apart. Raf edged closer.

"Well, happy birthday *again*!" he heard her say. "See you next year, *again*."

The woman stalked off. She got into her Jeep—the engine rumbled. She was gone. But he'd seen her expression when she'd turned—she didn't seem angry. She looked hurt.

Uncle stared at the empty road. When he turned, his eyes locked onto Raf's. Before Raf could take a step toward him,

Uncle raised a hand and shook his head. He walked back to the forest.

See you next year.

Again.

This wasn't the first time the woman had come. And it wouldn't be the last. But she couldn't have been his daughter. Shar had lost her leaf. And lost leaves were contagious. He'd never take such a risk. But staring at the empty space, Raf's heart raced—who else could it be?

ten

YAS

"I have news!" Yas sang out as soon as Marie stepped into the studio that morning.

Seeing Yas's expression, Marie raised a hand to her mouth. "Did one of the pieces *sell*?"

Yas gestured to her laptop. "I was cleaning up the back studio when I got a notification." She pointed to the piece directly across from them. "*Bay of Sunrise* sold!"

Marie hurried toward her to peer over Yas's shoulder.

"Yas . . . this is . . . this is incredible."

"Lowman's shared it on their platforms. They made a huge deal about how Mateo's work has never been available online until now—it got lots of traction after that. I can't wait until the buyer *gets* the piece," Yas said. "It's even more brilliant in person."

Marie clasped her hands together. "I figured it wouldn't hurt to try something new, but this was so fast! *Bay of Sunrise* is our most expensive piece."

"I found packaging paper while I was cleaning up," Yas said. "Happy to send it off for you."

"That would be wonderful," Marie said, recovering. "And as you know, you get a twenty percent commission for this."

Yas fidgeted. She knew Marie had mentioned a commission, but it wasn't as though Marie had money to spare.

"This is a professional gallery," said Marie, reading her expression. "A commission is your due. Besides, without you, we wouldn't have sold a thing."

Yas's heart fluttered; 20 percent was $350. "Wow, Marie," she managed to say. "Thank you."

"No, thank *you*, Yas." Marie's eyes glistened. "You're saving us. Really and truly."

Yas swung by the diner later that day to share the news.

"Congrats!" Raf exclaimed. "Was there ever any doubt you'd pull it off?"

"Plenty!" she retorted. "This wasn't a sure thing at all!"

"With you behind the wheel, it was." He grinned. "Marie must be relieved."

"Can you believe it, Raf? If I sell four or five more, I'll have enough."

"You're on your way. Weird for me to root for you to leave. But I am."

"Edgewood isn't far." Yas's smile faltered. "We'll see each other plenty."

But not like this. Not the seamless way they were melded into each other's lives like sand and sea. Yas studied the laminate countertop. Having hundreds of dollars newly to her name was exhilarating, but as the thrill wore off, reality swiftly kicked in. Edgewood was becoming real. Which meant she'd have to tell her family. Pack. She'd have to leave Moonlight. And Raf.

"What's the matter?" Raf asked.

"I don't know how to explain it." She shrugged. "I don't *want* to want to go. Hisae and everyone were plotting their departures since freshman year, but I always wanted to stay."

"You said it yourself, you need a break."

"If I deserve a break, don't you deserve one?"

"It's different for me."

"Raf. I know everyone relies on you." She leaned forward. "But what about you? Don't *you* need you?"

"I went to my father's grave to talk things out," he told her. "He'd want me to be where I'm needed."

"I knew your dad. He bought you your sketchbooks. Telling you to stay when you *want* to go to school? Doesn't sound like him." She hesitated. "It *does* sound like something Tolki Uncle would say."

"Yas," he sighed.

"I know you care about him. He's sweet. But . . . he puts too much on you. You know that."

"It's complicated. I've made my peace with it, though."

But he hadn't. She saw from his practiced nonchalance he was anything but at peace.

Before she could protest, Raf gave her a small smile.

"Haven't made peace with losing you, though."

She met his eyes. There it was again. He hadn't even touched her. This time, words alone made her body feel like a live wire.

"Nah," she said as lightheartedly as possible. "You won't get rid of me *that* easily."

Yas practically swayed as she walked home. Marie's smile, the sale and promise of sales to come, filled her with warmth. And Raf—seeing Raf always made her happy, didn't it? But her warm feelings vanished when she opened her front door. Her parents faced off in the family room.

"You're back for a night and want to call the shots?" her mother said angrily.

"I'm here for the weekend, and I'm trying to *help*." Her father's face was beet red. His eyes bright. "I am trying my hardest to help this family out."

"*This* family—as you put it—is *your* family."

"So we're playing word games now?"

Their words were darts laced with anger. They didn't notice Yas standing with the door ajar, steps away. She knew this argument practically verbatim. In the early days, it was the same back-and-forth, on repeat: They needed to cut their losses and move (her father). They could never leave—this was their home, their work, their life (her mother).

Now they lived three hundred miles apart. They each got what they wanted. Even still, they were angry. Looking at them, it was hard to imagine these two people had ever loved each other at all.

"Can you both *stop*?" Yas asked. "Even for a second?"

"Yas." Her mother abruptly turned toward her.

Her father's eyes widened. "We didn't see you there."

Yas closed the door and walked toward them. They had to make a truce. *We can't keep going on like this.*

Before she could speak, the doorbell screeched.

"Don't answer it," Yas said. "Please. We need to talk. Whoever it is, they can come back later."

Her mother wiped her eyes with the sleeve of her cardigan. Wind chimes sounded from the front porch when she opened the door.

"Olive," Yas's mother exclaimed.

"Sorry to bother." Their arms were wrapped around themself as though shivering. "Could use the star if it's ready, what with it being delayed a week."

"Finished last night," Yas's mother said, ushering them inside. Her father moved to the kitchen, pulling out a tin of teas.

Nothing to see here, Yas thought bitterly. *All is as it should be.*

Olive's eyes lit up at the sight of the square box imprinted with a stamped star Yas's mother brought over. Clasping the necklace, they closed their eyes and exhaled. "Better."

As soon as the door closed behind them, the doorbell rang again.

"What now?" Yas's mother murmured.

But it wasn't a customer this time. It was Ernie. He practically stumbled through the door as soon as Yas's mother opened it, carrying a wicker basket filled with chocolates.

"Thank God you're home," Ernie breathed out.

"Everything okay?" her father asked.

"Yes, yes," Ernie said. He walked to their sofa and sank into it, his arms wrapped around the basket like it was his favorite toy. His forehead was coated with sweat. "I came as soon as I could. I need to talk to Yas."

"Me?" Yas blinked.

"I heard from someone that you and the boy next door— you've become friendly?"

"Who told you that?"

"Have you spoken with him?" Ernie asked.

Yas rolled her eyes. Of course their tense exchange had been witnessed by someone and churned through the gossip mill, wringing out a tale of friendship. Of course.

"We spoke the other day," Yas said. "I wouldn't say we were friendly."

"Did he . . . did he say anything?" Ernie asked.

"About what?"

"Anything could be helpful. Their plans? Early impressions of the town?"

Cesspool. That's what his impression was. Looking at Ernie's earnest face, there was no way she'd ever tell him.

"He didn't say much," she said instead.

"Ernie," her mother said. "They're next door. Introduce yourself and ask them. You *are* the mayor."

"I tried." He gestured to the gift basket in his lap. "No answer. If they . . . if they stayed, they could change everything. They're the Naismiths."

"So the rumors are true?" her mother asked.

"Indeed. The pharmaceutical magnates themselves." Ernie nodded. "If they fell in love with our town, wouldn't it be perfect? The factory's *right* there. Needs a little spit and shine, but it could be put to use again. They're here for the water, right? Everyone's eager to get back to work. A more enthusiastic crew of workers they'll never find. This could save us."

"Do you think they'd come for the water?" Yas said doubtfully. "No offense, but it's not the same, Ernie."

"Yas." Her mother shot her a look.

"For people like them, it doesn't matter," Ernie said. "They swoop in when the market is low. Besides, the water isn't done—look at your mother's necklaces. Soon enough, it'll be back, stronger than ever. If we could charm them into staying, show them this is a place worth investing in, we could bring Moonlight Bay back to life. Tourism is done for." His shoulders slumped.

"Getting back to the manufacturing side is our only hope."

Ernie ran a hand through his salt-and-pepper hair. He was always so upbeat and energetic, but the light seemed to have gone out in his eyes. He seemed a decade older. Was the other Ernie, the one she saw most days, pretending?

"I aim to do whatever I can on my end," he continued. "But, Yas, we need your help. Their son. He's right about your age. Would be the most natural thing in the world for you to befriend him."

"Ernie." Her mother raised an eyebrow.

"That came out wrong," he rushed to say. "All I mean is, let's make him feel welcome. If you find out a bit about their plans or how we might make this town a keeper for them, let us know?"

"You want me to spy on him?" Yas asked incredulously.

"Since when did friendliness become spying?" Ernie chuckled. "Not asking you to interrogate the boy, but if in the course of being neighborly you learn some things that might help us figure out how best to get them to stay, it can't hurt. Maybe give him a tour? Talk up our small-town charm. I understand it's an unconventional request, but desperate times . . ."

Yas tried not to roll her eyes. She liked Ernie. Who didn't? But asking her to hang out with *Warren*? To sell him on the town she wanted to leave? She'd never been able to hide her feelings and she wasn't about to start trying now. Before she could respond, her mother spoke.

"Of course, Ernie. She'll do it."

What?

"Ernie . . ." Her father cleared his throat.

He was about to undercut her mother, and for the first time, Yas was grateful. *This is my choice. Not anyone else's.*

"Whatever we can do to help, count us in." Her father placed an arm around her mother's shoulders.

Ernie clasped his hands. "Yas, I owe you one. Really and truly, I surely do."

Standing, he balanced the basket in his arms. Her parents walked him to the door. Her father's arm still draped over her mother's shoulders.

As soon as it shut, his arm slipped away. Yas exploded.

"How could you volunteer me?" she spat out.

"I know it's an odd request, but the town needs you," her mother said. "He's right—manufacturing coming back could change everything. What Ernie is asking for is not the end of the world."

"The boy *is* your neighbor," her father said sheepishly. "All he's asking of you is to be friendly."

"*Now* you're both on the same page?" Yas folded her arms. "It's true. I met Warren the other day. He called Moonlight Bay a cesspool."

"All the more reason to befriend him," her mother said, unfazed. "Ernie wouldn't ask if he didn't truly need your help. Maybe by showing him some Moonlight hospitality, Warren could correct his misconception."

"I'm never going to like him!"

"Then pretend!" her mother snapped. "Honestly, Yasmine, it's not complicated."

"Got it. Be fake. Like you."

Her mother's expression fell.

"Yas," her father began.

"When someone knocks on the door, you're happy as can be together. As soon as they leave, you're back to *this*."

"It's not as simple as you make it out to be," her mother said.

"Not *that* hard to understand either," her father said. "People turn to your mother for comfort in difficult times."

"The work we do is important." Her mother nodded. "People won't trust us for peace when we have no peace."

So this is how it's going to be? thought Yas. Hot and cold. Tension and arguments, or distance and silence—or this third option: pretending all was well. Yas thought of the painting that had just sold; it brought her a step closer to leaving. To freedom. She was making the right decision.

eleven
RAF

"I have an idea," Yas said.

"Uh-oh." Raf took a sip of coffee. Save Kendall sitting by the window, the diner was in its usual late-afternoon lull.

"Hear me out! I'm heading to the gallery to package up an art piece—"

"You sold another one!" Raf exclaimed.

"Sold *two* more." She grinned. "I can't believe it. I know his work is incredible, but it *is* expensive."

"Not everyone's as broke as we are, I guess."

"Wonder what that's like. To scroll online and see a painting and go, 'Sure, my wall could use something that's the equivalent of two months' rent.'"

"That's got to be a relief for Marie."

"The specialty courier's not far from Edgewood. Come with? Diner's closed tomorrow, right? We could see Hisae's place and you could give me a second opinion." She grinned. "We could also check out other places too."

"Bura's got the truck tomorrow."

"Next Wednesday, then? With the way things are going, there'll be other parcels to send off."

"I . . . I'll check my schedule," he said. "But, Yas, I'm not going to stop by Surrey. All things considered, working at the diner is not that bad. It's fine."

"Not that bad?" Yas said with exasperation. "Is that what you dreamed of? A *not that bad* life? Raf—it's *me* you're talking to."

Raf sighed. How could he convince her when he couldn't convince himself?

"Hey." Yas swung around the counter. "I didn't mean to upset you," she said quickly. "It's just . . . you've talked my ear off about it since fifth grade. Remember the model town we made? Everyone was done in a day with their assigned building—you worked on it for weeks! I want you to do what you love because I want to see you happy. You deserve to be happy."

"I know, Yas. It's all right."

"I won't bring it up again." She bit her lip. "I don't want to be the reason you look this sad."

"You're looking out." He forced a smile. "I'd do the same."

Raf paced the nearly empty diner after Yas left. Dark clouds gathered overhead. Was it the absence of sunlight leaving him unsettled? The conversation with Yas? Or the vacant restaurant leaving too much space to stir up thoughts he'd rather not dwell upon?

He thought of Uncle and the mysterious woman last week. His leaf was fully intact at dinner that night, so it couldn't have been his daughter. But she'd wished him a happy birthday. Save the young who insisted on celebrating after picking up the habit from school friends, birthdays went unacknowledged in Golub. He had no idea it was Uncle's birthday. Who else but one's own child would remember that? Raf had approached Uncle after their meal that evening, and the following evenings, hoping for a moment alone, but each time Uncle had insisted upon a rain check—there were pressing matters surrounding the Hamra gathering. Tonight, Raf hoped, they'd speak.

Raf pulled out a spiral notebook from a drawer beneath the counter. A slow afternoon didn't mean he sat around—there were fridges to scrub, fryers to soak. Squeaky ice machines to fix. He could knock out a list of things to do so the day wasn't spent entirely in vain.

The front door chimed. It was Dena.

"Checking in on you," she said. "You've been here since open. Again."

"It wasn't bad," he said. "Fio better now?"

"He's fine." Dena rolled her eyes. "Gets into his moods, but Dar is with him now."

Raf thought of the woman in the Jeep. If anyone else caught wind of the encounter, it'd be Dena.

"Random question for you. Uncle never talks about Shar," Raf said. "Is it true she left the perimeter and never returned?"

"That *is* random indeed."

"Kot leaving the way he did got me thinking."

"None of us were around back then," she said. "Uncle said she stormed off after a quarrel."

"What sort of disagreement did they have?"

"From what I've heard, she had a thirst to see the world—to roam far and wide. Leaf be damned."

"So she *did* lose her leaf."

"It's just talk," she said. "Uncle's too broken up to get into the details, but it's probably why Kot and him had so many disagreements."

"Disagreements?" Raf frowned.

"You know Kot and his ideas." Dena shrugged. "He went on and on about his whole theory that perhaps we *could* go beyond the safety zone—stretch it, like a muscle—maybe the more we did, it could grow and expand."

"He never mentioned it to me," Raf said.

"No? That's right." She nodded. "Because of your closeness with Tolki, he probably didn't want to put you in an awkward position."

Raf gripped the counter. *My closeness with Tolki Uncle made Kot keep things from me?* What else did Raf not know?

What if Kot *had* taken a page from Uncle's daughter? What if he *didn't* return to Golub? What if he was out there somewhere? Wandering and alone?

"Easy, Raf," Dena said, reading his mind. "We know what happened. We saw the leaves—the fallen branches."

He nodded. He remembered that early dawn morning as clear as though it'd happened yesterday.

"I think some of us simply *wish* it was otherwise," said Dena.

Raf stared at her. "You'd rather he'd have wandered away and *lost* his leaf?"

"Then we could take comfort in knowing he was alive. Returning to Golub these days? I can't imagine it."

"I know Uncle's confident we'll go home. But . . ." Raf had never said this aloud. "Do you ever wonder if that'll actually happen?"

"Raf," she said. "All the time."

He wasn't alone in his misgivings. How many others felt this way too?

They were silent for a few moments; then Dena placed a hand on his shoulder. "All right. Time for you to go." Raf laughed, but Dena looked at him solemnly. "I'm serious. Dar is watching Fio." She waved at the near-empty room. "I can handle the throngs."

"I was going to check the leak in the fridge. I found a video on how to unclog the drain."

"Great, send it to me. I'll give it a go."

"Dena—"

"If I can't manage it, it can wait one more day." She took him by the elbow and ushered him toward the door. "You've worked ten-hour days for weeks. This cannot go on."

He tried protesting, but Dena cut him off. "Go be a teenager. You do a great job running the diner, but it's not healthy to be at this from open to close every single day. If you want to help, come back to help me close in a few hours, okay? See how generous I can be?"

"What am I supposed to do?"

"Read a book? Take a nap? Count the grains of sand on the beach? I don't know, Raf—but I trust you can figure something out."

Raf was the de facto head of the diner, but there was no arguing with Dena right now. The bells chimed overhead as he stepped outside. Salty air brushed against his face. Wind whistled through the trees of Willow Forest. Dark clouds moved briskly above. Raf pressed his back against the wall. A wave of exhaustion swept over him.

Now what?

This sudden pressing of the brakes threw his body off-kilter. Without tables to bus, windows to clean—with nothing to do—three words echoed in his mind. Three words he tried so hard to push away.

This is it.

Flipping the diner's CLOSED sign to OPEN. Cutting vegetables. Greeting customers. Wiping down menus. Busing tables. Hour after hour. High school was over, and this was his life. Day after day of sameness stretching into the horizon. And Uncle probably intended for him to take his place as leader of Willow Forest, didn't he? Until . . . when? They returned to Golub? All this sacrifice to hold on to a shred of hope that they'd return, a plan that Dena, at least, didn't believe would ever really happen either.

Raf traced a hand against his wrist. Kot had lived here less than a year and had questioned everything. Why hadn't *Raf* ever wondered about his etching? He'd never so much as stepped a toe past the safety perimeter.

He wandered to the parking lot at the back of the diner. He came here multiple times a day to deposit a new trash bag into the enormous green receptacle. But—he looked at their silver truck—when was the last time he'd taken it for a spin? When was the last time he did something *just because*?

Pulling out his keys, he walked toward it. His heart pounded. *Stop thinking. Stop thinking. All you do is think.*

In two seconds, he was in. The engine hummed. Moments later, he pulled out of the parking lot. Forty miles. He'd drive just past it. Just to see. Just to feel how it worked. It took time for the leaf to shout its warning. Hours for it to fade.

His breathing grew shallow as the odometer ticked higher and higher. The welcome board for Moonlight in his rearview, he braced himself for a call. For Uncle to sense something amiss. Familiar neighboring towns appeared every ten minutes. Ridgeview, with the enormous movie theater. Bennettsville, with the Shoe Depot his mother brought them to for new sneakers. Then Lipon. The last city.

The odometer climbed. Thirty-eight miles. Thirty-nine. Then, forty. A rush passed through him. He was on the other side. His leaf was still silent. Would it . . . ?

A burning sensation flashed through him. Raf gasped. As though on cue, his leaf flickered. Raf hit the brakes. The tires screeched. He pulled over to the side of the road. The terrain to his left was rocky. Bluffs overlooked a raging sea.

He leaned back against the car seat, breathing heavily. The leaf had illuminated. And it didn't send a gentle warming—it burned. Tolki Uncle's words echoed in his mind: *The leaf protects—it does so at all costs.* If Kot left the safety perimeter, it would've done the same to him. Reminded him how far he'd gone, and told him to turn back. He wouldn't have kept going if he felt this. He wouldn't have done that to Nara—risk losing his family and community forever.

How could he have even doubted it for a moment, when he'd been among the first to hear Uncle's cries the night Kot disappeared? The tree had been disturbed. There had been unmistakable signs of an opening.

Raf stared at his expression in the rearview mirror. He'd come all this way—why? Driven by rumors and idle chatter?

Or was it Surrey? Because even though he had told Yas that Surrey wasn't happening, when he closed his eyes and slept, all his dreams were about that university. Pulling up the truck filled with his belongings. Settling into a dorm. Walking across the campus. Deep down in the recesses of his mind, he was working himself into a pretzel trying to see if there *was* a way. That's what brought about this experiment, wasn't it?

Raf pulled out his phone.

Thanks for thinking of me, Raf texted Professor Singh. Please post the job. Unfortunately, I can't do it.

There. It was done. A chapter closed. But closure, Raf now understood as he drove home, did not always bring peace.

Save Kendall, the diner remained empty when Raf stepped in later that afternoon.

"My turn to kick *you* out," he teased Dena.

"There are only ten minutes left until closing," Dena said. "You have *got* to give this place a break. Get some hobbies."

"I added a new shoe rack to the Jugnus' entry two days ago!"

"Raf." She rolled her eyes. "I think we need to go over what the definition of a hobby is."

"Fine. I'll work on it, okay?" He smiled. "But I'm here now. Let me deal with the register and put up the chairs."

"You're really something," she told him. "We appreciate your drive, but try to relax once in a while—you're going to burn out."

"I'll take more breaks," he promised.

The bells above the doorway jangled when she left. Raf opened the register to count the till. A few moments later, the front door chimed again.

Warren. The boy from Holler Mansion. At least, Raf was pretty sure it was him, since he'd never seen this person before.

"This place closed?" Warren asked.

Raf looked at the clock. Almost. But he was a customer, and money was money. Besides, after Yas's blunt critique of him, he was curious.

"Come on in." Raf picked up a menu. "Lucky for you, you have the whole diner to yourself, so take a seat wherever you'd like."

"Counter's great." He settled down across from Raf and studied the menu. "What are the popular items?"

"We're known for our pancakes," Raf said. "Coffee's not bad either. I could whip up just about anything on the menu, except spinach quiche. We're out of spinach."

"Coffee sounds great." He shut the menu. "I'm not too hungry."

"To go?" Raf leaned down to grab a paper cup.

"Nah," Warren replied. "Doesn't taste the same."

"That's true." He poured Warren a cup and busied himself with the register.

Warren took a sip. "This coffee's great," he said. "Are the beans from the Suma region?"

"Yes." Raf tried not to look surprised. After what Yas told him, he'd expected insults, not praise.

"Any other good eats around here?" Warren asked. "Not much seems open."

"We're the only eatery in town. We *used* to be a big foodie destination, though. A great ice cream shop. A specialty fudge stand by the park. During the festival, there was more *food* than people . . ." Raf trailed off. Why was he rambling? Warren didn't need to hear all this. Except—Warren seemed genuinely interested.

"Festival sounds cool," Warren said. "When is it?"

"Oh . . . I don't see that happening this year." Raf tried to find something positive to say. "We *do* have a decent movie theater," he told him. "Gil and Finn don't change out the selection very often, but the popcorn is top-notch, and Finn makes great salty-sweet pretzels you won't find anywhere else. Otherwise, Ridgeview isn't far—they've got tons to do there. Good restaurants too."

"If your food here is as good as this coffee"—Warren nodded to the mug—"this diner'll be enough for me."

This was the same guy who'd insulted their town a few days ago? It was like Yas had described someone else entirely.

"We're only here a couple more weeks," Warren added. "I'll live."

The front door jangled. It was Ernie.

"Hello, you two!" In five long strides he was at the counter, settling onto the stool next to Warren. "I'll have what he's having." Ernie winked at Warren. "I don't believe we've met yet. I'm Ernie. The mayor. You must be Warren." He pumped Warren's hand vigorously. "Pleasure to make your acquaintance. Rang your house a little while ago. Wanted to welcome you and your folks to town personally. See if I can help with anything."

"My parents are out of town," Warren replied. "They'll be back tonight."

"I'll be sure to make time to swing by first thing tomorrow, then!"

Poor Ernie. Time was something he had plenty of these days.

"How are you liking it here?" Ernie asked. "Whatever we can do to make your stay more pleasant, say the word."

Raf winced. Ernie was a lot like the diner—a long-established part of this town. He'd been mayor since before Raf arrived, and it was hard to imagine anyone who would love this town with the devotion he did. Yet seeing him like this—the desperation leaking out of him—was painful.

The front door sounded. Raf froze. Was he seeing things?

Jake stood at the entrance with his wife, Skyler, who held their eighteen-month-old son, Ozzy. What was *Jake* doing here?

"Coffee," Jake said when Raf approached him.

Jake wanted to be served a cup of coffee inside *their* diner? Before he could respond, the front door chimed again. Crissy walked in. He followed her gaze, which was focused on Warren at the counter.

Warren drew them here. Their curiosity so intense, they were willing to enter the establishment they'd tried shutting down more than once since the seas grayed.

Raf gritted his teeth. He wanted the satisfaction of telling them he was allowed to deny service to anyone for any reason, and that he had more than a few reasons to see them out the door. But he held his tongue. He knew what Uncle would say.

Raf handed them menus and seated them at a booth as the door swung open again. And again. And again. Within minutes, half the diner was full.

Warren, it appeared, was good for business.

"Well, thanks again." Warren slid a twenty-dollar bill across the counter. "Keep the change. It was nice to meet you."

"Wow. Thanks. And likewise," replied Raf.

The crowd watched silently as he left. They waited for the door to properly shut behind him. Then—

"What did he say?" Bea said from her window seat.

"Are they visiting? Or planning to make it permanent?" asked another.

"Any plans on a factory?"

Ernie raised a hand as more and more people lobbed

questions at Raf. "Give the kid a break." Then, turning to him, he said, "Mind telling us what he said from start to finish? No detail too small. Just want to see if there's something we can work with as a community. We'd appreciate it, Raf."

This was so comical, Raf could have laughed. Except the hunger on Ernie's face wasn't remotely funny.

"He ordered coffee." Raf wished there was something more exciting or interesting he could pass on. "Tipped well. We didn't talk for long."

"He liked it?" Ernie asked.

"Liked . . ."

"The coffee. Did he like the coffee?"

"Yes . . ."

"Anything else?"

"They're not staying much longer. A few weeks, he said."

Ernie paled. "But they only just got here!"

The gathered crowd murmured worriedly.

"Did he say what brought them here?" Ernie asked. "Anything at all spark his interest? Something we could work with to convince them to give us a chance?"

"I can't think of anything." Looking at Ernie's crestfallen expression, Raf added, "I did tell him about the festival we used to have. He said it sounded cool." He regretted the words as soon as they left his mouth.

"The festival?" Crissy paled.

A hush fell over the diner. Was he the first person to utter the word *festival* since last year? Every festival had been a joyous celebration since Raf had arrived to Moonlight, but the only festival that came to mind nowadays was the one they all most wished to forget.

"Well." Ernie slowly nodded. "If it's a festival he likes . . . it's a festival he'll get."

All heads swiveled toward him.

"Ernie," Jake said. "You cannot be serious."

"Serious as can be," Ernie said. "Who throws a better one than us?"

"After what happened," Jerry said slowly, "we can't."

"There's no way to put one on that fast in a good year, much less *this* year!" Crissy exclaimed. "Have you *seen* the park? It's in shambles."

"We need to clean it up either way, don't we?" Ernie said. Raf could see he was pitching this idea not only to them, but also to himself. "The Moonlight Bay Festival was our crowning glory. This one would be simpler—but we're a scrappy bunch. We can pull it off."

"Even a pared-down festival takes time," Crissy said. "And who's *coming* to this festival? Just us? An empty festival will be more depressing than none at all."

"We'll reach out to Ridgeview. Mill Creek. All our neighboring towns. They'll want to show support. Our success fed into their own when things were riding high here."

"And money?" Jake said. "Painting. Fixing up the swings. Repaving the cracked concrete walkways."

"And the Ferris wheel," Jerry said. "After the storm ripped into it—I'm not sure how it's standing. All of this costs money, Ernie."

"We can't fix it all, but what we can, we should. It'll be an investment," Ernie said firmly. "We need them to stay. You agree, don't you? Isn't it worth a shot?"

The crowd murmured. Were they actually considering

this because of one offhand remark from Warren? This town wasn't ready. Not this soon.

"*If* they stay, and *if* they repurpose the factory," Jake said slowly, "that *would* change everything."

"If things have gotten this bad in a year"—Bea was nodding—"how will Moonlight Bay look a year from now if we don't do something? This is the first real opportunity since everything fell apart."

The crowd murmured. Were they serious? A festival with three weeks to go?

"This could be good for all of us. After everything we've been through," Ernie said, "we've got to get on with the business of moving on."

"No!" A chair scraped roughly against the floor.

Kendall? Other than his meal orders, Raf barely heard him speak. He stood up. His six-foot-three frame towered over everyone.

Ozzy began to whimper. Skylar picked him up and rocked him.

"Kendall." Ernie put his hands up. "Pardon us over here, going on and on with all our yammering. We'll just continue this conversation outside."

"You think restarting the festival will help anything?" Kendall said in a low growl. He gripped his mug tightly in his hand.

"Easy there, friend. We're only trying to figure out how to fix things around here." Bea spoke to him as though trying to talk down an angry and wounded tiger. "You see it, don't you? It's been hard going lately. This town is circling the drain."

"The festival isn't the answer," Kendall said. "The easy way out isn't always the solution."

"Now, what does that mean?" Crissy frowned. "How is a festival the *easy* solution?"

"None of you want to do the work. The *actual* work. We're the only ones summoning the sea." Kendall glared at them. "We're the only ones doing what the elders laid out for us. You want to chase the newest, shiniest thing—not what actually works."

"The elders passed down a bunch of contradictory gibberish, and you lot decided to read into it what you wanted. Besides, it's been almost a *year*," Crissy shot back. "Pray tell, what do *you* have to show for all your work?"

"Everyone, let's take some deep breaths." Ernie rose.

"If you wanted a say on things," Crissy continued, unfazed, "you could've stayed on the council instead of quitting when the going got tough."

Kendall's face grew bright. He raised his mug. Raf flinched as it torpedoed across the room. It slammed against the back wall, shattering. Everyone gaped at the splintered remains.

"No one is ready to start feeling better," Kendall growled. "After what happened? No one *should* be moving on."

Without another word, he stalked out.

Crushed porcelain and splattered coffee dripped down the back wall.

"Sorry, kiddo," Ernie said as Raf walked over with a broom and dustpan.

The council members spoke as Raf swept up the shattered cup. Their words indecipherable through Ozzy's full-throated wails. Kendall had always had a hotheaded streak, which had vanished since the oceans grayed, but Raf knew how quickly fixed realities could change for both places and people.

Raf grabbed the carafe and doled out coffee. He looked around at all the animated faces. A busy diner, even if it was only for coffee, wasn't nothing. He'd share this at dinner tonight, and Uncle would be happy. At least there was that.

"No, thanks," Crissy said when he approached with an empty mug.

"On the house," he offered. "We also have fresh-squeezed orange juice."

"Did you not hear me?" Her lips pressed into a thin line as though the act of speaking to him was painful. "I said no. Thanks."

Her words landed like a slap.

So what? Tolki Uncle often said in the face of such accounts, *We are here temporarily, and we must bear it until we leave.* Brevity was relative, though. For Tolki Uncle, eleven years was a blink of the eye. For Raf? Practically his entire life. And the look in her eyes just now? Whether he liked it or not, it mattered.

twelve
YAS

"Don't move!"

"I'm not!" Raf protested.

He was in her room, sitting on her bed. She stood at her easel. It'd been only twenty minutes, and he was already squirming like a toddler. *Predictable.* She pushed back a smile.

"Can't you take a photo of me, and use *that* to paint me?"

"Raf, this was *your* idea," she reminded him.

"It's been a while." He gave her an apologetic grin. "Nice to see you painting again."

"Thanks for the push."

"Tackling the mural today?"

"As long as the rain clouds hold off from pouring down, I can at least go out and assess it. Raf! Hold still!"

Raf groaned, but he put his hands on his lap again. He looked out the window. His bare feet tapped against her bedroom rug. His hands clasping and unclasping. *This is just like last time,* she wanted to tease him.

Except this wasn't at all like when they were nine.

It was a strange task before her. The very real job of taking in Raf. She saw him all the time, but now she could simply stare at him openly. When was the last time she'd truly *seen* him? His jawline. The slight stubble along his chin. The smile playing on his lips. His warm brown eyes. Which turned from the window and now looked directly at her. He looked at her intently. So intently, for a moment she forgot to breathe.

"Yas?" He bit his lip and cocked his head to the side.

"Yeah?" Her brush grew still in her hands.

"What's that noise? I thought they were done next door."

"Oh, that." What'd she *think* he was going to ask her? "Sounds like Jamal, the repair guy from Mill Creek, is here. He's checking out the oven and the guest room lighting. Our house is falling apart more and more each day. My mom says I'm imagining it, but I swear I heard a mouse squeaking somewhere in the walls last night." She shuddered.

"Can I see the painting yet?"

"Not until it's done. That's the rule."

"Just a peek?" He rose and angled toward her.

"Hey!" She swung the canvas away.

"It's my image!" he protested.

She pushed her hand against his chest, playfully shoving him.

"Whoa!" He tilted backward.

"Sorry!" she said. "I didn't mean—"

He grabbed her arm. They tumbled onto the bed.

Yas laughed until she had tears in her eyes. "I can't believe this, but you're *more* obnoxious to paint now than you were nine years ago."

He propped his hand under his head, watching her with a grin. "You sure you're not painting me as a troll? Because I'm starting to suspect something suspicious is going on."

"You suspect something suspicious, huh?"

"Don't make fun, you know English is not my native language."

She gave him a look and laughed.

"Can I see the other portrait?" he asked. "You never showed me."

"I didn't finish that one either."

"Come on, there's got to be a statute of limitations for this sort of thing. I should be able to see it *now*."

"Fine." She rolled her eyes. Yas pulled out the notebook and brought it over. Sitting next to him, she blushed. It felt so serious and important at the time, but looking at it with Raf, it seemed so silly. The nose blocky, the curls across his forehead a swirly storm of pencil.

"I barely remembered that day," Raf said. "But now it's all coming back to me. We were right here in the same spot."

"Yep."

"Why'd you draw me off to the side? There's all this blank space."

"You don't remember *that* part?"

"Were you going to make a backdrop? I was *really* into spaceships back then."

It was so long ago. A lifetime ago. "I was going to draw myself in it. Next to you," she said, trying her best to sound casual. "I said it would be a portrait of us so we'd be together forever, and you said . . ."

"Right." Raf straightened. "Yeah . . . sounds like me. Awkward as ever."

"It's okay. Statute of limitations expired on feeling embarrassed about things we said as kids."

"Do it this time." He looked at her. "Draw both of us."

"Not sure I'll get *you* down, much less myself."

"You're leaving," he said. "Something to remember us by."

You won't need to remember me. I'll always be in your life. We'll always be us, she wanted to say. *Whether I move away or stay. No matter what, that doesn't change.*

She'd have said it without a thought normally. But lately she felt inexplicably shy about saying the simplest things to him. *Snap out of it,* she told herself. If she was going to feel awkward around him, what then? Raf was her best friend. The one person who made life make sense.

Later that day, paint supplies nestled in her bag, Yas set out for the pier. Even from this distance she could see cracks spreading like spiderwebs across the concrete mural. That was fixable, though. Some plaster, a bit of sanding and elbow grease. This would be her farewell present for her town.

Walking down the beach, she stopped short. A sandcastle sat along the shoreline. Any other year, it would have been nothing to remark upon in the slightest. But there were no tourists on the beach. So who made it? Certainly not Patty, who sat in her chair with a book in hand off in the distance. Nor the Weepers.

She moved closer to it. It wasn't a sprawling creation like Raf once made, complete with drawbridges and moats and watchtowers. This one had four crudely built towers. A shallow moat. Seeing it, Sammy's laughter rang in her ears. She remembered how he bounded out of his house pleading with Raf to help him. Together they'd smoothed out edges and shaped watchtowers. Later, he'd gleefully stomp his creation before the ocean's tide so much as lapped its edges. Why couldn't *these* be the memories running in a loop in her mind? She'd give anything to erase the still frames of Sammy's blue lips. Tears sprang to her eyes. She knew this was how grief worked—it found its hook in you when you least expected it.

"Collecting time again?" A voice jarred her from her thoughts.

Warren. He stood behind her, watching her. She tightened her grip on her tote bag. This was the *second* time he'd snuck up on her.

"Did you make that?" She nodded toward the creation.

He followed her gaze and smirked. "Yep. What else is there to do other than dig around in the sand?"

Aaaand there it is. Ernie wanted her to befriend *him*? Shaking her head, she walked away.

Approaching the mural, the situation was worse than she'd expected. Sections along the bottom were on the brink of crumbling off. Some already had. She ran her hand along the rough exterior—it wasn't great—but she felt more determined than ever to repair it.

Yas took the steps onto the wooden pier. She stepped over the missing planks. She and Raf had come to this pier nearly every day when they were little. It stretched hundreds of feet into the sea. Once there had been cotton candy and ice pop stands at the far end. Revelers in flip-flops posed with the ocean backdrop. Raf and Yas would cannonball from the edge into the ocean and race each other to shore.

Yas pulled out a brush. *The past is gone.* She couldn't heal any of that—but she *could* fix this. Just then, she heard movement. Turning, she saw Warren walking toward her.

"Can I help you?" she asked.

"I didn't mean to be rude back there." He walked up to join her. "We keep starting off on the wrong foot."

"How about you do your thing and I do mine? You'll be leaving this cesspool soon enough, right?"

"Do you ever let anything go?" His eyes narrowed. "I get it. I offended your delicate sensibilities, but I'm trying to be civil."

He had the nerve to try to make *her* feel bad? She took a step back, ready to tell him off, when her foot bumped against something. She tried to regain her balance, and gasped. The paintbrush. It slipped from her fingers. Dropping to her knees, she reached out to grasp it, but it was too late. The brush plunged into the sea. Yas groaned. Mateo didn't have any more brushes of that type.

Add another twenty bucks to the shopping budget.

Between that and the cost of the sanding material, plaster, and white paint she'd need to redo this wall, her good deed was getting costlier and costlier. Trying to move to Edgewood felt like taking one step forward and two steps back.

"I got it," Warren said. Before Yas could reply, he jumped into the water.

Yas gasped—he'd dove in with his polo shirt and shorts. His shoes!

A few seconds later, he reemerged. He held the brush in the air and grinned at her. Yas stared at him. How had he gone from mocking her about sandcastles to diving into the water to grab a paintbrush for her?

"There's a ladder. To the left." She pointed. He swam to it and climbed up, grunting as he made his way back onto the pier. He dripped from head to toe. He looked like a soaked poodle.

"That water's intense!" He glanced down at his clothes. "How ridiculous do I look?"

Yas laughed. "Thanks for that. I just—"

Her words evaporated. Over his shoulder, there was a flash of something in the water. She was dreaming. Hallucinating. Maybe it was how the light hit the sea, drawing her deepest wish into a mirage. It couldn't be what she thought it was.

Yas took a careful step to the edge of the pier. It *was* there. Rolling with the waves. A few hundred feet away. A spot of pink. A stretch no wider than the pier: definitively, unquestionably the color of before.

Yas dove into the sea. Salt water filled her nose. Stung her eyes. She swam toward the color. Coming up for air every few seconds, scanning the horizon. Would her splashing about scare the color away? Her arms strained against the fierce current.

Closer, she made out the colors more clearly—a hint of pink threaded with lavender. Yas paddled faster and faster. She was almost there. A few strokes away. It was painfully close. Real.

Is it true what everyone says? The water will return?

At last, nearly an arm's length away, her hands trembled as she reached out her fingers, straining to graze the surface.

She heard it before she saw it. The six-foot surge careening toward her. Yas dove into the sea a flash before the wall of water crashed down. She counted to fifteen before kicking herself up. Yas panted as she resurfaced. Her stomach dropped.

No. No. No.

The patchwork pink was gone. Endless gray stretched all around her.

"You okay?" Warren swam toward her.

"I'm . . . fine," she managed to say.

After swimming to shore, Yas stumbled onto the beach. The

Weepers. Did they see it? They were closer to the forest today. Dots in the distance. Their shoulders were bowed, but there was no sign they'd seen a thing.

Warren walked over, his wet clothing clung to his body.

"Did you see it?" she asked.

"The color?"

Tears sprang to her eyes. It *had* been there.

"Thought I was imagining things," Warren said. "But then— the wave. It came out of *nowhere*."

"And now the color's gone."

"It looked incredible."

"It used to look like that all the time," Yas said. "Not just a smidge. The entire sea, pink and lavender practically to the horizon."

Back then, did she ever stop to think about how beautiful it was? It was the background of her life. As ordinary as the sun or the sand. She'd barely noticed it. If Warren hadn't been there, if he hadn't confirmed it, Yas would've thought she'd imagined it. It *had* been real though. Even if for a moment.

"By the way," Warren said. "The sandcastle. I *did* make it, you know."

"Oh," she managed to say. She needed to apologize for snapping at him, but her throat felt like it was closing up. "I . . . I gotta go." She raced toward home.

She stumbled through the back door, dripping water on the hardwoods, her boots pressing wet prints on the floor. "Mom?" she cried out.

She checked the guest room. The back nook with the velvet couch. She was not home. Of all the days!

I need to see you, Yas texted Raf as soon as she'd changed

116

into dry clothing. Warren and I saw something today. I have to tell you in person.

I'm at my usual spot, Raf replied. And then—

Forgot to tell you! I met Warren the other day. He was actually . . . nice?

Yas reread his text. Warren dove into the frigid sea to rescue her brush. He'd swum out to help her. He'd gazed with awe at the pink stretch of water. *Did I have him all wrong?* she wondered.

Pressing her palm against the window, Yas stared at the ocean. She wanted to go to the diner. To see Raf. Or find her mother. But what if she looked away and the water returned? What if she missed another sighting?

For the first time, Yas understood why the Weepers leaked their tears into the sea, praying for the color to return, day after day. Why Ernie wandered through town desperately calculating how to persuade Warren's family to stay.

She'd do anything—no matter how outlandish—to see the pink again. The spot of pink in the ocean made her drunk with hope.

"Pink, huh," Raf said for the tenth time.

They sat at the shore's edge watching the sun begin its slow descent. The tide inched toward them bit by bit. Yas hugged her knees, impatiently scanning the water. Her hair brushed against his shoulder. He inched imperceptibly away.

"Maybe there've *been* pops of pink showing up, and we never caught them," she said.

"The Weepers never said anything," Raf said. "If anyone would've noticed, it'd be them. And if they saw it, they wouldn't shut up about it."

"But they never look up!"

This was true. They were huddled in the distance. There were more today. Seven.

"It was the smallest of patches, Raf." She turned to him. "I probably only saw it because of where I was standing. Does make you wonder, though."

"Wonder what?" Raf cocked his head.

"Wonder doesn't mean knowing! But fine. I guess it did make me think, maybe . . ." Her words trailed off.

"That maybe . . . I'm right?"

"I knew you'd gloat!" She elbowed him.

"Have you told anyone else?"

"I was going to tell my mom, but she was out. Now I'm not so sure anymore. What if it's nothing? I hate getting my own hopes up—don't want to put more on her. She acts like everything is fine, but I know it's harder than she lets on. Can you imagine if I told Ernie?"

"Do *not* tell him. He'd park himself at the beach and never move. Speaking of Ernie." Raf smacked his head with his hand. "I forgot to tell you what happened."

"Uh-oh."

"He was at the diner the other day. It's a long story, but he wants to put on the festival."

"What?" Yas's face drained of color. "That's impossible."

"He was dead serious."

"*This* year? There's only a few weeks to go!"

"Warren came by the diner right around closing time, and Ernie asked for a play-by-play of our conversation. It's not like I had amazing insights to share, but when I mentioned he thought our festival sounded cool . . ."

"He hopped on a roller coaster and ran with it," Yas finished. "It won't happen. There's no way. Has he seen the park? There's no time to fix it up, get the vendors in order—and isn't he always saying we don't have any money?"

"Most everyone there, including the council people, seemed on board."

"So we're the only two who feel like this is a bad idea?"

"We're definitely not the only ones." Raf told her about the heated debate. Kendall's outburst. The broken mug. "His meltdown had the opposite effect. Everyone got *more* into it."

"I loved the festival like everyone else, but . . ."

"I know."

Yas hugged her knees tighter. "This festival is going to bring back so many painful memories. I almost wish I hadn't seen the spot of color. It's like I'd finally gotten comfortably numb. Now I can't stop remembering what was. Everything hurts again."

Raf longed to put an arm around her. To comfort her. He understood the double-edged sword of hope. There were so many things he hoped for. For Kot to come back whole. For Nara to find peace. For their lands to be safe again. For forgiveness.

"Turning our town upside down because Warren made a random comment isn't rational," Yas said. "I love Moonlight, but . . . it's starting to feel toxic here."

"Good thing you're leaving."

"We both should." She uncurled herself and turned to him. "Let's not pretend it's not way harder for you here than for me."

"Yas," Raf began.

"At least come with me to see the co-op? Let's take a mini-break from this place. I need to check out what kind of job opportunities there are too. No matter how much I save up, I'll need a steady gig there if I want to *keep* paying the bills. A day with just the two of us . . . how amazing does that sound?"

He glanced at his leaf.

"We'd be back before anything could happen." She nodded at his wrist. "It's not far."

She was right. They wouldn't be gone all *that* long. And he wanted to spend time with Yas, especially since she was leaving soon.

She scooted closer. "If you say yes, I'll let you choose some of the music for the drive."

"Well, this changes everything."

"I can be generous," she teased. "Come on, Raf." She pursed her lips, her hands pressed together, mock pleading with him. Raf shook his head and laughed. How could he not go? It was something any friend would do.

"Fine," said Raf. "Let's do it."

Her mouth parted. "Did you say *yes*?"

"I'll have to check with Bura," he said. "But should be enough notice to work something out."

Yas hugged him. They hadn't embraced in nearly a year. When he pulled away, he realized Yas wasn't looking at him. She was looking down.

"Your leaf." She took his hand. "It's glimmering. Doesn't it only do that if you leave the perimeter?" She traced a finger over it. "Does it hurt?"

Raf swallowed. His sweatshirt had scrunched up and there was his leaf, flickering its warning.

"It does that sometimes." He yanked his sleeve down. Tried to pretend his birthmark wasn't cutting into his skin as though attempting to draw blood. It'd been a hug—nothing more. He and Yas were friends. The sooner his brain could let his heart absorb this and let go, the better off he would be.

"So this playlist offer," he said. "How much control are we talking about?"

"Let's be clear." She pointed a finger at him. "I said *some* music. Can you bring some Golub music too? If your mom could spare a CD or two? I'll figure out how to get them added into the playlist."

"I feel like I hear that music so much, it's vibrating in me at all times."

"I *love* Golub music. But you do realize you can't change your mind now, right?" she told him. "I'm holding you to this. What's the Golub word for 'won't let it go'? Because that's me."

He actually wasn't sure what the Golub word for "won't let it go" was. Before he could think of a reply, a voice cried out in the distance. Raf and Yas leaped up as Dena raced toward them.

"The tree!" she shouted. Her face was ghostly pale. "Raf. We need you!"

Raf took off in a run before Dena finished speaking. Adrenaline coursed through his veins. The tree. No one had stumbled out since Nara and Kot. Had someone new arrived?

He tore through the brambly bushes; thorns dug into his jeans. Yas raced close behind. Nearing the tree, he saw Nara. Her face was streaked with tears. Her arms were wrapped firmly around the trunk. Tolki Uncle knelt by her, whispering. Whatever he said simply made her cling tighter. Seeing Raf, he rose and hurried toward him.

"Can you try to speak with her, Raf? She can't hold on much longer before she loses a finger. We don't know what else we can say to her."

Everyone turned to him. What could *he* say? Her brother was missing. Words wouldn't erase her pain.

Tentatively, Raf approached her. Leaning down, he placed a hand on her back. Her entire body was trembling. "You need to let go, Nara. Your hands are turning blue."

"Not until he tells me."

"Tells you what?" Raf asked.

"I've already told you all." Her lower lip quivered as she turned to the gathered people. "I will not move until *someone* tells me how to return home." She looked at him. "Ask him, Raf. Please. Make Uncle tell me. After all this time—he must know *some* way to get past that door."

"Nara," Raf said. "We've tried to figure it out many times before. These days—ever since things turned—it glimmers at will."

"That cannot be true. When have we observed it glow the most? At night? Morning? Is there any sort of pattern? I want to return. I want to be with my brother."

"I don't know the rhyme or rhythm to the door anymore, child." Uncle shook his head frantically. "I swear on my life."

"That's impossible!" she cried out, clinging tighter to the trunk. "You are the leader of the community!"

"Even if he did, Nara," Raf told her, "it wouldn't be wise to open it. It's not safe when we can't be certain of what's on the other side."

"I'd rather be there with him than here alone."

"You're not alone," Tolki Uncle said.

"There's nothing for me here."

"We can't take Kot's place," Raf said. "But we love you, Nara. The longer you cling to the tree—"

"You will die!" Dena shouted. "That's what you're going to do!"

"He'll come back," Raf said. "The Kot I knew would do everything in his power to return to you. You know how stubborn he is. Remember what he did for the family of chinta right before you left for Moonlight? The ones that got stuck in the barbed fencing? It took him the entire day, he said, but he managed to get them out by sheer will."

"*And* our father's clippers."

"That too." He smiled. "Didn't you keep them in your care until they healed enough to leave?"

"He loved those creatures." A tear slipped down her face. "Made them a nest in a dresser drawer."

"The way he told it, he was ready to stick them in strollers and call them his own."

To his relief, Nara laughed a little.

"And if he loved those chinta, think about how he cares for you," Raf said. "He wouldn't leave without a plan to return. Whatever he went for—he'll come back."

"I know how much it hurts," Tolki Uncle said somberly. "I know what it is to not have any family here. Not a day passes when I don't miss my daughter. But we must continue on. Sitting in grief eats you alive."

The memory of the woman Tolki Uncle chased away days earlier came back to him, but Raf pushed it away.

"I miss Kot too," Raf said. "I won't pretend it's the same. But he *was* my friend. He told the best stories. He made Golub come alive. It's hard to imagine life without you both." He looked at the ground. "I can't stop turning the day over in my mind. What I could've done differently so he was still here."

"Me too," she said softly.

"Tolki Uncle?" Raf asked. "Is there any way to try the signals again? I know they haven't worked in years—but it might be worth checking if we can get word. Even if there's a small chance."

"That's a good idea." Uncle nodded quickly. "Nara, I give you my word, I'm doing everything in my power to make sure he is all right."

The tree pulsed from the cold. The lowest branches were

bare like it was the middle of winter. Nara needed to move away from the trunk before it was too late.

"See?" Raf said. "We have reason to hope."

Nara said nothing. Then—she bowed her head as though in defeat. Raf leaned over and gingerly helped her disentangle her clothing and hands from the tree. He winced at the burn marks along her palms and arms.

Raf's mother approached them. "Why don't you stay with us tonight?" she asked. "I don't want you to be alone."

"Of course," Raf said. "Nara can take my room."

At home, her palms resting on the kitchen table, the full extent of Nara's injuries came to light. Her sweater and clothing were singed from the cold; her palms were red and blistered. Her left cheek was injured, her arms coated with fresh wounds.

Raf finished cleaning up his room while Yas, who had been hovering by the door, hurried over to fill a bowl with warm water. His mother simmered precious herbs and minerals from back home. With a gentle touch, she cleaned Nara's burns and wrapped them in a gauze. These injuries would take weeks to heal. Nara kept her gaze fixed to the table—her eyes were dry now.

"I'm going to get the boys ready for bed," his mother said once she finished. "Raf, put some tea on the stove for Nara. Add imrata and cinta—drinking it helps with healing."

When his mother left the room, Raf moved to stand, but Nara put a hand up to stop him.

"I don't want tea," she said.

"I'm so sorry, Nara," Yas said. "This is so hard."

"The days blend into each other. It's an endless waiting I cannot escape."

"Our necklaces—some say they help," said Yas.

"Uncle said they don't work for us."

"I don't know how powerful they are for *anyone*," Yas said. "But it can't hurt?"

"I can go with you," Raf said. "Early morning, before people are up and about. We can go the back route. Along the shore. I can scout it first to make sure the beach is clear."

"And I can text you how things look on my end," Yas said.

"I'll think about it," she said. "Thanks, Yas."

Raf sat next to Nara. She rested her head against his shoulder. He looked down at her and felt relief—she was thinking about stepping foot outside the forest. It was the first time she hadn't shut it down.

There was a knock on the door. Uncle. He stepped in, resting a hand on his cane. Nara moved to stand, but he put a hand out.

"No, child," he said. "I came to see if you are okay."

"I am sorry, Uncle."

"I know how much you grieve," Tolki said. "Perhaps you should begin taking some steps out of the forest. Wounds fester when they don't get air."

"Might get a necklace made with Yas. Raf said he'll walk me over," she said. "Would that be all right?"

"Whether they imbue anything for us is questionable, but they are lovely to behold. This is good news. Thank you, Raf." Uncle nodded to him. "We really needed you tonight."

Raf looked out at the darkening forest. He couldn't argue with this, could he? But were these words a badge of honor? Or shackles?

fourteen
YAS

Focus, Yas told herself.

She stood by the mural, her paints laid out by her side. She traced her hand over the slab of concrete, trying her best to avoid gawking at the water. She hated this. How hope raged inside her like an infection, making her palms go clammy, robbing her of sleep. Filling her with want. She'd been right not to tell her mother. If hope hurt this much, she didn't want anyone else to catch it.

The last few days working on this project were busy and exhausting. Her arms ached from plastering and spackling and smoothing the broken bits of mural. As tiring as this was, the next part of the project felt more complicated. She'd thought she could retrace the old drawings and repaint them like an oversized coloring book, but the storm had done a number on the wall. Much of the art had faded or crumpled. Even if she dug up old photos for reference, she couldn't recreate what he'd once made.

And—did it even matter? Who came out this way anymore?

Heading home, she passed Patty reclining in her beach chair with her oversize umbrella.

"Hey, doll." Patty waved as Yas approached.

"Not exactly the best day to be sunbathing." Yas nodded at the dark clouds overhead.

"Those *are* the strangest things, aren't they?" Patty squinted up. "You can't beat this ocean breeze, though. Saw you by the mural just now—thinking of redoing the wall?"

"Maybe. Not sure I can make it look the way Mateo had done it."

"Nor should you," Patty replied. "Paint it white and start over, darling."

"Start over?"

"Mateo had his spin at it." Patty nodded. "If you're going to take it on, you ought to give it your own. A mural is no joke—have fun with it and make it yours."

"Are you an artist, Patty?" Yas asked. She realized with a start that though she'd known Patty all her life, she didn't really *know* her.

"Not at all." Patty chuckled. "But I appreciate good art when I see it."

"Hope there's some artistic bones left in me," Yas said.

She looked again at the water. *Snap out of it,* she chided herself. They'd joked Ernie would camp out at the beach and never leave if he heard about the water—but Yas was at that point herself.

After tucking away her art supplies beneath her bed, Yas set off for the diner. Her thoughts drifted to Raf. That moment a few days earlier when they'd sat side by side on the shore. The sea inching toward them bit by bit. His smile when he said he'd go with her to Edgewood—bright and beautiful like the sun. Later, when she'd hugged him, she hadn't realized that they didn't hug anymore. She never hooked her arm in his while they walked around town like she once had. And this hug had felt different than the ones before—like electricity crackling through her. Through *them*?

Later, she'd watched Raf race to Nara's side. His entire body tense as he begged her to let go of the tree. She saw the easy way they spoke to each other. The two of them made sense. How she'd leaned against him that evening. Even in the middle of her pain, he'd made her smile. Yas couldn't wave away how Raf had looked at her.

Raf and Nara.

Nara and Raf.

But Raf told Yas everything. Why hadn't he told her this?

Approaching the diner, she slowed. Ernie stood smack in the middle of the road. His hands rested on his hips as he studied the boarded-up shops with a resigned expression.

"Everything all right, Ernie?" she asked.

He gave a weak smile. "It's nothing. Getting a bit of push-back is all."

She saw now. Flyers. There were flyers stuck on each and every boarded-up window.

FORGET THE PAST
AT YOUR PERIL
SAY NO TO THE MOONLIGHT BAY FESTIVAL

"The Weepers?" she asked.

"Mainly Kendall," Ernie said. "He's trying to rally opposition. Most people are understandably emotional at the prospect of the festival after last year, but plastering the town? I suppose we can't please everyone, but this is . . . This is excessive."

"There aren't all *that* many Weepers, how much damage can they do?"

"Their membership is growing. Octavia and Miko have also joined back up. Who knows who else these flyers will attract?"

"Ernie . . ." Yas hesitated. "Are you sure the festival is a good idea? When I found out it was back on, it threw me for a loop too. There's a reason we weren't doing one this year. After everything that happened—"

"But we don't have time to wait around. We need the Naismiths to stay. I've traveled practically the entire continent looking for investments into our factory. I applied for government funding to tide us over. Nothing came through. I know it's a long shot for a festival to turn things around, convince them to stay, but *if* it could, it's worth a shot. I'm not sure how long we can hang on. They have serious money. Went down the rabbit hole last night. They're not only pharmaceutical magnates. They've got their hands dipped in everything. They buy up places, invest in towns. Revitalize them. It's like lady luck landed in our lap. We have to make them see this town is worth the investment."

She looked at his tense expression. She understood why he wanted them to stay, but she hated how badly he needed it.

Clearing his throat, Ernie quickly added, "Besides, our festival goes back over a century. Fixing the park back up, stringing lights, it might be good for everyone to remember what normal felt like."

Normal. A cleaned-up park, lights, a newly painted Holler Mansion—none of that would make her feel normal. They'd been living the new normal so long, it had calcified against her skin.

"Have you learned anything else from the boy?" he asked her. "Any insight?"

"Nothing useful. If I find out anything, you'll be the first to know."

"Thanks, Yas."

She continued to the diner. She wasn't about to start putting up flyers, but there was no way she'd have anything to do with this festival.

The diner was slammed when she stepped inside. Every booth occupied. Nearly every table too.

What on earth? Scanning the restaurant, she paused. Two people she'd never seen before sat at a table by the broken juke-box, studying their menus. The woman was tall and slim like a number-two pencil, her hair piled up in a twist. The man's dark hair was slicked to the side. Sitting in the other occupied chair was Warren.

Ah. Yas took in their clothes—a cream-colored blouse and slacks for the woman, a periwinkle-colored polo and jeans for the man. The Naismiths. The locals around them tried—and failed—to appear busy while stealing glances in their direction.

Raf approach them, a pad in hand.

"Hey, Raf." Warren smiled.

At this, the man looked up at Raf and then at his son.

"Do you two know each other?"

Warren nodded. "Came by a few days ago. They make some good coffee."

"Thanks." Raf smiled. "No need to rush on deciding. I can come back."

The woman dropped the menu on the table. "More time won't fix this menu. Beggars can't be choosers, I suppose. Eggs, poached. Coffee, black."

"Make that two," the man said.

"French toast and breakfast potatoes for me, and you know I want coffee, right?" Warren grinned and handed him the menus.

Blood rushed to Yas's face. The Naismiths' money didn't earn them the right to treat those who prepared their meals and waited on them as though they were nuisances to be endured. And to insult the establishment they were *sitting* in?

Yas slipped into the bustling kitchen and tied on an apron as Raf handed Bura a list of supplies.

"Task me up," she said.

"Yas!" he said, relieved. "You're a lifesaver."

"Those people!" She fumed. "Not enough things on the menu? There's three pages! Every single breakfast staple is on here."

"Can't take it personally." Raf shrugged. "Warren's nice, though."

Well, she could admit that this much was true. Heading to the main floor, Yas wiped down the counter and refilled the coffee carafes. She eyed the Naismiths as their food was set before them. Would they raise a fuss about the quality as compared to whatever fancy establishments they preferred? But nobody spoke. Not to Raf. Not to each other. Their eyes remained fixed on their glowing devices.

As they wrapped up their meal, the woman pulled money from her purse and tossed it on the table.

"Hope you enjoyed your breakfast," Dena said as they walked past.

None of them replied.

The chimes above the door jangled. Ernie hurried in. He beamed from ear to ear, beelining for them. "It is an absolute pleasure to make your acquaintance!" He stuck his hand out. "Ernie—I'm the mayor, and I do hope you're liking your stay here."

His words punctured the anticipatory air buzzing in the room. A group gathered around them.

Crissy held her hand out, introducing herself. "I own the antique store up the road and I'm on city council."

"Pleased to meet you," Gil said. "I'm also a member of the city council. My husband, Finn, and I have the theater past the gas station."

"Nice to meet you all," the woman said. "I'm Siobhan. This is my husband, Peter."

"Are you enjoying your time in Moonlight?" asked a local.

"The pace is quieter than we are accustomed to," Peter said. "But coming from big-city life—quiet isn't bad."

Others interjected. Introduced themselves. The couple shook hands. Laughed. Their stony faces from earlier gone.

Gross. This was her community? Groveling at the feet of people who probably looked down on all of them? How could she unsee this? Their desperation wafted off of them like a stench.

Yas felt sharp relief stepping into the art gallery a short while later. But cracking open the back door to the workspace behind the gallery, her jaw parted.

What on earth?

She'd cleaned up this space two days ago, but now the

worktable was splattered with paint. Watercolors were stacked haphazardly on shelves and tables. Dirty paint-brushes languished in the sink, the paint caked thick on the bristles.

Yas turned on the faucet and rinsed the brushes with soap and water. Rivers of color filled the sink. She patted the brushes dry and stacked the paints where they belonged. Was Mateo painting again? Had he been inspired by the sales to return to the studio?

She scanned the back space. Propped open the dusty closets. Whatever he was creating, he hadn't left it behind.

Locking the gallery door a few hours later, she saw Warren standing alone on the other side of the road, his back turned to her, looking out at the sea bordering Willow Forest. He glanced back at her. Their eyes met. He raised a hand in greeting.

He'd rescued her paintbrush. He swam to help her when he thought she needed it. He hadn't done anything wrong at the diner. It wasn't his say who his parents were.

"Did it happen again?" he asked.

She almost asked, *Did what happen?* Except she knew. This strange thing they now shared.

"No." She crossed the street. "Have you seen anything?"

"Nope. But not from lack of trying. Can't look away now, hoping I'll spot it again."

"Me neither." She felt relief at his admission.

"You'll be the first to know if I do."

"How are you liking it here?" she asked. "Any better?"

"Eh." He shrugged.

Ernie would wince at her saying this, but . . . "Not that Moonlight isn't a riotous good time, but all you have to do is go to Ridgeview or Mill Creek if you need something to do—they've got pretty much anything you could want. Restaurants. Cafés. Bookstores. *Stores*, period, really."

"No big deal," he said. "We're not here much longer."

"This used to be a great town," she told him. "You missed us by a year."

"The Hollers leaving ruined everything, huh?"

Yas blinked. Why was she surprised he knew this? Of course he knew. The news of Holler Candy closing up shop made national headlines for weeks.

"That and the seas turning. You wouldn't recognize this place."

He read the signs of the shuttered stores. "Tilted Tales. Cake Story. Doggone Treats. Sounds like it was a quirky town."

"Little bit." She laughed. "We were a bit anti-establishment. Everything had to be solidly Moonlight Bay."

She remembered the last town hall—fighting over a new hotel being planned kitty-corner to Main Street Park. "We aren't like the other towns," Kendall had shouted angrily into the microphone, as he did whenever a proposal arrived for a hotel or restaurant chain.

"Tourism," Ernie pleaded. "Lodging is constantly sold out—why not accommodate more people instead of letting Ridgeview and Mill Creek get the dollars when they're really there for Moonlight? It's only good for our economy."

"We don't *need* more tourism!" Crissy retorted.

"That's right," Kendall interjected. "Tourism is a plague—clogging up the roads and establishments. The Hollers do right by us."

How confident they'd been that day. How sure that each

day that followed would be the same as the last.

Warren's eyes swept over the closed shops, the Ferris wheel in the distance. "Too bad I missed it. Looks like it used to be pretty great." He tipped an imaginary hat toward her.

Watching his retreating frame, Yas thought of Ernie's desperate plea for her to befriend him. Warren *had* come across horribly when they first met—but considering his parents, he didn't have much in the way of role models either.

"Warren," Yas called out. "Wait up."

He stopped and looked back at her curiously as she approached him.

"It's not like we have *nothing* going on here," she said. "We've got a movie theater. The pharmacy has a good selection of trading cards if you're into that. I could . . . I could show you around?"

"Really?" He seemed as surprised by her offer as she was in making it.

"You'll need to keep your expectations low," she warned. "There's not a whole lot, but we're not a ghost town either."

Not yet.

"Maybe you could give me a used-to-be tour?" he said. "Show me what the town was? *Before* things changed."

"Yeah?" She nodded. "That sounds like a plan."

She wouldn't be here much longer, but she could do this. She'd help if she could.

fifteen
RAF

When Raf stepped into his house after closing, for a split second he thought he'd stumbled into someone else's residence. Every shoe was in its space. The floors freshly scrubbed. There was not a crumb to speak of on the rugs. Even the windowsills were dusted.

His mother valued a neat home, and back when his father was alive, the home looked mostly presentable, but these days she'd justifiably given up in the face of his little brothers and their blizzard of toys, crayons, and half-finished crafts.

Nara sat at the kitchen table with his siblings. The trio colored and spoke in hushed voices.

"So this is what it's like to see a miracle unfold," Raf marveled. He sat down at the empty seat next to her. "Nara, the place looks incredible, but you came here for downtime. Plus your hands are recovering."

"Your mom is taking a much-needed nap, so I thought I would be useful. And my hands are better—see? Our herbs still do the trick."

Indeed, her bandages were already off. Though angry pink scars ran along her palms—they would take time to return to normal—she looked far better off than he'd expected.

"Well, thanks. Nice to see the floor."

"I think being in my empty house all day got me twisted up in my thoughts." She handed Louk a purple crayon. "My head feels clearer here."

"Stay, then."

"Raf."

"I love our couch. It's more comfortable than you'd think."

"I don't know about that." She smiled a little. "But a few more days *would* be nice."

There was a knock. Tolki Uncle.

"What happened here?" he asked, glancing around.

"Nara happened," Raf said.

"Just the person I was here to check on!"

Nara gave him a hug. "I'm sorry about yesterday." She reached into her dress pocket and pulled out three leaves. "I had a chance to do these too."

"Wonderful." Uncle took them from her. "I will hang them right away. And I have leaves from everyone in the community with prayers for Kot. It was Raf's idea," he said in response to her surprised expression. "How are you now?"

"Better," she said. "Finishing the leaves helped."

"And the plan for the necklace?" he asked.

"Day after tomorrow. As long as I can work up the nerve."

"Leaving the forest will do you good. I have been wanting to protect you, but cloistered like this—it's not good for anyone." He looked at Raf. "I had something I wanted to talk to you about. When you have a second, come by my place?"

"Go on." Nara waved a hand. "I can look after the boys."

—•—

The gravel path leading to Tolki Uncle's home bloomed on either side with yellow and red flowers. A gust of wind whipped against Raf's hair. He studied Uncle's profile. Had Dena complained about how understaffed the diner was as she'd been threatening to do for so long? With Ernie's frequent meetings, and the eavesdroppers part and parcel with them these days, the diner *was* busy. They couldn't do it with their skeleton crew alone anymore.

Or—Raf wondered—was this about the woman he'd seen the other day? The one with streaks in her hair who sped away just as quickly as she'd arrived. He'd promised Raf they'd talk about it later, and this was the one spell of calm since.

Uncle walked to the kitchen, filled the metal teapot with water, and placed it on the stove. He crushed cloves and cardamom and set out a bowl of tea leaves and almonds. The last time he'd made tea for Raf was nearly one year earlier. Raf studied Uncle. His expression was unreadable.

"Have a seat." Uncle gestured to the kitchen table overlooking the window.

"Is everything all right?" Raf asked gingerly.

"Thanks to you, yes." He turned off the stove and pulled out a jar of sugar. "Did me good to see Nara smile. It's good for her to have company."

"I told her she could stay as long as she wanted. The boys love having her there."

Tolki Uncle strained the tea and brought the steaming cups to the table.

"I wanted to get your thoughts on Nara. I'm glad she is planning to leave the forest. The best way to wash away people's fear of us is to show that there is nothing to be afraid of. It's good for the community."

Raf shifted. Uncle was right. Nara was sweet and kind; no one could be afraid of her if they knew her. But the way he said it—Nara's presence being good for the community? So *the locals* could feel less afraid?

"I'd thought about asking her to work at the diner," Raf said. "But I don't think—"

"Certainly not," Uncle interrupted. "The town is not ready yet. Baby steps."

Raf blinked. He'd meant to say he wasn't sure if *Nara* was ready.

Uncle was their unofficial leader; he was the one who spoke to Ernie and other council members on their behalf, which meant he knew more than the others in the forest. What were people saying about Nara that made him this adamant?

"Sugar." Tolki Uncle tapped the table and stood up. "I left it on the counter."

Raf's phone buzzed. A text from Yas. Don't forget to ask Bura about the truck.

"Interesting email?" Uncle asked as he placed the sugar jar on the table.

"Sorry. Just a text." Raf stuck the phone in his pants pocket. Tolki Uncle was not a fan of technology, least of all the ones with the glowing faces that kept people numb, as he often said. In fact, it was only Uncle, Raf, and Bura who had phones. Uncle found it a needless expense for everyone to have one when they lived close enough to one another to speak in person as needed.

Uncle took a sip of tea. "Perhaps it's my advancing age. Lately I keep thinking of home. Miss it more and more with each passing day." He contemplated the wooded forest out the window.

Raf missed it too. Or at least the *idea* of it. He certainly wanted to see Golub again after hearing the stories Kot shared of maneuvering down crushed-ice rivers that were once thermal and warm and the mountain peaks that stretched into the clouds. The windswept valleys. But the longing of the elders like Tolki Uncle was different from his own. Raf's warm feelings were based on the memories of others; his own had long begun fading. Uncle knew *exactly* what he was missing. Would Uncle live long enough to return? His father hadn't.

Raf watched Uncle sip his tea. He knew he hadn't been brought here to wax philosophical. Uncle looked thoughtfully at Raf.

"You are young," Uncle said. "Too young for all you've been asked to carry. When your father was here, it was his confidence I sought. You have his calmness and wisdom."

Raf shifted in his seat. His father *had* been calm and wise. Nothing ever ruffled his feathers—even when Louk and Mac were having full-on meltdowns. Raf? He was good at keeping hidden what he did not want others to see.

"I suppose this is why you have ended up becoming my number two," Uncle continued. "And why I wanted to tell you"—he looked down into his teacup—"Kot has been found."

Raf nearly dropped his cup. A rush of adrenaline swept through him. Nara would be weak with relief! Their prayers finally answered! Why was Uncle telling him instead of Nara?

"I'm afraid the news is not good," he said, not meeting Raf's eyes. "He didn't return to Golub."

"I . . . I don't understand."

141

"I'm still gathering information, but from my understanding, he left the perimeter. He stayed out too long, so he . . ."

"Lost his leaf," Raf said in a hushed voice.

Uncle said nothing. Raf's head spun at this silent confirmation. "Isn't there some way to reverse it? Someone's got to have come up with some healing medicine. Something can be done, can't it?"

"I'm sorry, Raf. It is irreversible."

A gust of wind rattled the windowpanes. Raf tried to still his shallow breathing. One mistake. An emotional decision by Kot. And he lost everything and everyone?

"What now?" Raf asked shakily.

"I'm getting him situated."

"Situated? Where?"

"There are contingency plans I set up for moments like this," Tolki Uncle said. "He's no longer part of our community, but he is ours. We will watch out for him."

He's no longer part of our community. The words hit him like a ton of bricks.

"At least Nara will know where he is," Raf said in a hollow voice. "Maybe she could see him from a distance. Talk to him on the phone. At least she can know."

"That's where it gets complicated," Uncle said. "Any contact will erase her leaf."

"Not even a phone call? A letter?"

"Nothing."

"There has to be an exception!"

"I am afraid there is not."

"No." Raf stood up. He paced the kitchen. His mind swam with a million thoughts. How could Nara *never* speak to the only surviving member of her family? There had to be some way around it! "That *can't* be right, Uncle. Let's review the details. There have got to be some caveats built in. How can a letter—"

"Raf! Enough!"

Uncle's face was flushed. Raf grew still. Had he ever raised his voice at *anyone*?

"I am sorry, Raf," Uncle said. "I have turned it over in my mind ever since the day I learned the news. I wish it could be otherwise, but there is nothing that can be done."

"What about the woman who came in that Jeep?" Raf asked. "She was your daughter, wasn't she?"

Uncle's eyes widened.

"Sh-she looked so much like you . . ."

Uncle studied the table. "You are correct. That was Shar. My daughter."

Deep down, Raf'd known it, of course. Still, he felt too stunned to speak.

As though anticipating Raf's next question, Uncle continued. "I am, as of this year, able to connect with the leafless." He gestured to the leaf glowing against his wrist. "Once one enters their seventh decade of life, the leaf cannot fade. It's why I've been able to make arrangements for Kot. Why I was able to, after decades, speak to my daughter."

"But you sent her away," Raf said. "I saw you speaking with her. You were angry."

"She endangered everyone by approaching the forest," he said. "I'm grateful you had the presence of mind to stay a safe distance away. The well-being and safety of my community is the most important thing to me."

But that was your daughter. Couldn't he have met her somewhere else? In Ridgeview or Mill Creek? Somewhere at a safe distance, to be with the child who'd left all those years ago? Raf didn't know how to ask without sounding accusatory.

"If you can leave the perimeter now," Raf said, "that means you're the only one who can. Why didn't you tell us?"

"As a leader, I set an example. Though I suppose my example did not serve to deter Kot." He sighed. "If only he had listened. I warned him. I told him to give it time—the locals would come around. Kot was too free-spirited. Alas, what is done is done," he said. "And we cannot tell Nara. Not yet."

"But she's his sister. How can she not know?"

"I will tell her," he said. "Once she is able to take the news . . . but she is not ready to hear this, you know that, Raf."

Raf thought of the pink scars along her palms and hands. How could he argue with this? Kot was both found and irrevocably lost. If they were lucky, he and Nara would have to wait for most of their life to pass them by before they could reunite. His eyes filled with hot tears.

"Why not give her the choice to join him, then, wherever he went?"

"So she loses her leaf too?" Uncle stared at him incredulously. "I cannot have two leafless children. I *will not* have it."

"What is the point of keeping her leaf if she can't be with her family?"

"She has you."

"It's not the same. It's not family."

"Perhaps one day it could be."

Raf looked up.

"She is a nice girl, isn't she?" Uncle asked. "You like her, don't you?"

"I do," he said slowly. "It's impossible for anyone to not like her. But I don't feel that way about her."

"You could learn to," Tolki Uncle said. "Love does not always strike like a bolt from the sky—sometimes it blooms when we water and nurture it."

Raf's own parents had married in this manner, their union suggested by their elders, and they'd been blissfully happy—but Nara was like a sister to him.

Tolki Uncle leaned forward. "Hearing the news, I cannot help but worry. We cannot change the fact that she has lost her brother. But she does not have to be alone in the world."

Raf heard the other words that Uncle hadn't spoken: *She's alone because of you. We lost Kot because he worked at the diner, because you pushed to let it happen. She lost her brother because of you.*

"You . . . you want me to marry Nara?"

"No, no. You're both young. I'm only bringing it up. An idea to consider," Uncle said. "I'd never ask you to do anything you didn't want to do. You know that. Keep it in mind, that's all."

Raf set his cup in the sink. Numbly he walked outside. He stepped down the flower-lined path. Gravel crunched beneath his feet. Warm lights glowed inside his home.

An idea to consider. Tolki Uncle always spoke like this. Gently. Never any pressure. He only gave suggestions. But Raf knew.

Walking home, he thought back to their conversation. All this time, Raf had never questioned Uncle. Never once. How long had Uncle known where Kot was? How long had he kept it to himself? What else did Raf not know?

sixteen
YAS

"I'm off to complete my homework assignment," Yas said when her mother walked into the kitchen.

"Homework?" Her mother looked at her, puzzled. Her hair was tied up in a messy bun. "Last I checked, you graduated."

"I'm showing Warren around town."

"Really?" Her mother's face exploded into a smile. "That's great!"

"Trying to be helpful," Yas said. Though now that she was getting herself ready to actually do it, she was starting to dread it more and more.

"Ernie will be ecstatic."

"He owes me." She slung her satchel over her shoulder and tried to play it cool. A smile from her mother—after so long in the cold, she savored the warmth.

Her mother took a sip of coffee and gestured toward the pier.

"The mural is coming along nicely."

"You saw?"

"It's only *right* there." Her mother laughed. "It has real promise."

Yas had been working on it so up close, it was disorienting

to see it from this angle. For now, it was just a sketch. Charcoal clouds and shoreline. Four divided squares that would house the images she hoped to create. Her eyes drifted to the sea. Gray as ever.

"Is everything okay?" her mother asked.

"Yes. Why?"

"You've been looking out at the water a lot," she said. "You combed for shells much longer than usual this morning."

"I've been thinking about the sea lately." Yas wanted to tell her mother the rest of it. The words heavy on her tongue. But with each passing day, the moment felt smaller and smaller—an aberration, nothing more.

"Makes sense," her mother said. "We're coming up on one year."

"And this festival Ernie's planning." Yas moved closer to her. Relieved they were talking. Relieved she could share some of what had been weighing on her. "Bea and a few others were talking about the musical lineup. Food stalls. Kendall's going ballistic—he's got flyers up all around town."

"I wasn't sure about a festival at first either," her mother said. "Most everyone seems to be coming around, though. It's all anyone who comes through talks about."

"Is it worth bringing up all those painful memories just in case the Naismiths are festival freaks?"

"Maybe it'll be a jolt of joy for us also? It's important to have things to look forward to."

Yas checked the wall clock. It was past ten. Her mother was usually in the back with a client by now, but she was grateful for this uninterrupted time.

"I pulled some decent enough shells today," Yas said.

"Define decent," her mother groaned.

"I guess decent is a bit generous," Yas said. "I say we should start harvesting the broken shells and figure out how to use them instead."

"I'm thinking that's where we're heading at this rate." Her mother laughed.

"Want me to help you sort through the inventory?"

"They'll be here when you get back. Now go." She shooed her. "And if you can, try to have fun!"

Warren leaned against her mailbox at the end of the gravel driveway. He wore dark jeans and a pale blue shirt; a black notebook peeked out from beneath his arm.

"A notebook? How quaint," she said.

"Wanted to show you I was taking the tour seriously." He grinned.

"I'm pretty sure you won't need a notebook. This town is one square mile of abandoned buildings."

"This isn't the usual direction," he said as they walked past Holler Mansion toward the edge of town a few blocks south.

"We may as well start at the beginning," she said. They stopped at a faded welcome board. *Welcome to Moonlight Bay: When you're here, you're home.*

There was an empty parking lot behind the sign and vacant storefronts that were once dubbed "tourist square." She hadn't come this way since the before times. There was a busted window in the old trinket shop. Debris from the storm last year still littered the sidewalk. This parking lot once teemed with cars, angling for a spot. Each shop filled with Moonlight-branded wind chimes and mugs and towels. Families and couples once sprawled on the grassy median in the center with cheap slices of pizza from Joe's. Music blaring from idling RVs. Now silence roared in her ears. She thought she'd grown used to the empty buildings and boarded-up bed-and-breakfasts. Now Yas realized she hadn't gotten used to it—she'd grown numb. Seeing this place after so long, through Warren's eyes, her self-protective remove wasn't strong enough armor to stop tears from filling her eyes.

"Is this a second town square?" Warren asked.

"We called this *tourist* square." *Get it together,* she chided herself. "The city council forbade souvenir shops in the main part of town because it would mess with the 'true Moonlight charm.' Joke's on us, huh?"

She waited for a wry remark. He'd called this place a cesspool and, well, she was proving him right. But Warren looked sympathetic, not smug.

They walked past an overgrown space filled with weeds that had once been a community garden. The abandoned bike rental lot. Dry vines wound up metal light posts. The brick stand-alone that had once been the local bank—the first to leave town.

"This art gallery is technically closed." Yas gestured to Mateo's. "But it's hanging in there." She felt a swell of pride knowing she helped make that happen.

The door to the gallery opened. Mateo? It'd been ages since Yas had seen him up close. His dark hair was rumpled—more gray than black now. His jeans and shirt too big for his dwindling frame. He'd always been a bit taciturn even before things changed, but he would've paused to say hello. To nod in acknowledgment at the very least; now he walked by them as though they weren't even there. *It's not personal,* Yas reminded herself. This was the way of the Weepers.

Continuing on, she pointed out the historic bed-and-breakfasts overlooking the sea to Warren—they'd once had two-year-long waiting lists. Sandpiper Inn and Iguana Motor Lodge flashed red VACANCY signs a few paces away—they were the only two somehow keeping their lights on, housing travelers heading to other places along the eastern shore. She showed him the theater—known for its popcorn more than its movies. Warren said little, but he *did* seem to be taking it all in. It was strange—to match the person she'd first met to the person next to her now.

"How do we stack up to the other towns you've bought?" she asked.

A flash of surprise crossed his face. "Where'd you hear that?"

"It's the talk around town," Yas said. "It's not true?"

"Sort of. My mom's hometown was going under for years, so we helped fix things up there. When Hurricane Jessi hit the barrier islands, we made some hefty donations."

Ah. The rumors—as rumors tended to be—were only partly correct.

"Why, hello there!" a voice called out.

Crissy. Yas slowed down as she crossed the street and joined them.

"What are you two up to?"

"Showing him around town," Yas replied.

"Yas is a great tour guide," Warren said smoothly.

"What have you enjoyed seeing so far?" Crissy asked.

"The movie theater looks top-notch," Warren said.

"It really is." Crissy beamed. "We hope you're enjoying your time here."

We. Yas looked around self-consciously. Jake peeked out the grocery store window. A handful of people across the street eyed them. Skyler with her toddler in the stroller a few paces ahead. Ernie by the park. He shot her a thumbs-up.

"I'm sorry everyone's being so weird," Yas said once she'd extricated them from Crissy.

"Why's it weird they're into me? Maybe I'm just super magnetic." Warren grinned.

She laughed. "That's it."

At the end of the sidewalk, the park lay ahead. Neighbors stopped to smile. Wave. There was a time when a new boy walking about would have been as ordinary a sight as seashells on the beach. Sure, Kendall once took tourism and the factory for granted, but Yas had taken all of it as a given too, hadn't she?

"I'm afraid that's the extent of our tour," she told him. "Not much else to see here."

"We haven't visited Willow forest." He pointed toward the trees. "The Golub tree's there, right? Could we see it?"

"No," she said abruptly. "I mean . . . that's probably not a good idea, to head in unannounced."

"Why not? I'm sure the leaf people won't mind."

Leaf people. Yas gritted her teeth. He didn't mean anything by it. He didn't know this was how the townspeople referred to them to insult them. And how could she fault him for his curiosity about the tree? The tree *was* special. "The Golub," she said, correcting him. "I just . . . I don't think they'd be expecting anyone right now."

"But it's public land." He raised an eyebrow. "They can't stop us from coming in."

"It *is* public land. But they've lived there for nearly two decades. It's *their* space. Things have been tense here lately. I wouldn't want to show up unannounced."

Warren looked at the diner. "Raf—he's one of them too, isn't he? I could tell he wasn't from around here and I *thought* I saw a tattoo on his wrist. Must've been the leaf."

Casual, laid-back Warren was gone—this Warren stood straighter. His blue eyes brighter. What could she accuse him of? Of being curious about a beautiful tree rising above the tree line, visible from his home?

"You're right, it *is* rude to barge in," Warren conceded. "I didn't realize there were local dynamics at play. Why don't we ask Raf? He lives there. If he says no, it's a no. I'll respect that." He opened the door to the diner. "After you." He bowed with a mock flourish.

Yas studied him. *It's normal to be curious,* she reminded herself. Who *wouldn't* want to go and take a peek? But this didn't change the *feeling* inside of her that, no matter how hard she tried to talk herself out of it, wouldn't stop burrowing deeper into her skin.

seventeen

RAF

Volunteers were in full swing in Main Street Park. Gil trimmed branches from the overgrown myrtles that had been left to go wild this past year. Bea and others sanded down the exterior of the bandstand. Raf marveled at how one offhand comment had led to all of this: the town's emergency budget deployed to string up lights, paint the bandstand, and sand down and repair the awnings by the picnic table. At least it was paying off. The park *was* looking better.

Raf checked the clock. It was nearly closing time, and he couldn't wait to be done. It was painful to be here today while Uncle's bombshell roiled inside of him. Knowing was worse than not knowing. Kot was alone. Nara was alone. Definitively, absolutely alone.

How could Raf keep this secret from her?

He thought of Uncle's nudge. Nara and him. But his feelings weren't like a light switch, turned on and off at will. That wasn't how love worked. At least, it wasn't how Raf worked.

And Raf still couldn't stop wondering: What other secrets was Tolki Uncle keeping for the "safety" of the community? He wished he had someone to share all this with. His mother had enough on her mind. He couldn't burden her. He missed his father so much in these moments.

Kendall walked by the diner. He hadn't returned since the day he'd broken the mug in a fit of outrage. Today, he walked swiftly past the diner, his movement swift and limber. He beelined toward the park. Other Weepers joined him. Olive and Mateo. Laura— the local preschool teacher. Eight in total. They wore gray today. Every last one of them. From head to toe. Ernie spotted them, and even from this distance, Raf could see his expression pale.

Raf watched Kendall speak to Ernie—he jabbed an arm in the air. Then Raf leapt off the stool; Kendall shoved Ernie squarely in the chest. Mateo grabbed Kendall, pulling him away. Kendall struggled, then straightened. Mateo released him. As quickly as they arrived, the Weepers left.

There was the old Kendall. Not the one hunched by a window with cold coffee, but the opinionated, outspoken one—the one who needed to have his way. Except this time he wasn't a council member. And he was angrier than Raf had ever seen him.

The front door bells jingled. Yas and Warren stepped inside. He looked at Yas quizzically. She shrugged. Ah. Raf remembered the promise Ernie finagled out of her.

"Hey, Raf. Yas was giving me a tour of the town," Warren said. They sat at the counter. "She saved the best for last."

"That's right," Yas said. "They have the best everything, but their strawberry milkshakes are my personal favorite. The best in the world." She winked at Raf.

"Because you've sampled them all, right?" Raf grinned.

"Don't need to. Frimos, remember?" She wrinkled her nose at him. "Perfection is perfection."

"In that case, I'd like one," Warren said. The bells chimed

again. In came Gil. Ayo. Finn. Tomorrow was Wednesday, which meant the diner was closed, but maybe they should stay open every day while the Naismiths were in town, thought Raf. It was proving to be a more profitable summer than expected, thanks to their presence.

Raf slipped new orders to the kitchen. He handed Warren and Yas their milkshakes. He'd have to ask Yas how it'd gone—if her thoughts on Warren had changed. Judging from how she sat on the stool, though, her body curved just the subtlest bit away from Warren—the worry lines creating the number eleven on her forehead—she wasn't fully sold.

"The park looks good." Warren nodded toward the window.

"And we have you to thank for it," Yas said wryly.

"Me?"

"I accidentally mentioned to Ernie that you thought festivals were cool," Raf said.

"I did? Huh. I forget we tend to cause a stir wherever we go."

"When you're in a town sinking into the sea, any lifeline looks appealing," Yas retorted. There was an audible gasp. Yas quickly added, "Kidding, of course."

When the clock struck five o'clock, Dena flipped the sign to CLOSED. Warren leaned forward as customers reluctantly began filtering out.

"I had a question for you, Raf. The tree. The huge one. I can see it from my bedroom window. It's in your forest?"

Raf nodded.

"Could I see it?"

"Warren." Yas grimaced.

"Right." Warren raised his palms up. "Sorry if I'm not allowed to ask."

"No . . . it's not like that," Raf began. No one came by lately except Yas, but that didn't mean it was off-limits. "I need to close up," he said. "But sure, I'll show you around."

Raf felt eyes trailing them as the three of them headed toward the forest.

A swirl of wind snaked past once they crossed the tree line. Raf never thought much of it—it was as remarkable as commenting on the green of the grass or the tint of blue in the sky. With Warren there, though, he was newly aware of everything. Their homes, wooden cabins set in a semicircle, with flowers lining the gravel pathways connecting them all to one another. The long pine table in the distance with lanterns strung around it.

How *did* this all appear to an outsider?

"Why is it so much colder in here?" Warren hugged his arms to his body. "I know it's shady since we're surrounded by trees, but . . ."

"It's the Golub tree." They were approaching Raf's bungalow, the first in the clearing's circle of homes. He pointed to the enormous tree in the distance—close to where the brush met the sand beyond it. "It lets off a coolness—keeps us up-to-date about how things are on the other side. In Golub."

Warren stopped walking. "It's . . . it's huge."

Raf smiled at Warren's unconcealed wonder. He remembered when the locals used to come and go. Tourists. They'd all regarded at it with the same awe.

"Is it okay to go near it?" Warren asked.

Before Raf could reply, his brothers rushed outside.

"Yas!" cried the littler one. He lunged toward her, giving her a hug.

"Whoa! Relax!" Raf nodded to Warren. "These are my brothers."

"Nice to meet you." Warren smiled.

Noticing him now, his brothers grew shyer. They exchanged curious looks. Raf saw Warren eye the tree again.

"I can take you closer," Raf offered. "But it's frostier than usual today. Let me grab you a sweater." He opened his door. "Come on in."

"Wait," Yas said, stepping inside. "Are we at the right house?"

"Why does everyone keep saying that? It wasn't *that* messy before," Raf protested.

"Clutter is in the eye of the beholder, I guess." Yas winked.

"One sec," Raf said. "I'll grab the sweater for you."

Slipping off his shoes, he heard the sound of crying. Raf raced up the steps two at a time and down the short hallway toward his bedroom.

"Nara?" He tapped the half-opened door.

She sat on his bed, her back against the wall, wrapped up in a blanket. Her eyes and nose were red.

"Did something happen?" he asked.

"I changed my mind." She sniffled. "I don't want to get a star made. Tell Yas I appreciate the offer, but I'm not ready."

"Nara!" Yas scooted past Raf and settled by Nara's side. "What's wrong?"

"It's nothing." She wiped her eyes with the back of her hand. "That is the problem. It's *nothing*. Some days I can deal with it. But putting on a smile? Trying to pretend everything is fine? Right now that feels impossible."

"Of course," Yas said. "Things aren't fine. So how can you feel fine?"

And things would never, ever be fine again for Nara, thought Raf. Why did Uncle share this burden with him? But he saw how she grieved. She couldn't take the news.

"What am I supposed to do?" she asked softly.

"You find the center of peace in the storm," Yas said. "You breathe in and out. You don't demand any more of yourself than you can give. If you don't feel fine, then don't act fine. You don't owe anyone a happy face."

"Do you think we will ever find him, Raf?" she asked.

Raf felt his insides constrict at the direct question. She looked at him earnestly. Because she trusted him. But he couldn't tell her the truth. She was already so heartbroken. How could he share what Uncle had told him?

"Uncle's got more resources and connections than anyone else," Raf said. This was the truth. A version of it, anyway, even if it didn't answer her question. "He's doing everything he can to make sure Kot is safe."

"You are right." She wiped her eyes. "I need to take this day by day."

Heading down the stairs with Yas and Nara, Raf was startled to see Warren on the sofa in their main room. Raf had forgotten he was there. Forgotten to warn Nara, who paused now at the foot of the stairs.

"Nara," Raf said in a rush. "I completely forgot to tell you—"

"Hi, I'm Warren." He rose and flashed a thousand-watt smile as he approached her.

"Nara," she said cautiously.

"Sorry for spooking you," he said. "I invited myself over. Yas was giving me a tour of the town, but how can a tour be complete without visiting this amazing stretch of forest, you know what I mean?"

"I wouldn't know," Nara said. "I have not left the woods since I arrived about a year ago, which—" Nara faltered. "When you say it aloud, it sounds . . ."

"Reasonable," Warren finished. "I'd say the forest is the best part of Moonlight Bay."

"That is nice to hear." Nara smiled.

"But you're leaving the forest tomorrow, right?" Yas reminded her. "I know you said you didn't want to get a necklace made, but I hope you'll reconsider."

"What's the saying? The only thing to fear is fear itself, right?" Warren winked.

Yas shot him an annoyed look, but Raf couldn't stop focusing on the fact that Nara had smiled. The smallest bit.

"Let me grab a sweater for you," Raf said. "We can all go check out the tree."

"Maybe another time," Warren said. "My parents texted while you were upstairs. I have to run." He smiled at Nara. "It was lovely to meet you."

"Where did *he* come from?" Nara asked once Warren left. "He's definitely not a local."

"He's new here," Yas said.

"Is he a Naismith? He is *their* son?" Nara exclaimed. "To hear Dena describe them, they were ice figurines. Warren seemed nice, though."

"Jury's out on him," Yas said. "He's nicer than his parents, though. I'm sorry," she told them. "I didn't know he was going to invite himself over like this. One minute I think I'm wrong about him, and the next minute he proves me right."

Raf waved a hand. "I told him he was welcome. By now the whole town probably knows he came. That's good for us."

"Hope he didn't freak you too much," Yas said to Nara.

"I've not been outside, and now the outside came to me," she said. "Good practice run for tomorrow."

"So it's a yes on the necklace?" Yas asked.

"I'll try my best." Nara smiled.

Raf grinned. He knew Yas was wary of Warren, but moments earlier, Nara had been weeping upstairs. Now, thanks to Warren, she was smiling.

eighteen
YAS

Yas stretched and yawned. Her arms ached. Her shoulders were sore. The sun had barely risen into the sky when she'd begun painting. She'd underestimated how hard painting the mural would be. She'd also underestimated how good it would feel. Working on it each morning beneath the rising sun, her mind cleared. Of the festival. The shells. Her father. It was her and the wall. Nothing else.

Each section was a memento of their town. A sandcastle by the shore. The view of Main Street in better days.

Rinsing her brush, she mentally tallied how much money she'd saved so far. She was almost there. About $130 shy of her goal. Posting Mateo's art a few pieces at a time had been a smart strategy. No one knew how many more paintings would go up for sale. Or when they would be posted. Everyone wanted to be one of the few to own a masterpiece. They'd even doubled their prices, but the brisk business continued. Still, paintings were a finite resource. They'd eventually need more to sell to keep them afloat. Luckily, Mateo *did* appear to be painting again, though she'd yet to have glimpsed anything he was creating. Maybe there would be more inventory soon.

Her phone buzzed. Picking it up, she saw it was from Raf.

Just left.

Raf and Nara were on their way. They'd be at her house in less than ten minutes.

Yas gathered her supplies and hurried toward home.

Stepping onto the porch, she scanned the horizon. The shoreline was empty, save the Weepers. Yas counted ten. Was the anniversary bringing people back? Or were they responding to Kendall's flyers?

Raf and Nara emerged into view. Passing the Weepers, Nara's pace slowed.

It's okay, Yas murmured. They wouldn't do anything. Until Kendall's outburst, she'd hardly heard any of them speak. Raf whispered something in Nara's ear. He placed an arm around her. Nara looked at him gratefully.

Was there something between them? Yas wondered. Was this why he flinched if Yas's shoulder so much as brushed against his?

It made sense. Raf was there for Nara. A light in a dark year. She was so sweet and helpful—always watching out for other people and their feelings. What *wasn't* to like about Nara?

What *didn't* make sense was how this was making Yas feel. He was her friend—always had been. Always would be. This didn't change anything between her and Raf.

"Nara, you did it!" Yas welcomed her as they came up the porch steps. "I hope it wasn't too bad."

Nara's cheeks were flushed pink. "Feels good to breathe open air. The water seems different up close. *Everything* seems different."

"Come on in." Yas waved them both inside.

"Your home is beautiful," Nara said.

"That's nice of you to say." Yas eyed the scratched-up wooden floor. The faded couch, fraying at the seams.

"It's true. There's a warmth here," Nara said. "Those decorations over there—are those the stars?" She pointed to the wall by the front door, where customers came through. It was a floor-to-ceiling display of necklaces on hooks.

"You'll be getting one handmade especially for you," Yas told her.

Nara drifted toward the art as Yas's mother stepped into the room.

"Good morning!" she said with a huge smile. Her work apron was on over her flowery skirt. "Honored you chose us as your first visit beyond the forest."

"Thank you for seeing me," Nara said shyly. "It felt like a good first step."

"Do you want some coffee?" Yas's mother said. "I know it's early."

"I'm too nervous to eat or drink a thing."

"How about we get started, then?" Her mother gestured to the hallway and the room at the end of it with the velvet sofa overlooking the sea.

"You got this," Raf assured her. "I'll be here when you get back."

"*I* could use some coffee." Yas yawned. "You want some?"

"Sure." Raf settled on a stool on the kitchen island. He watched her pour coffee grounds into the coffee maker. "Hey, this is a nice change."

"What's that?"

"You making me coffee. Not often I get to have someone make something for me."

"Why stop there?" she said. "How about some pretzel brownies?"

"Don't joke about such things!"

"Who's joking? You know, I actually bought the ingredients a little while ago." She poked her head into the pantry and pulled out a bag of pretzels.

"Do we have enough time?"

"It'll be an hour at least, considering it's Nara's first time and all."

Raf hopped off the stool and riffled through the pantry, pulling out flour and sugar.

"I thought you wanted to be waited on?" she said.

"It always tastes better when we make them together."

"Facts." Yas grinned.

Soon the smell of coffee filled the room and the heat from the oven filled the space with warmth. Yas rolled up her sleeves and pulled down two coffee mugs.

"You and Warren bonded the other day, huh?" Raf pulled out measuring cups and spoons from the drawer by the stove. "You were like old pals at the diner."

"Bonded?" She snorted. "I'm still irritated about him steamrolling his way into the forest yesterday."

"I invited him," Raf reminded her.

"You did. Because you're you, Raf. The way he went about it, it rubbed me the wrong way."

"It's great he came," Raf said. "You know how word travels.

Yesterday evening, when I swung by to get gas, Oscar smiled at me. Warren's rubbing off on us."

"You're too good for this town. Oscar should be nice to you because you're *you*."

"At this point, we'll take what we can get."

"It's weird to see everyone transfixed. They're ready to do cartwheels if Warren deigns to look their way."

"Or throw an expensive festival because he said he liked them."

"Exactly." Yas leaned her elbows on the counter, watching him measure out flour. "Remember Kendall at city hall? The last one?"

"It's a privilege to be in this town!" Raf mimicked him, banging his fist on the counter.

They both laughed.

"He's ramped up the campaign against the festival." Yas pulled out the mixer and set it on the counter.

"Yeah, he got into it with Ernie at the park when people were cleaning up," Raf said. "Mateo had to hold him back."

"I get it. It *is* hard to see them going through with the festival. We're not ready."

"Lots of people *look* ready," Raf said. "They're fixing up the park so fast, it seems like Ernie really might pull off a smaller-scale festival in time."

"Money motivates."

"The Naismiths aren't just rich, though," Raf said. "They're stupid rich. I looked them up the other day. They'd be one of the richest countries in the world if they were their own nation-state. Considering that, Warren is pretty chill."

"I guess," Yas said. She didn't want to spend their time together discussing Warren. She wanted to be here with Raf.

They mixed sugar, butter, eggs, cocoa, and flour. They lay down the crushed pretzels in a layer and slowly poured the batter over.

"Think we got carried away?" Yas looked at the mixing bowl. "There's enough for two batches."

"You know me. I can always eat."

"Um, no way you can eat all that."

"Then we'll save some for our road trip."

"Right!" She grinned. "Raf, thanks so much for going with me!"

"Thanks for being patient while I worked it all out in my head. Sorry I couldn't make it work sooner."

She hugged him. She didn't realize she'd expected him to pull back until he didn't. She felt the light stubble against her face. His warm cheek against hers. A funny feeling roped through her. She wanted, in this moment, to never let go. When they parted, Yas felt heat rising to her face. She searched his face.

Do you feel it too? she wanted to ask. But as close as they were, she didn't know how to ask him this.

The oven beeped. Yas placed the baking dish inside the warmed oven as the back door creaked open and Nara emerged. She looked different—like a weight had been lifted. Without the constant tension lining her face, she was even more beautiful.

Raf called her over to the kitchen. "Nara, you've gotta try these sweets. Should be ready in twenty minutes."

"What are they?" she asked.

"Pretzel brownies," Yas said. "A little salty, a little sweet. So basically . . ."

"Perfect," Raf finished. "They are basically exactly perfect."

"Not sure I like to confuse my taste buds." Nara scrunched her nose.

"It's entirely possible they are palatable to an audience of only two," Raf said sheepishly.

"Nara, you did great today," Yas's mother said. "I'm going to put yours up to prepare first. Should be done within four days."

"Four days?" Nara's expression fell.

"The shells aren't as sturdy as they once were," Yas explained. "We have to make sure they're properly reinforced to keep their shape. I can bring it to you when it's ready."

"Thank you," she said. "It's strange, but I feel a bit better already?"

"Unburdening oneself can do that," her mother said. "You've been through far more than anyone should ever have to go through."

Stepping onto the back porch, they saw Patty was set up on the shoreline, but otherwise the coast was clear.

"Patty is a sweetheart," Yas assured Nara.

"And the people by the shore didn't do anything either. It wasn't as bad as I had feared," Nara marveled. "I had built it all up in my mind—but it was . . . fine."

"How about we head to the main drag next?" Raf teased.

"I don't know about that," Nara said.

"One step at a time." Yas swatted him.

When they got to the beach, Yas groaned.

"Warren!" Nara waved. "Nice to see you again."

"Likewise." He approached them. "Thought you didn't leave the forest."

"Baby steps." She smiled.

"Guess my pep talk helped, huh?"

Pep talk? *This* was Warren. Smug. Arrogant. Yas rolled her eyes at Raf, but he smiled at Warren too.

"Yas's mother is making a necklace for me," she said.

"I should get one made too. I do happen to live right next to the legendary place where it happens."

You mean the arts and crafts project? It wasn't fair. He'd apologized. And yet.

"You should," Nara said. "Yas's mother is so easy to talk to. I shared things with her that I hadn't voiced aloud before. I have no way to know if the necklace will work for me, but just sitting there and speaking with her helped."

Because it was therapy, Yas thought.

"It's gotta be tough," Warren said. "To leave Golub and come here."

"Leaving was not the tough part." Her smile faded. "Staying is."

"I heard about the wide-domed mountain dwellings—the warmth inside of them worked in direct correlation to the cold outside, right?"

"You know about that?" Raf asked.

"I've read everything there is to know about Golub life. It's fascinating. Are the solar windmills still there?" he asked.

"Unfortunately, they were close to buckling when I left," Nara said. "And the mountains are not well either. With the rising cold, heat also rises. So we cannot live outside, and we cannot live inside."

Warren had acted like he'd just wanted to admire a beautiful tree he'd seen poking out beyond the tree line. Now he sounded like a Golub expert.

He looked at Nara's arm. "And the leaf. This connects you to your home, right?" He grazed a finger against her wrist, causing Nara to inaudibly gasp. "The pathway home to Golub is through the tree?"

"Both to arrive and to return, yes," Nara said. "My brother left before you arrived. It's been . . . a difficult time for me, waiting to see if and when he will return. We can't know when the tree will glimmer again."

His eyes filled with concern. "Is there anything I could do to help?"

"Not unless you can tell us when the tree glimmers for an opening."

"Maybe I could help you figure that out."

"What do you mean?" Nara stared at him.

"Is there record keeping for when people have seen the door glimmer long enough to open?"

"There must be." She nodded. "Tolki Uncle would have it."

"He does keep notes," Raf said. "I don't think anyone's seen any pattern to predict when it would open lately."

"I could put it forth to a gifted statistician. Give us some educated guesses, at least. Worth a shot?"

"Warren, thank you," Nara said. "It would mean so much."

"My pleasure," he said. "Looking into this beats my sand-castle pastime." He gestured to the mound of sand to the right.

Nara looked at it. "That is a . . ."

"A disaster?" he finished. Nara clasped her hand over her mouth, but Warren was smiling. They both burst out laughing.

"You should have Raf help you," Nara said. "I have heard he is the best there is."

Yas looked at Raf. He wasn't smiling anymore. His eyes were fixed on Warren's hands lingering against Nara's wrist.

"Raf?" Nara nudged Raf. "Do you want to show him?"

"Sure," Raf said. "I'd be happy to."

They walked to the misshapen mound of sand. Raf kneeled to the ground. His expression was normal now.

But Yas had seen the way he looked at Warren. The pained look that flashed across his face.

Jealousy.

So it *was* true. No matter how she looked at it, they made all the sense in the world.

nineteen
RAF

"Raf! Mind coming here a second? Quick question for you."

Raf shut the register and walked over to Ernie and the other council folks camped out at their usual booth. Even Crissy was here today, though she studiously avoided looking at Raf. The table was cluttered with notebooks and balled-up scraps of paper.

"We needed a young person's opinion about something," Ernie said. "Are you all into fireworks?"

"Fireworks?" Raf repeated. "At the *festival*? We never had fireworks before."

"You see?" Bea said triumphantly.

"Sounds to me like a comment in *favor* of fireworks," Ernie said. "Kendall and the others are upset about everyone remembering too much . . . but if we do things *differently*, it can pacify them, hopefully, and get us what we need. A win-win."

"I'm pretty sure Kendall won't care if there are or aren't fireworks," Gil said.

"Sorry, Ernie, but I agree with Gil," Raf said.

Ernie's face fell. "It's possible that there's no pleasing him, but maybe it might help *others* who are having a bit of a hard time. With a different tone, the festival won't feel like . . ."

A haunting, thought Raf. Ernie wanted to separate what happened that night from the festival, but the two were inextricably tied together. Fireworks, different food stalls—these wouldn't erase the memories of what happened.

"Will you be ready in time?" Raf asked.

"We have a few vendors lined up." Ernie beamed. "I talked to Jeff, and the Backyard Bandits are offering their services pro bono. And the mayors of Ridgeview and Mill Creek said they got an enthusiastic response from their communities— we'll have a decent turnout after all. Just got to finish fixing up the park, but we've got shifts working to get it back to good. I daresay we'll get there soon."

"I have an idea that might help the Weepers get behind things," Raf said. "How about before the festivities begin, there could be a moment of silence?"

"Silence?" Ernie's smile wavered.

"That's a big part of our own Hamra gathering each year. We remember the good and the bad of the year that came; we write down our difficult moments and speak of the lighter ones as well. It helps us let go. Maybe that would appease the Weepers," Raf said. "If we did something to remember what happened."

Ernie looked like a deer in headlights.

"It's a great idea," he finally said. "For later. If we go down that road at the festival, it won't be much of a festival at all. Reminding the Naismiths about . . . *you know* . . . it'll only make it worse. They live in the house where it happened. We don't want them to get fixated on all the things that went wrong here."

What about the rest of us? Raf wondered. There was a reason no one had planned to put it on this year.

When Raf walked back into the kitchen, his phone buzzed. It was a text from Yas.

> Look at the inside of the
> apartment! Hisae sent me
> a million photos.

There were three bubbles. And then another batch of photos.

> Wait, how'd these Surrey
> pics get in here? ☺

She hadn't brought up Surrey lately, but of course she hadn't forgotten. He scrolled past the science building with the mustard door. The concrete pathways across from the grassy open courtyard. He'd looked at the website so many times, he'd memorized these images. The cozy suite with twin beds and matching nightstands. The stock images of students with textbooks spread out on benches and smiling.

Look at the library! She texted another photo.

The interior looked like a painting. Students absorbed in work at wooden tables with a warm glow overhead as multi-colored spines were displayed all around.

> They got great marketing and
> promotion. You know it's all

> photoshopped to full saturation
> to look amazing, right?

> We could see it for ourselves
> and get to the bottom of it
> once and for all!

Less than a week to go. He glanced at his leaf. He'd broken down the trip in increments. He'd set an alarm once they left the perimeter. Plus, the leaf was its own warning system. It burned. It reminded. Just like it had the night of the Moonlight Bay Festival last year.

"Earth to Raf."

Raf blinked. Warren. Had he been so distracted, he didn't hear the front door chime?

"Hey, Warren," Raf said. "Coffee?"

"You know it." He nodded. "Do you work here *all* day?"

"I did for a while." Raf poured him a cup and slid it toward him. "I'm trying to take more breaks when things slow in the afternoon, though. Dena's pushing me to take more and more time off."

"You should take her up on it," he said. "I told Nara to come over and check out my pool tomorrow. My mom is making a brunch. Well, 'making' a brunch." He put up air quotes. "Our chef is making it. Swing by around eleven or so?"

"Nara?" Raf frowned. "When did you see her?"

"A few minutes ago. She was by the shoreline near your forest."

Nara, outside? Alone? And going to Warren's? It was one thing to sit by the shore and another to go to Warren's home.

"Thanks for the invite," said Raf. "I'm working, and Nara—I'm sure she'd love to, but—"

"She said yes."

She said yes?

"It's cool, right?" Warren asked, studying Raf's face.

"Yes, of course it is," Raf said. Warren wasn't a local. He didn't blame her for the town's circumstances. She didn't have a reason to worry around him.

"I didn't mean to offend," said Warren.

"Nara's not under my guardianship," Raf told him. "I'm glad she said yes, but don't be offended if she changes her mind."

"She said the same thing." He laughed.

Raf went into the kitchen to check on orders. His thoughts were a jumble. It was great that Nara was leaving the forest—this was good for her. Healthy. Even Tolki Uncle now understood that remaining within the confines of the forest wasn't healthy.

Raf's worries were rooted deeper. He'd seen how she'd lit up when Warren approached them the other day. How she'd startled when he touched her. Nara didn't love Warren. Of course not. But was she starting to like him? The last thing he'd want was for her to plunge down the same rabbit hole he had. The one that went nowhere because it couldn't. The one that could exact costs greater than she could imagine.

It's probably nothing. He had no way to know what was in Nara's heart. After all this time, she saw a friendly face. Someone who saw her as *her*, not a harbinger of all that had followed. Why *wouldn't* her eyes light up? That's all there was to it.

He was simply projecting. Not all were as foolish as Raf.

"Want an omelet?"

Yas's father pulled out a carton of eggs from the fridge. He'd been home less than forty-eight hours and was packed up to leave already—back to Yaksta. His new job. His new life.

"Not sure I'm hungry."

"I'm adding sautéed shitake." He raised his eyebrows. "Can't say no now, can you?"

He looked at her so earnestly. How could she say no?

"Omelet sound great."

Her father set the table with plates. A carton of juice. The coffee carafe. Her favorite mug with rainbow glitter.

"These are good," she said, taking a bite.

"Glad I still got it," her father said. "How's your summer going?"

"It's been busy with the art gallery, but it's definitely quieter than usual *here*. Not a single souvenir moved."

"That's rough. Hopefully things pick up."

It's July. She bit her tongue. He'd checked out. She had to accept that. The sooner the better.

"How was your walkabout with Warren?" he asked.

"You know about that?"

"Word gets around." He smiled. "Thanks for doing it. Meant a lot to the council."

"You mean to Ernie."

"To Ernie." He laughed.

When they finished eating, her father took their dishes. Yas helped him clean up the table. She tried not to fixate on the fact that her mother hadn't joined them. Her plate was untouched. The dishwasher was humming in the background when her father cleared his throat.

"I wanted your thoughts on something," he said. "Your *honest* unfiltered thoughts."

"Okay," she said slowly.

"If Yaksta ended up becoming my permanent home base . . . would you visit me?"

Permanent. Home base. The words hit like a bullet train through her heart.

"You said you'd keep searching," she managed to say.

"I am. It's not looking good, though."

By that, did he mean the job hunt? Or his marriage?

"You can't give up, Dad."

Her father sighed.

"If you stay in Yaksta, then what happens to our family? Just come back. Maybe Ernie's plan works. Manufacturing returns. They'll need a sales team. Pharmaceutical reps make way more than candy reps, I bet. I'm sure Ernie can put in a good word about the work you used to do for the Hollers."

"No," her father said with a sharper tone than she'd ever heard him take. "We can't wait the *rest* of our lives waiting for what *might* happen. I *have* to make decisions based on the facts I have right now. And this is our life right now."

Tears pricked her eyes. She'd grown cynical too. Wasn't she *also* planning to leave? Wasn't she also struggling to breathe beneath the weight of all the memories? But Yaksta? A day's drive away?

"The color could return," Yas said.

"Yes." Her father nodded. "And the Hollers might come back. And the latest grant Ernie applied for might get approved."

"When did *you* get so cynical?"

"Not cynical. Pragmatic," her father said. "Change is a part of life. Once, the place we now stand upon was beneath the surface of the ocean. Before that, volcanoes bloomed. For all we know, tyrannosaurs stomped along these shores. Things change and there's nothing you can do about it. That's the only reality that's true. We must change with it."

"What if I told you it did come back?" She'd only told Raf, but her father needed to hear it. "What if I told you I saw a hint of pink in the sea?"

"It's a nice thought," he said. "But—"

"It's not a hypothetical. I saw it. Straight out that way, about a hundred yards from shore."

He looked at her calmly. Considering it. "Then I would tell you the mind is a powerful thing. It can conjure up what we want most." He pressed his fingers against his temple. "This is what I'm talking about, honey. It's unhealthy here. To keep searching for what isn't coming back."

Yas's head throbbed. He'd entertained her tales of visiting fairies and gnomes as a little girl more than he'd bothered to consider this. The way he looked at her now, it was how she looked at the Weepers.

"It wasn't a trick of the mind." Her voice rose. "I saw it! You don't want to believe me because if you did, then you wouldn't be able to justify what you're doing. You *need* to believe Moonlight is over—our business is over—so you can sleep at night! What I don't understand is why you even bother to come back!"

He flinched as though she'd slapped him. She trembled with anger.

"I'm sorry." He sighed. He leaned down and kissed her forehead. "I really and truly am, Yas."

He told her he'd call when he reached Yaksta. In a few steps, he was out the door, down the stairs. The engine rumbled outside. He was gone.

She looked out the window at the gravel parking lot. The empty space with marks where the car sat moments earlier. Who was that person who'd just driven away? Could he still be the same father who'd rescued her kite each time it got stuck in a tree in Main Street Park? Who carried her, racing all the way to the nearby clinic, when she'd fallen and broken her arm? He'd always been there. He'd never looked away. And now he hadn't just looked away, he had left.

Things change and there's nothing you can do about it. Yes, she thought, her father was right about that.

Yas gathered her supplies and threw them in a bag, along with a bottle of water and snacks. The mural. It was nearly done—it would be complete before she left for Edgewood.

Walking toward the beach, she heard the sound of laughter. A familiar voice. Yas frowned. It couldn't be . . .

Nara?

Yas strode toward Holler Mansion. Toward the opened gate. When she got to the entrance, her hunch was confirmed. It *was* Nara. She wore a yellow sundress and reclined by the aquamarine pool. Warren sat next to her, wearing swim trunks and a rash guard.

"Yas!" Nara waved her over.

Yas tentatively approached her. "Didn't expect to see you here."

"It was nice to get out of the forest and visit your home the other day." She chewed her bottom lip. "I hadn't felt so peaceful in a long time. But I'm not sure this was the best idea."

"I didn't mean to make you self-conscious," Yas rushed to say. "It's good to be out."

"Grab a chair," Warren said.

Yas did *not* want to grab a chair; she was on her way to paint the mural. But something about leaving Nara alone with Warren made her uneasy.

"You were okay walking over?" Yas asked her, settling down.

"Warren met me by the forest. I was finally able to show him the Golub tree!"

"It was incredible. Almost a spiritual experience." Warren's eyes brightened. "No. Not almost. It *was* a spiritual experience. When you're right up against it, you might as well be an ant. Something about it just really makes you stop and think about everything."

"It puts the world in perspective, doesn't it?" Nara nodded. "You feel how inconsequential you are."

"I'd say you're pretty consequential," Warren teased.

Is he flirting with her?

"Was everything all right walking over here?" Yas asked.

"I saw a few people, but they just *smiled*."

Of course they smiled, Yas thought. She'd been with Warren.

Yas looked at the pool. She hadn't been here since it had been redone. She braced for memories to flood back, but it looked different now—mosaic tiles at the bottom of the pool were in the shape of a peacock. A lot of effort for a family planning to leave. Maybe Ernie was in luck after all.

"Who's ready for snacks?" a voice called out.

Warren's mother strolled through the opened French doors in dark sunglasses, wearing shorts and a sleeveless blouse. She held a tray with two pink lemonades and tea sandwiches.

She set them down on a low table and glanced in Yas's direction.

Her eyes were concealed behind the sunglasses. "I'll get another drink," she said.

"No, thank you, I'm good," Yas replied tensely.

"Hope you're all enjoying yourselves." She patted Nara's shoulder.

Yas remembered Siobhan from the diner. The way she'd coolly regarded Raf and Dena. What changed? Yas's head throbbed. She hated feeling suspicious all the time. Wasn't it possible Nara simply won this woman over? Nara didn't have a mean bone in her body—there was no reason to dislike her in the first place, though this never stopped people from hating the Golub anyway.

Yas knew Raf would tell her to give them a chance. This was a big step for Nara. To be out of the forest. And being seen around town with Warren, of all people? It could shift things for her. For their people. Yas sat back in the seat. Maybe she'd grown so jaded, she was unable to see anyone's intentions as pure.

twenty-one

RAF

"Tell me why we're doing this, again?" Yas said, wiping sweat from her brow.

"I'm sorry," Raf told her. "Uncle roped me into it. I couldn't say no. I was really looking forward to heading to Edgewood today."

"It's okay," she told him. "We'll go next week."

Raf checked his watch and grimaced. It was four o'clock in the afternoon, and he was exhausted. This felt particularly unfair since it was Wednesday, his *one* complete day off. Not only was the trip out of town pushed out—again—he didn't have a chance to sleep in or catch up on other tasks that had waited until today to be attended to. Instead, Raf was in Main Street Park, helping with the community cleanup.

At present, he mulched the flower beds and bushes alongside Yas. "The final blitz," as Ernie had put it cheerfully that morning, before the festival's launch a week from tomorrow. Practically everyone in town was here. Vendor booth tents were being erected along the perimeter of the park this very moment. A new welcome sign was being hammered next to the entrance.

"Heard from your dad lately?" Raf asked Yas.

"He called last night, but I didn't answer. If he wants to be on his own, he should just be on his own."

"Aw, come on, Yas," Raf said. "Your dad—he loved working for the Hollers. The way they left all their employees in the lurch probably felt like a personal betrayal."

"We *all* feel betrayed, don't we?" Yas gestured to the people in the square. "I know I'm leaving also . . . but I'll be back every weekend. I'm not giving up on my family. My dad? At this point, I hope he stays gone forever."

"Not forever, Yas," he said gently. "Trust me on that."

"Oh, Raf." Yas winced. "I'm sorry."

"No, I get it . . ." His voice trailed off. Tolki Uncle approached them, his shirt and pants damp from power washing the concrete walkways.

"You are making wonderful progress," Uncle said, nodding approvingly.

"I understand why you wanted us to help, but I'm tired, Uncle."

"I know this was a big ask from me. Everyone is here. It felt important that our community represent as well."

Ernie approached them. "Thanks for the pressure washing, T." He patted Uncle on the back. "The sidewalks are gleaming. The rosebushes—they're beautiful. Look like they've been there all along."

"It was my pleasure. I will try to remember to water them regularly," Uncle said.

Ernie clapped a hand on Raf's back. "Now, son, can I possibly bug you about something?"

Raf smiled weakly. He was almost done mulching and wanted to head home, but Tolki Uncle watched expectantly. "Sure, Ernie. What's up?"

"I was remembering your sandcastles. Maybe you could

create some to showcase on the beach ahead?" He pointed to the thin stretch of sand bordering the park toward the ocean. "Might be fun? Heard you were helping Warren with one the other day."

Raf did not want to spend hours putting together sand-castles. Even seeing Warren's lump of packed sand the other day had made him feel nauseous. There were too many memories tied to it. Before Raf could figure out a response, he heard a sound in the distance. Chanting.

Looking past Ernie's shoulder, he saw Kendall. Olive was with him too, as were Laura, Mateo, John, Betty, Sebastian, and Rodrigo. There were twenty people in total. Once again, they wore all gray. They marched toward the park. Their mouths moved in unison, as though they were one person. One voice. Booming into the air. Two words that sent a chill straight down Raf's spine.

"REMEMBER WHEN!"

The words, spoken like a ceaseless drumbeat, practically vibrated the ground beneath him.

Ernie broke away from Raf and hurried toward them.

"Come on, everyone," he protested. "We understand your pain. We do. We're trying to do something nice. I understand you don't agree, but—"

"REMEMBER WHEN! REMEMBER WHEN! REMEMBER WHEN!"

With each chant, their cries grew louder and louder. Jake stormed toward them.

"Remember *what* exactly?" he shouted.

"Jake, I can handle this." Ernie hurried after him. "Kendall. Please."

"Give it a rest," Jake growled at Kendall.

"Jake's right. We're trying to help this town," Crissy said.

"If you wanted to help, you'd join us, by the sea," Kendall said. "You would do the work. It's not too late."

"Help? You're not helping *anything*!" Jake barreled toward Kendall until their faces were inches apart. Ernie jumped in, pushing him back. "You're just getting in the way!"

Kendall watched Jake struggle against Ernie's restraint. His lips curled into a smile as the chants continued. "Remember," Kendall said evenly. "Or be sorry."

With a clap of his hands, the procession fell silent. They filed down the pathway, out of the park, out of sight.

"Are they a cult now?" Yas whispered. "Matching clothes. A chant. Charismatic leader."

"Kendall? Charismatic?"

"Fair point. It's weird, though."

Clearing his throat, Ernie glanced around the stunned crowd. He plastered on a huge smile. "Let's not let an interruption mess with our flow!" He addressed the crowd. "Gil—why don't you crank up the music? We'll have this park ready to go by dinner, won't we?"

The radio crackled on. Music filled the air. People warily returned to their work, but the Weepers' words still echoed.

"Kendall's acting more and more unhinged," Yas told Raf. "It's like he *wants* to get a rise out of everyone. Ernie keeps tearing down the signs, but there's double the number today."

"It's not just him," Raf said. "There are a *lot* more Weepers. I wonder if we should be worried."

"The festival's sparked something. Like they're zombies coming to life."

An upbeat song came on the air. Raf grimaced. "Not this one again. Like I haven't been through enough today. It played nonstop last year. I'm over it."

"Well, bad news, I added it to our playlist. That feels like a sign."

"From the woman who doesn't believe in signs? I'm noticing a trend here, Yas."

"It's just a saying," she retorted. "The pieces are fitting together. No one better come up with some other idea we can't say no to next Wednesday."

"I hope not. Leaving for even a little while sounds nice."

"Speaking of leaving," Yas said. "Nara was at Warren's the other day. Holler Mansion."

Raf nodded. "He invited me too. I was working. I'm shocked Nara went. It's a huge step."

"He knew you'd be busy, didn't he? Couldn't he have picked a different time?"

"It's fine. I'm not a big pool person."

She nodded, but her brows were furrowed.

"Did something happen?" Raf asked, growing tense. Nara hadn't said a word. In fact, she'd been nothing but smiles all through dinner.

"Nothing happened. It's one of those things you feel more than you can put words to. Did you know he ended up seeing your tree?"

Raf nodded. "Nara checked with Uncle beforehand, but there's no reason to stop him from seeing it."

"Yeah . . ."

"Is there something else? You can tell me."

"It's just, his mom was so . . . nice."

"Nice?"

"She was chatting up Nara. Super cheery. All smiles."

"I can see how that's weird," Raf said flatly. "Seeing someone speaking to us like actual human beings in this town has got to be surprising."

"Raf!" She gasped. "That's not what I meant! You remember the diner last week. Where was all the sweetness then? How do they go from cold to hot so quickly?"

"They *were* snooty, but it's good for Nara to see that not everyone thinks she's the grim reaper. Having powerful people like them on team Nara—that's a win."

Yas moved to reply, but then she paused. Raf realized the entire park had gone quiet.

Was Kendall back? What now?

But it wasn't Kendall. In fact, for a moment, Raf wasn't sure *what* he was seeing—his brain unable to process it: Nara. And Warren. Walking down Main Street.

The pair seemed oblivious to everyone as they walked past the stores in deep conversation. They slowed outside Mateo's gallery. Warren leaned close to Nara and whispered something. She laughed. It was only when the street ended at Main Street Park that Nara looked up.

Her shoulders hunched up to her ears. She moved to turn. What was she *thinking*? Raf's heart raced. How could Warren have let this happen? He took a step toward her. He had to go to her. Before Raf could do anything, Warren touched her elbow. He leaned in and spoke. Nara gave him a tentative smile. She nodded. Instead of turning away, they walked toward the park.

The townspeople stood unmoving as the pair approached. *They have a calculation to make,* Raf realized. How much they hated the Golub, and how much they needed the Naismiths to stay. The two stepped into the park. Breaking free from his trance, Ernie hurried toward them.

"Hello, Nara. Warren." He stuck his hand out and heartily shook their hands. "Glad to see you both out and about."

"This is serious teamwork," Warren said.

Ernie nodded. "Finishing touches for the festival."

Crissy glided toward them. "It's going to be wonderful! We think you'll—" She caught herself. "*Both* of you will like it."

Where was Uncle? Raf scanned the crowd until he saw him off to the side. He looked as relieved as Raf felt.

"Anything I could do to help?" Warren asked.

"Thanks, son! We've got it taken care of," Ernie assured him. "A few things can't be helped, like the god-awful Ferris wheel, but otherwise it'll be good as new shortly."

Warren studied the Ferris wheel. "I can probably help with that."

"Thoughtful of you to offer." Ernie chuckled. "We've got a pretty tight timeline at this point, so I'm not sure it's possible."

"Do you like Ferris wheels?" Warren asked Nara.

"I have never been on one." She self-consciously ran a hand across her newly made star necklace.

"That settles it. I'll get this taken care of," he said.

"Really?" Yas crossed her arms. "In a week?"

Warren shrugged. "I like a challenge."

"Warren . . . we're speechless. We cannot thank you enough," Crissy said. "Even the thought is so generous."

A crowd gathered around Nara and Warren. Nara eyed

them nervously. Warren placed a hand on Nara's shoulder. She smiled at him.

"Raf?" Yas touched Raf's arm. He flinched—the leaf on his wrist burned. Looking at Yas, a sensation much like dread rose within him. *This* was what was happening to Nara.

"I'll be right back," he told her.

He strode toward Uncle.

"A quick word?" Raf asked.

"Certainly," Uncle said.

Once they were out of hearing range, Raf turned to him. "You're seeing this, aren't you? Nara and Warren?"

"Wonderful, isn't it?"

Wonderful? "It's nice she's out," Raf said, "but . . ."

"You think you can predict something, and life reminds you we have no idea what even the next moment will bring." Uncle was beaming. "This is a very good development."

"Uncle," he said slowly. "Does Nara know?"

"Hmm?"

"About the rules around developing feelings for someone not of our world."

"That's not what is happening here." Uncle looked at him askance. "It's good for her to be out—you and Dena were always so concerned about her isolation, and now she's done it. She is stepping outside and making her way. And being with a Naismith, of all people—this is a good thing for us, Raf. Even Jake's astonished."

"I understand, but we could warn her. What if they develop feelings for each other?"

"I hardly think there's any worry of that. It's all right, Raf."

Uncle laughed. "Having a friend is a good thing—no rules against it. I *will* talk to her in due time, but in the meantime, I'd say friendship is important. Sometimes it's the only way to see things through."

This made no sense. How could Uncle not worry? How could Nara not be warned until she was in too deep?

twenty-two

YAS

Walking home from the park cleanup, Yas felt the strangest sensation. It took a moment to recognize it. Lightness. It was cleaning up park with Raf, their hands digging into long-neglected soil to unroot weeds, put down new flowers, and mulch the beds. It was seeing sweet Nara outside the forest, walking through town freely. It didn't matter if the locals behaved themselves purely for Warren's sake. Today was the closest in forever that Moonlight *felt* like Moonlight. Maybe Ernie was right. Maybe Warren and his family *were* the key to turning things around here.

And next week! Next Wednesday, Raf and Yas headed off to Edgewood. Maybe he'd decide to check out Surrey too. Maybe if he saw it in person, it would sink in. That he couldn't walk away from what he was destined for.

"Well, hello!" a bright voice called out.

Patty stood on Yas's front porch in her trademark pink top and floral shorts.

"Hi," Yas said. "I didn't see you there."

"Lost in your thoughts." Patty chuckled. "You've been that way since I first met you . . . when was it? About fifteen years ago, I wager."

"Has it been that long?"

"Believe so. You could barely toddle in the thick sand, but you managed to introduce yourself to me my first week here. Showed up with a shell, painted and sprinkled with glitter." She smiled. "Still got it on my bookshelf back home."

"I haven't decorated shells in a while."

"Busy with the mural." Patty shaded her eyes with her hand and nodded toward the pier. "It's shaping up nicely."

Yas glanced over at it and felt a touch of pride; it *was* coming together.

"Your style reminds me of DeMoi."

"Ha!" Yas laughed. "I don't know about that."

"I'm serious," Patty said. "Her earlier works were very similar in brushwork."

"You sure you're not an artist, Patty?"

"I told you, I can't draw worth a lick—but I know good art when I see it."

"Thanks, Patty—that is high praise."

"I call it like I see it." Patty winked. "I came over this way because I had a question for you, actually. Would it be okay for me to get a necklace made?"

"You want a star?" Yas asked, surprised. Patty on her beach chair with a mystery book in hand seemed to not have a care in the world. But there was no telling what people showed and what they kept hidden.

"I know, I know," Patty said quickly. "It's a local thing, but . . ."

"You're as local as they come, Patty."

"Thanks, doll. Could use a pick-me-up. Didn't want to barge in to your residence unannounced, though."

"Let's see if my mother has room to fit you in," Yas said.

"Patty," Yas's mother greeted her when she stepped inside. "Good to see you."

"She wanted to get a star made," Yas said. "What's your calendar like this week?"

"As luck would have it, I have time right now," her mother said. "Just hang tight a minute? I'll tidy up in the back."

"Those are some pretty necklaces." Patty nodded to the display by the front door.

"Thanks," Yas said. "I made these last summer. Yours will look similar."

When Patty left to join Yas's mother in the back room, Yas lingered by the necklaces strung along the wall. She remembered each of them. The yellow shell with pink waves. The lavender one with swirls of red. The one to the right with blue feathering. That was the last one she'd made.

Wandering to her room, she opened her top dresser drawer and plucked out the gray box to the side. She sifted through the childhood trinkets, faded photos, and the shell. The perfect one, with ribbed edges and a smooth interior, the size of her palm, that she'd been unable to part with. Pulling her scissors from their felt case, she sat at the desk by her bed. Snipping the edges of the shell, her heart skipped a beat. It was so familiar. Intimate. The weight of the scissors. How the tiny triangular discards of shell tinkled when they fell upon the table. She sanded and polished the edges. It'd been so long, but her hands still knew what to do. Relief passed through her. It was all there inside of her still.

Yas pulled out a bowl in the kitchen and filled it with warm water and crushed limestone before plunging the star inside.

A wave of grief washed over her. Had things not taken the turn they did, she'd be doing this work as an apprentice— fine-tuning her skills for actual work with actual customers and learning the way to blend the work of the water with words to heal. Had things not taken the turn they did, she'd have believed that they could.

Something wet landed on the kitchen table. A tear. She wiped it away and retrieved her case of paints. The brushes of all different sizes, different from what she'd used on the mural. These were used only on shells. For priming them. Painting them. Detailing them. She dried the shell and laid it against the table. The base was yellow like their picnic basket, stored in the attic. The green edges for the trips to the cliff-laden hills where they picnicked, three towns over. One memory unlocked the next. Her father's knock on her door on Sunday mornings for breakfast, her mother sleepily walking over in her robe and slippers as they ate waffles and scrambled eggs, the soccer games they'd put on after. The way her father cheered loudest when he attended her own soccer games, so embarrassingly proud, she'd blush.

It hadn't been perfect. Yas had held worries before. The tourists *did* blast their radios. The lines were endless and everywhere all summer. It wasn't until her world ended that she understood how fragile it'd been.

Dipping her brush in gold, she painted MB along the lower edge. It would need to dry, followed by a second limestone wash to finish. But it was a star now. *Their* stars. Yas had pulled out paper towels and laid them flat to dry the shell on when the door opened.

"Thank you so much," Yas heard Patty say as she and her

mom walked down the hallway. "That chat did me a world of good already."

"I'm glad I could help." Her mother slowed as she neared the kitchen. Her eyes drifted to the star. "Yas, you did that just now?"

"Yes." Yas rushed to add, "But it wasn't a usable shell."

"It's . . . it's beautiful," her mother said.

"Absolutely," Patty marveled.

Yas looked at the shell, a mixture of joy and sadness entwined inside of her. Who knew what any of the work did— but this star she was looking at? Yes, it was beautiful.

twenty-three
RAF

"Just me, or did the movie go way faster than usual?" Raf asked as lights flickered on in the theater. He rubbed his eyes. As usual, they were the only ones there.

"Movies must go by faster when you're reciting every line out loud," Yas commented.

"Hey! Not true!" Raf protested.

"Are you not even aware you're doing it? This means we've officially entered the 'too many viewings' territory."

"We crossed that bridge weeks ago." He yawned.

This *was*, after all, their fifth viewing. Luckily, the quality of the caramel pretzels and buttered popcorn hadn't changed either. And an evening spent with cold air blasting them in a darkened theater was reason enough to be here.

And the quiet.

Not the physical quiet of the space around him, but the quiet that happened in Raf's head when he was at the movies. When the loudspeakers came to life, the constant churn in Raf's mind emptied. A welcome relief.

"What had you so distracted?" he asked Yas as they exited the theater.

"How could you tell?"

"I wasn't sure," he admitted. "But *now* I am."

"You tricked me." She poked him. "I *am* a little distracted. Just the usual. My dad. The festival. All sorts of fun stuff. I'm excited about our trip, though—it's almost time!"

"Me too." He *was* looking forward to it, but he still hadn't told his mother—only Bura knew he needed the truck, though not what for. He'd arranged for Dar to watch the kids that day so his mother wouldn't be burdened. But what would his mother or Bura say if they knew the real reason he needed it? What would Tolki Uncle think?

"I already grabbed chips and soda for the drive," Yas said. "Also downloaded a campus map this morning. *If* you're up for it." She laughed at his side eye. "They're not doing tours during the summer, and classes aren't in session, so I thought it best to be prepared."

"You sure you're not planning to dump me there and make a run for it?"

"Can't make any promises."

Raf shook his head and laughed.

"And for a plan B," Yas continued, "they have a theater a few miles from Edgewood. It's got more than one movie playing, believe it or not—*new* movies."

"Oh," Raf began. "I'm not sure—"

"It's a *really* nice theater. Remember? We went there for a school field trip in sixth grade."

"I didn't go."

"Of course you went! It was the shark documentary. Lilah screamed so loud, they called her Shark Attack the rest of the year."

"I don't think so."

"Wait." She frowned. "You ended up getting sick. Right?"

Raf nodded. It was the culmination of a whole semester of underwater science studies. The leaf would be safe, his parents had told Uncle. There'd be no harm—the buses would be back well before the etching was in any danger. Tolki Uncle had been adamant: It wasn't worth the risk. Vehicles could break down. Delays happened. Raf didn't know how to tell his teacher or Yas that he'd be the only one not going. So he pretended—until the very last moment—that he was.

"Well, now we can make up for that," Yas said.

"I probably need to get back as soon as we're done. My leaf gets funny if I go too far for too long."

"Right. Sorry," Yas said quickly.

Her arm brushed against his as they walked. He thought of Nara and Warren.

"Has Nara been by again?" Raf asked Yas. "To Warren's?"

"Not that I've seen."

"It was weird, at the park—seeing them together."

"That *was* surreal," Yas said. "I wasn't sure if I was crashing a hangout or a date when I saw them by the pool."

"Date?" He stared at her. "What about it seemed like a date?"

"I don't know." She eyed him curiously. "He *seems* into her, doesn't he?"

Uncle had dismissed it, so Raf began doubting his own intuition, but it *wasn't* in his head. Yas saw it too. There *was* something brewing. Nara had no idea what the consequences could be.

"Raf?" Yas touched his elbow. "You still there?"

He felt his leaf warm. Was this happening to Nara too? He

hated how much she didn't know. The truth about Kot. Now this. Uncle was trying to protect her—but did there come a point when protection was more harmful than the truth?

Uncle couldn't see past how their friendship benefitted their community, but Raf *knew* how difficult it was to push away what one felt. He also knew the consequences. If Uncle wouldn't tell her, Raf would.

Nara knelt over the flowers in her garden, watering them with her gardening pail. She glanced back at the sound of his approaching steps.

"Hey, Raf." She smiled. "How was the movie?"

"It was the same as last week," he replied.

"Maybe next time I could join you."

"That would be nice. I've been trying to get you to check it out forever."

"Warren's been a godsend," she told him. "I cannot tell you how it feels to be able to walk about and feel safe."

She was happy. Here came Raf to destroy it.

"Nara," he said. "There's something I need to tell you."

She set the pail on the ground. "Sure, Raf."

They sat on her front stoop, overlooking the other homes. She watched him expectantly.

Just tell her. He swallowed.

"I'm not sure how much Uncle told you about our leaf and how it works on this side of the world."

"He told Kot and me some of it. About the safety perimeter," she said. "It can risk us losing our leaves and our ability to return home should such a day ever arrive."

"But there are other ways to lose a leaf."

"What other ways?"

There was no easy or gentle way to put it.

"Love."

"Love?" She frowned.

"If you fall in love with anyone who is leafless—and you act on it—the leaf vanishes."

"Fall in love?" Nara repeated. "But what does that have to do with anything?" She took in Raf's drawn expression. "Oh." Her eyes softened. "Oh, Raf."

Just as he'd feared, her smile was gone. Raf felt a rock in the pit of his stomach. He was right to tell her, after all. He hated having to break her heart, even if it *was* a necessary breaking.

"I'm so sorry, Raf," she said. "This must be so difficult for you."

He frowned. Had he misheard? "For me?"

"You and Yas. This can't be easy. I can't begin to imagine."

Heat spread across his face. "No, that's not what I meant," he said quickly.

"It's okay," she said. "I know."

"Yas and I. We're friends. We've been best friends since grade school. There's . . . there's nothing to know," he sputtered.

"All I know is what I see. The way you both look at each other."

Raf moved to deny it, but then—

Both?

He tried to find the right words. To deflect. She looked at him intently, with genuine concern. What was the point in hiding it from her?

"I do love her," he said quietly. The truth. Spoken aloud for the first time. He felt light-headed. Exposed. "But the feeling is not mutual."

"I wouldn't be so confident."

Raf almost laughed. From an outside perspective, it was possible that someone could see their togetherness as a sign of something more—but he knew how Yas still thought of Moses, checking his social media feed surreptitiously. They were friends. She saw him as a friend. Nothing more.

"Even though you love her," Nara continued, "your leaf is there, isn't it?"

"It's not the feeling that's the problem," he said. "It's if you act upon it. If you say the words. When you're with Warren, does your leaf ever act funny?"

"Not really."

"Never? Not even a flicker?"

"I suppose it does flicker *sometimes*." She frowned. "But the leaf can be finicky . . . that's how it is."

"That's a signal it sends. A warning system to protect itself. To protect you."

Nara shook her head firmly. "Warren's been kind to me. After so long locked up and hidden away—he sees *me*. And I have Warren to thank for helping me feel like I can safely get out of the forest. I appreciate him a great deal. But I don't love him, Raf."

"Maybe you don't know it yet," Raf said. "The leaf flickering means *somewhere* in you the feeling is there—it knows before you fully become aware. That's why I wanted to warn you—the leaf is our one connection back to Golub—to each other. Without it . . . we lose everything."

"Why wouldn't anyone have mentioned it to me before?"

"You've been dealing with enough as is," Raf said.

She nodded, considering all he told her.

"I'm sorry, Raf," she finally told him. "It isn't fair, not that fair has anything to do with anything, right?"

The sun lowered in the distance. Lights blinked on in the homes around them—music sounded through half-opened windows. Soon it would be night.

Raf thought about what Nara said. Yas feeling the same toward him as he did? She didn't. He knew this. And he wasn't sure what would have been worse—for how he felt to be unrequited, or to know his feelings *were* reciprocated and he couldn't do a thing about it.

twenty-four
YAS

Yas yanked and yanked—until, finally, her faded green back-pack and thermal lunch box that had been shoved into the recesses of her closet since the last day of high school popped out.

Setting them on the kitchen island, she smiled. After what felt like forever, it was *finally* here! Wednesday. Raf had to watch his brothers for a short bit in the morning, but they'd be on the road by lunch. He promised he'd bring his famous turkey paninis, and she was gathering the rest of their stash. Playlist? Check. Drinks? Snacks? Check and check. She packed in fresh pretzel brownies she'd gotten up extra early to bake as well.

"Where are you off to?" her mother asked.

Yas froze. She'd hoped to slip out before having to say anything. But there was her mother. Standing in the hallway. Watching her. She'd been meaning to tell her by now. She just didn't know *how*. But if today went according to plan, she left in just over a month.

"I have some paintings to mail off for Marie—and Raf is joining me," said Yas. "We thought we'd get out of town for a little while."

"That sounds fun!"

Since Patty came by, things had grown less tense between them. If it'd been this way from the start, would Yas have even considered leaving? She looked out the window. The Weepers were gathered not far from where she stood.

"When will they give it up?" Yas asked her mother. She pointed outside. "There are more people there than ever."

"The festival's stirred up a lot of emotion."

"Raf told Ernie he should do a moment of silence, but Ernie's too busy pretending last year didn't happen. Don't get me wrong, the flyers *are* obnoxious. You know they papered them all over the bandstand and stapled them onto the trees around the park last night?"

"Poor Ernie." Her mother sighed. "And poor Kendall. This is all so difficult."

"Kendall doesn't help his case acting the way he does."

"It's been a difficult year. We're all finding our own ways to cope."

Yas looked at the gravel driveway. The empty space where a car should be. It *had* been a hard year for everyone.

"He called an hour ago," her mother said. "He's coming by after work. He took a few days off."

"He wants to attend the festival?"

"He's coming back for *us*. He's imagining the one-year anniversary might bring up a lot of things. I think he may be right."

Yas felt a lump in her throat. "Seeing the festival prep ramping up lately, it's been . . ."

"A lot," her mother said. "I know. That's why I'm so glad you're getting out today. You both need to do it more often."

Yas worried the edge of her shirt. This was her opening. As perfect a chance as there ever would be.

"Mom. There's something I need to tell you."

"I'm listening."

Tears formed in Yas's eyes. "I'm . . . I'm thinking of leaving."

Her mother's expression was impossible to decode.

"I've been saving up money from the gallery, and I've got enough now." The words tumbled out of Yas in a torrent. "Hisae lives at Lowman's. Remember the collective? She needs a roommate, and I've started to feel like I could use a break. Not from our work—but from the town. It's not like I'd be far from here—I'll still come to help with all of that."

Yas waited for her mother's response. She clenched her palms so tight, her nails dug into her skin.

"Yas." Her mother drew closer to her. "Leaving isn't the worst idea in the world."

"What?"

"It's actually a great idea."

"I'll be back, though," Yas said weakly. "I'll still collect shells. I'll still help you with what you need. I'm not . . . I'm not abandoning you like Dad did."

"Yas, your father didn't abandon us."

"Seriously, Mom?" She wiped her eyes. "What do you call *leaving*? He didn't consult us—he made a choice and went with it. You can't make excuses for him."

"I'm not. I haven't been thrilled by the choices he's made. But . . . Yas—he's supporting us." Her mother closed her eyes. "Haven't you noticed? Things are slower. It's a struggle to sell our services to a community where money is tight."

"We're busy. People are here every day."

"I'm not one to turn anyone away because they can't afford it."

"They're not *paying*?"

"Some do. Most give me IOUs. It's fine. The work matters more than it ever did—but promises to pay don't cover the bills. Between that and zero tourism, we can't afford to keep it up. Your father saw the writing on the wall before I could properly face facts. How do you think we managed to get the stove fixed? How are we paying for groceries?"

Yas's head spun. All this time she'd thought he was running away. But her father *had* to go. He *needed* to search for work. It'd been a matter of literally putting food on the table. All this time, she'd blamed him.

"You've been fighting from the start. Why are you defending him now?"

"It's taken me longer than I care to admit, but I'm starting to come around. I'm finally hearing what he's been trying to say. Staying feels more and more like a fool's game each day."

"Wh-what are you saying?" Yas sputtered. "You want to leave all of this? Our home?"

"This place is a house of cards—prop one thing up, another one falls. You know there's a slight tremble in the pipe above the guest room? That's what's been making the shells crack from the ceiling." Her mother massaged her temples. "I'm not even going to tell you how much that'll cost to fix. Looking at the books, I can't argue with your father. We'd be better off shuttering things."

Shuttering? Their business? Their life's work? Yas's head throbbed. "Mom, our family's worked too hard for this. This is our legacy."

"No one in generations past ever had to deal with what we are."

"Maybe the water will return."

"This is *you* saying it?" Her mother gave her a crooked smile. "I'm afraid I'm no longer quite so hopeful."

Her father had dismissed her. But—

"What if I saw the water turn pink?" she asked.

"Best not to engage in hypotheticals. Not good for the heart to play 'what if' scenarios."

"Not *if*. I *did* see the water turn pink. A patch of it. For a short while."

She waited for her mother to frown. To wave it away like her father had. Instead, she looked at Yas curiously.

"Yas. What are you saying?"

"A few weeks ago—I was by the water. Painting on the pier. Out of nowhere, there it was. Pink. Just a spot of it, in the water." Yas told her mother how she swam toward it. The swell that bore down on her, forcing her underwater. "Once I resurfaced, it was gone."

"Why didn't you tell me earlier?"

"Because it never returned. Why get your hopes up the way mine did?"

Her mother didn't speak.

"It sounds hard to believe, I know," Yas said quickly. "But Warren saw it too. If he hadn't been there, I'd have thought I made it up. But I'm not making it up. It was there."

"I believe you."

Tears filled Yas's eyes.

I believe you.

Yas hadn't known how much she needed to hear those words from her mother until this very moment.

"Is that why you peer out so much these days?" her mother asked.

"Keep hoping I'll see it again. Haven't yet, though. And, well, the Weepers, they'd have the best access. You'd think if it was a thing that happened more than once, they'd have said something."

"They tend to look down . . . not ahead," her mother said.

"Maybe Dad's right. Maybe all things must end—even our work. But maybe don't make plans to close shop. At least not right this minute. Please?"

Her mother kissed Yas on the forehead. She didn't say no. Right now, this was enough.

"Surrey's close to Edgewood," her mother said. "You and Raf would be minutes from each other."

"He's written it off. There's no getting through to him. It makes no sense."

Except—Yas realized—it did make sense. Was Nara the reason he didn't want to go?

"I should've invited Nara to come with us," Yas said, almost to herself.

"Nara?" Her mother looked at her quizzically. "Why?"

"He likes her," Yas said nonchalantly, as though it didn't faze her at all. "So an endorsement about attending Surrey coming from her could have gone a long way. I know she'd support his dream."

"Raf likes Nara?" Her mother raised her eyebrows. "That's news to me."

"He doesn't broadcast it or anything." Yas laughed a little. "It's obvious, though."

"I'm pretty certain that's not true."

"How would you know?"

"Because I'm fairly certain there's someone else he likes."

Yas frowned. Her mother raised her eyebrows and looked at her knowingly.

Yas's stomach did a backflip. "Mom," she said quickly. "No!"

"You sure?"

Yas's face grew warm. "We've known each other forever."

"Doesn't mean things can't change," her mother said. "Raf's feelings about you are as plain as day."

Raf liking her? *Liking* her? He was her friend—and lately he seemed uncomfortable at even the slightest touch. But . . . Yas paused. What about how he *looked* at her? She thought back to when she'd painted his portrait—still half-finished in her room—and the day on the beach when she told him about the colors shifting. In those moments, she'd be lying if she didn't admit a part of her *had* wondered. But she'd seen him with Nara. Her mother hadn't seen that. She hadn't seen the way he draped an arm around Nara when she shivered along the shoreline. Her mother didn't know that Raf told her nearly a decade ago that he couldn't be with someone who wasn't Golub. She didn't know the things Yas did.

"What about you?" her mother asked.

"Me?" she sputtered. "Raf's . . . he's *Raf.*"

"Of course," her mother said. "Your mural made me wonder, is all."

The mural? The mural was a tribute to the town. Walking up to the windowpane, she looked at the sandcastle on the shore, the pink dolphins that swam in the bay. The town square was painted a dazzling mauve, but the movie theater and Tilted Tales were illuminated in their own colors, set apart.

Yas grew still. The sandcastles. She'd made them with Raf. Helping him smooth the edges and scrape the sides. The dolphins, Hira and Mira. The ones she and Raf would swim alongside in the sea. The town square—the movie theater and the bookstore—the two places that had always felt as though they belonged to just the two of them.

The mural was an ode to her community. It was also an ode to the two of them. But why wouldn't it be? He was her best friend. They spent nearly every day together. Of course they shared memories.

Except—a shiver ran through her—it was more than that lately, wasn't it? He was still the shoulder she wept on. The person she shared everything with—nothing ever felt actually real to her until *he* knew. And lately . . . there'd been subtle shifts she hadn't dwelled too long upon. Like noticing in a wholly new way the honey brown of his eyes. The dimple on his left cheek. How a casual brush of his arm made her feel like a live wire of electricity. Sometimes even a look could do it. He was everything to her. She loved him. Was she also *in love* with Raf?

And was her mother right? Did Raf feel the same?

Suddenly, everything felt different.

Raf's truck idling outside her home. The passenger seat, cool to the touch as she settled in. And the smile he flashed at her as he switched from park to drive. None of this was unusual. It was all the same. And it wasn't.

"Can you believe it's happening?" he asked. "Kept thinking *something* would come up. A last-minute emergency. Dar needing an extra set of hands with the boys."

"I'm not sure what's harder to believe," Yas said. "The fact that we're going, or that it's taken this long for us to leave."

"Before I forget." He looked at her. "I meant to tell you that I checked out the mural today."

"You . . . you did?"

"You never told me how far along you were. It's amazing, Yas. I'm glad you're painting again."

Did he see what her mother saw when she looked at the mural? Yas studied his profile and shook her head. She had to get out of her thoughts. They were finally taking this trip—she couldn't cloud it up by overanalyzing things.

"It's time for some music," she announced.

"Hey!" Raf exclaimed as she connected the phone to the car. "My favorite song."

"Told you you'd have a say in the music selection."

Raf grinned, and Yas felt herself relaxing. As they turned down Main Street, she tapped her foot. This was happening—after weeks of hypotheticals, she was going to see Hisae, check out the collective, and meet her future.

At the stop sign, Yas glanced out the window at Main Street Park. "Look at that!"

A cluster of construction trucks and cranes crowded along the edge of the park. The golden Ferris wheel was gone.

"They took it down?" Raf stared at the empty space.

"The new one's not far behind." Yas pointed to the chrome-gray circle glinting against the sun, in the process of being lifted up.

"But it's not the same. It's all sleek and shiny, like some kind of futuristic thing."

Yas nodded. "It's not ours." She was glad the teetering wheel was being replaced, but it was still an ending. The wheel of their childhood, another memory of the past, gone.

"I can't believe Warren actually did it," Raf said. "Who knew you could do something like that so quickly?"

"Money makes you a magician."

"Hey, is that . . ." Raf leaned over and traced the necklace against her collarbone. "You're wearing it again."

"It's a new one." She pretended his touch against her skin did nothing. "I made it a little while ago."

"Does that mean you believe again?"

"I don't know. This one isn't even 'from the sea,' as my mother requires. Even though my faith in everything I believed about my work feels shattered, when I put this necklace on—it feels right. I guess right now that's enough."

They drove past the faded Moonlight Bay sign—COME BACK AND SEE US SOON, it beseeched. As they got on the highway, Yas watched Raf check his wrist.

"Are you worried about timing?" she asked him.

"Hmm?" He looked at her. "No—I mean, a little. It would be good if we came back by five o'clock."

"It won't take long. I'm really glad you're coming. I'd hate to do this alone."

A new song came on. Yas tapped her fingers and sang along. Raf laughed.

"I haven't heard you sing in forever," he told her.

"You missed it?" she teased him.

She waited for him to tease her back. To say something like how her singing made him nostalgic for cats screeching from fences.

"Well, yeah, I did."

She looked at him. *Stop,* she told herself. Her mother's words were *not* going to get in her head. She wasn't going to read into his movements, his words, his smile to decipher how he felt about her.

But taking in his profile, his eyes fixed on the road ahead. The set of his mouth. The shadow of stubble along his jaw. Yas felt light-headed.

How did her mother notice what she only realized now?

She loved him.

She always had, hadn't she? Ever since that first day in Ms. Stein's class, Raf's eyes nervously scanning the room until they settled on Yas—the shy smile spreading over his face when the teacher seated them together. When he saw the leaf she'd drawn on her right wrist to match his, his face breaking out into a grin. She'd loved him since then. But the love had shifted. Evolved. He'd been such a part of her life, she hadn't realized what those particular and new feelings were. Until now.

I love you.

The three words a wonder to her.

She looked at him and tried them on again, like a brand-new dress at a department store.

I love you.

I love you.

I love you.

The words fit. Perfect and true. It felt like a trapdoor opened inside of her and Yas was falling. What was she to do with this newfound revelation?

"Mmm, this song reminds me of Ms. Ho's class. Remember chemistry?" Raf asked her. He raised the volume of the song. The bass shook the windows.

"Yeah." She felt her face warm. *He can't see inside my head,* she reminded herself. "Don't know how this song snuck in. I'm sick of it."

"Sick of it?" He side-eyed her. "You set your ringtone to it and always forgot to silence it."

"She had my phone in her desk drawer more than I ever had it in eleventh grade."

"And remember the snacks—"

"Okay, *that* wasn't my fault!" she protested.

"Just saying, you really *had* to pick the crunchiest things to sneak in? Admit it. You liked trolling her."

"A girl wants what she wants. And speaking of snacks." Yas dug into her old book bag. "Ta-da!" she triumphantly held up the bag packed with pretzel brownies. "Freshly baked!"

"Yas! You're the best."

"I agree, I *am* pretty prachin."

"Good job with the Golub there."

"It's a beautiful language," she said. "I feel lucky you've taught me so many words."

After dropping the packages off at the courier, they headed onward—the sign welcoming them to Edgewood appeared quicker than she'd have liked.

"It's a bigger town than I remember," she reflected.

Cars sped up and down the four-lane road. Streetlights blinked green, yellow, and red every few paces. There were outdoor patios with folks drinking wine and chatting.

"Fredrick's." Raf pointed to a building on their right. "Bura comes here for our groceries."

"That thing is enormous," Yas said, taking in the parking lot and supermarket next to her.

"It's a chain," he said. "There's fifty of them in this state alone."

"So Edgewood is anti-anti-establishment. Kind of like a fun house mirror of Moonlight Bay."

"Uh, okay, Kendall," Raf teased. "Is there not enough small-town charm for you?"

"Hey!" She shoved him. "No fair!"

"I'm kidding!"

But the truth was, there really *wasn't* much charm here. The beige strip malls. The square parking lots every few minutes. It was disconcerting.

Heading toward Lowman's Collective, the scenery shifted to green and lush. When they arrived, Hisae swung open the door and hurried toward them before they'd even locked the car.

Her eyes twinkled. "I can't believe y'all are here!"

It felt like an out-of-body experience walking through Hisae's apartment. Everything was just as it had been in the pictures. The same couch with the flowered rug spread over wood flooring. The identical bedrooms were across from one another with a shared bathroom. After all this time singularly focused on earning enough to make this moment a reality, she was finally here.

"And the best part"—Hisae beamed—"Surrey's down the road. You both won't have to deal with the long-distance thing. I know it's only fortyish miles, but I've seen people break up over less distance than that."

Yas wanted to sink into the flooring. People assumed they were dating in high school, but they'd simply rolled their eyes and shrugged it off back then. Now? She didn't dare look at Raf. Was he too mortified to correct her too? Raf laughed awkwardly but said nothing.

When they were back in the car, Raf turned to her. "So? Thoughts?"

"Hmm?"

"You haven't said much," he said. "Hisae's room is a mess, but the rest of the place was in decent shape."

He was right. Everything was as advertised. So why wasn't she excited to see what would soon be her brand-new life?

Raf looked pensively out the window.

"What's up?" she asked him.

"Nothing."

"Raf . . ."

He looked at her sheepishly. "We got done faster than expected. Surrey *is* the next exit down. Maybe after we grab some job applications, we could head there to check it out?"

"Raf!" She clapped her hands. "I was trying so hard not to bring it up—but yes! Please! Let's do it!"

"Just to see it," he clarified. "It can't hurt, right?"

He looked so nervous. So sweet. "It wouldn't hurt at all. Let's go."

twenty-five
RAF

What. Are. You. Thinking.

Raf's heart pounded in his chest, thumping against his rib cage. The car was back on the highway and heading west. Away from Moonlight Bay. Toward Surrey. He knew seeing it would make what he was letting go of hurt all the more. But he couldn't help it. They were so close.

He checked the time. They had two hours to spare—the leaf would warn him if it got too late. And so far, it had stayed surprisingly quiet—flickering here and there, but not dramatically so.

Yas pointed out the exit. "We're here."

Taking the ramp, Raf pressed the brakes at the sight across from him.

"Look!" He rolled down the window and stuck his head out, pointing to the circular four-story building across from them. The staircase wound around its exterior.

"The weird white building?"

"Weird? That's the Sphere!" He turned to her. "You know that's a house, right? The owner asked the architect to make it feel infinite, so he designed loops and loops outside and inside too. Professor Singh wrote about it in the last edition of his textbook, *Local Marvels and Oddities in Architecture*. Can't believe one of the pieces I read about was within driving distance of home!"

"I'm sorry, but you geeking out over a house is proof you're meant to do this sort of thing."

As they continued on, the next song began. She sat up straighter. "Raf. This song! Wasn't this the one your mom *always* played?"

"*Plays*." He laughed. "Present tense."

"It's about chasing dreams, right? Can you believe it's playing right now?"

"I can. *You* put the playlist together!"

"The timing is still pretty amazing. A great note to end on," she said. "Come on, you *have* to sing along with me."

"You think you still know all the words?" He looked at her, astonished. "I'm not sure *I* even do."

"I might. Sing it with me. You know it's your favorite!"

Raf rolled his eyes, but as she began to sing, he joined in. It turned out she *did* remember all the words. He hadn't sung along to this song since he was in elementary school, but like muscle memory, the lyrics came back to him. He remembered every word, and Raf felt a funny feeling he hadn't felt in a long time.

Happy.

Really and truly happy.

The feeling filled up every nook and cranny of his truck. In this moment he knew one thing: It couldn't get better than this.

Or could it?

Stepping onto the grassy campus, Raf couldn't stop staring. He knew the photos of Moonlight Bay didn't compare to the actual thing. You couldn't capture with a camera how the pink of their sea in years past had glinted against the sun. How the sparkle within the folds of salt water shimmered with hints of the coral below. So why would this be any different?

Sure, it was the same tree-lined walkways, the same cobblestone steps leading to enormous buildings that seemed older than time itself that he'd pored over incessantly online over the years. But you couldn't hear the brick clock tower chiming on the hour with a melodic twang. You couldn't capture a feeling through a screen.

They strolled past the empty student union. The closed bookstore. Past a pond with picnic benches spaced around it before stepping back onto the grassy median. A few students passed by, but otherwise it was deserted. Like the campus belonged only to Raf and Yas.

At last they approached the College of Architecture. White steps led to a set of locked oak doors. He peeked in the windows and took in the framed posters of famed architects. The tables in the classrooms were wide. Angled up just so—for blueprints and sketching. For measuring and planning. Dreaming. Raf pressed his palms against the glass. That was what architecture was for him—it was about dreaming up what didn't exist, seeing it come to life.

"Is that a sculpture garden?" Yas pointed to a fenced-in space off to the side of the architecture building.

"That must connect to the fine arts building," Raf said.

They wandered through the mazelike gardens. Marveling at metal sculptures and porcelain elephants. Glass raindrops strung from above.

"Charan," Yas said quietly.

She was right. Surrey *was* extraordinary.

"Makes *me* want to apply to Surrey."

He could feel her eyes on him. He knew the question playing on her lips. Was this affecting him? Was it working?

It was.

He wanted to be at Surrey more than ever.

"Doesn't it *feel* different here?" he asked her. "It was the same in Edgewood. There's a different vibe. I know we're coastal and this is more inland and, sure, it's great not to see Crissy or Jake shooting darts with their eyes at me, but there's more to it."

"It's true." She nodded. "Look at everyone. Look at their faces."

A couple reclined on a picnic blanket a few steps away, chatting on the plush green lawn. A professor hurried past them, his attention fixed on his phone. It wasn't that anyone was grinning from ear to ear or anything—

But they weren't grieving. There wasn't the feeling of being suspended. Of *waiting*. There wasn't the *want* that consumed Moonlight Bay.

"I guess I never realized it," Raf said. "How heavy things have gotten. It's all around us back home. It crept on slow enough, I got to thinking it always felt that way."

"Like humidity, right?" Yas said. "A billion invisible heavy drops pressing against you."

The weight of grief, Raf thought. The weight of every soul in Moonlight Bay yearning for a time that was gone. What was the personal cost of putting one's life on hold?

"Even with how tense and strange things are lately, I never think of Moonlight as grief-stricken."

"The Weepers are the most *obvious* with their grief," Yas said. "But Kendall, Olive, Mateo—they'd been dealing with things before the waters had even turned. Olive with the divorce. Mateo never fully recovered from his mother's passing. And Kendall, he was always a bit . . ."

"Volatile?" Raf finished.

"Exactly." Yas nodded. "In a way, the water gave them a reason to come together. So they didn't have to be alone with their pain. But *everyone* is grieving in some way. We lost so much."

"And all those emotions, they're leaking into our atmosphere. I've never understood why anyone stays in Moonlight Bay if they could leave."

"It's not so simple. You can't just run away from grief. Moses is on the other side of the continent, and—" She stopped herself.

"You keep in touch with him?" he asked.

"We haven't spoken since . . ." Her voice trailed off. "But I do look him up sometimes. I don't know why I can't stop checking his social media. It's a compulsion. His feed hasn't changed. It's stuck to that day. I can't stop wondering if he's okay. I mean, he's not okay. How could he be?"

Of course. Raf looked at her pained expression.

"I like to imagine there's a parallel universe out there." Yas looked out at the handful of students sprawled on the lawn. "Some physicists say the multiverse is real. Maybe there's one unfolding right this minute where none of it happened. Where we're just living our lives and Sammy is there. You're building sandcastles. I'm polishing stars. Nothing changed, and we're complaining about how boring it all is."

"How do we get out of this simulation and over to that one?"

"Wish I knew," she said. "At least we're away for a little while. This little bit of a breather feels good. Didn't know how bad I needed it."

Raf agreed. It was good to see the world had in fact continued spinning, even if things remained stuck in Moonlight Bay.

They hopped onto the back of Raf's flatbed and pulled out their packed meals. She swatted Raf's hand away as he dove for the pretzel brownies.

"You know those were meant to be dessert for *after*! Between all the bites you snuck on the drive up and now, I think you've finished most of them at this point."

"Why save the best for last?" Raf retorted. "I say we treat ourselves."

"*I'm* treating myself to this *amazing* panini." She took a bite.

"I had to hide the smoked turkey in the back of the fridge to make sure no one else used it. Our vendor is having a shortage."

"You saved it for me? I feel special."

"Well, you *are* special."

"What's the Golub word for 'special'?"

"Craoin."

"Oooh, that's a nice one." She smiled. "I'll have to write it down so I don't forget it."

They sat next to each other, their backs reclined against the truck bed, taking in the landscaped campus across from them. Despite the summer heat beating down from the waning sun, in this moment Raf felt absolutely, undeniably happy.

A group of cross-country runners raced by on the sidewalk across from them. When Raf looked at Yas, her expression grew drawn.

"What's wrong?" he asked.

"Nothing."

"Yas . . ."

"It's stupid," she said. "Moses ran cross-country. I wonder if he does anymore."

There it was again. Raf put his sandwich down. He knew what it was to care for someone who was out of reach. She was hurting. He would support her. Be the listening ear she needed.

"You . . . you miss him," he said.

"What?" She looked at him funny. "No. Not exactly. It's not like we spent much time together over the years." She took a deep breath. "But that night. The night of the festival . . ." Her voice wavered. "I'm not sure how to say it. I've never told anyone before."

Raf's heart grew heavy. "I know, Yas."

"What do you know?"

"That night." Raf cleared his throat. Would she hate him for it? Would she accuse him of spying? "I was on the beach. I saw you. And Moses."

For a moment, she simply stared at him. "You've never mentioned it."

"So much happened after that. It was none of my business anyway, and . . ."

And it was all my fault. Everything that happened was because of me. Those were the words he *wanted* to say. Needed to say. What better moment than now? The words wouldn't form on his tongue.

"I can't remember how we ended up there," she said softly. "We were at the festival, and it was so noisy. Melinda had walked Sammy back hours ago. He was supposed to be with her. She was supposed to have tucked him into bed. I still don't understand what happened. What was Sammy thinking?" She moved to say more, but she squeezed her eyes shut.

Raf looked at her drawn expression. He placed an arm around her.

"I'm fine," she said. "I never said it to anyone before, so I guess it's got me a bit choked up and . . ." Her lower lip quivered. Her shoulders began trembling. She began to cry. She pressed her head against his chest. Tears soaked into his shirt.

"How does everything change completely in *one* day?" she whispered into his shirt.

"I know. One minute you're living your life—and the next minute . . ."

"Boom."

They sat quietly for some time, neither speaking.

"I miss Sammy. So much," Yas said.

"Me too."

"He was so cute."

"He was." The past tense of Sammy was hard to process, even after nearly a year.

"I loved babysitting him," she said. "I taught him Go Fish, and he made me play it for three hours straight one day."

"I remember. I got roped into that marathon somehow."

"Right." She smiled.

"He had the best giggle."

"He did. Whenever he won, he'd spin and get so dizzy, he'd fall on me." Yas smiled at Raf. "It feels good to talk about him."

"No one talks about him. No one talks about *anything* that

happened. It's like we're powering through. Except we're not powering through. We're drowning."

"Yep," she said softly. "That's exactly it. But you're the reason I've made it through."

"Same," he said. "I don't know what I'd do without you."

She looked at him. A funny look crossed her face. As though she saw something in his eyes she'd not noticed before.

"Raf." She hesitated. "I have something I wanted to tell you."

"You can tell me anything."

She bit her lip. "I don't know if I can say this."

"Why not?"

"Once I say it, I can't take it back."

She looked vulnerable. Nervous. And the *way* she was gazing at him—her eyes locked into his own—his thoughts stilled. Had Nara been right? Were his feelings not one sided after all?

She touched his hand. They looked at each other silently. She sat so close, he could smell the sweetness of her breath. Her mouth inches from his. She scanned his face.

Raf's breath caught in his throat. Was Yas about to kiss him? If so, Raf knew as certainly as the moon reflected the sun, turning from her would be just as impossible.

Yas leaned closer. Raf felt unable to move. To breathe.

Suddenly, her phone rang.

Loud trills echoed against the truck bed. Yas gasped as they sprang apart. She picked up her phone. "It's . . . it's my mom."

Raf tried to still his breathing. What just happened? What *almost* happened? They had been about to kiss, hadn't they? It had *seemed* so in the moment, but he must have imagined it.

Because if she *had*, his leaf would have warned him. It warned him against the slightest touch, and it hadn't burned at all. Not when she'd taken his hand. Not when she'd scooted so close, there was no space between them. Not this entire trip.

"Mom? Everything okay? . . . Yes, Raf is here. What? Just tell me!" Her face paled. "I'll be there as soon as I can."

"What was that?" Raf asked as she shoved the phone into her pocket.

"I have to get home." She hopped out of the truck bed.

"What's wrong?"

"She won't say. Just that we had to get home right away." He knew what she was thinking. Whatever it was, it wasn't good.

Raf pulled out his keys. "I need to get gas when we get closer to town, but—"

Raf looked up at the horizon. His entire body went cold. The sun. It was setting.

"Yas. What time is it?"

"Eight thirty." She startled. "Raf. We lost track of time, didn't we?"

Raf couldn't reply. His whole body felt made of lead. Five hours. They'd been outside the perimeter for five hours. His timer hadn't gone off. What about his leaf? It didn't burn. It didn't flicker. It had done nothing to warn him of the approaching time.

Yas was saying something to him, but her words sounded as if they were underwater. His heart thudded in his chest. He felt cold. Then hot. Beads of sweat formed across his forehead as he felt the weight of his carelessness. The far-reaching consequences for this risk he'd taken—this selfish mistake.

It was over. Everything. His brothers. His mother. He'd

never see them again. What would happen to the diner? What would happen to everyone who relied on him and needed him? His chest burned with shame. One trip out of town. And now his leaf—irrevocably and permanently erased.

He needed to see it. He had to force himself to see the space where it had been. Pushing his sweatshirt up his arm, he grew still.

It was there. The golden etching. Shaped like a leaf, glowing on his wrist. Same as it ever had.

Raf felt dizzy. His head throbbed with one question: *Why?*

twenty-six
YAS

If the ride up had been light and full of air, the ride back was its opposite. The sky outside was dark. No music played. There was only the hum of the truck barreling down the highway.

It was hard to believe a short while ago, they'd sat side by side. Talking at last about that night. As they spoke, something shifted between them. Like they were finally seeing each other.

They'd almost kissed.

Hadn't they?

Looking at him now, she marveled again at the new revelation: *I love him.* It wasn't anything like the burst of desire that drew her to Moses. Her feelings for Raf had shifted so imperceptibly, like the subtle drift of sand dunes, bit by bit and day by day, until she looked around and suddenly saw another landscape entirely. But now it was as clear as observing the flares of the sun. And in that moment in the back of his truck, she had been convinced Raf loved her too.

But now? It was hard to say. Raf gripped the steering wheel so tightly, his knuckles were white. What happened in the span between that moment and her mother's call? It almost felt like the flash of pink she'd seen that day. Certain and true. Then gone.

He'd been there, on the beach. He saw me with Moses. Yas shivered. Did he blame her for Sammy's death? Did he regret what almost happened between them? Is that why he'd seemed so shaken?

"You see it, right?" Raf asked. His eyes on the road, he held out his arm toward her. His jaw was clenched tight. "My leaf."

Yas inched up his sleeve. "It's there," she said. "That's good, right?"

"Is it faded? Changed?"

Yas traced a hand over the outline of his leaf. It looked as beautiful as ever. "I— I can't tell a difference."

She waited for him to say something, but he simply shivered. No words came.

"This is a good thing, right?"

Is it really about what nearly happened between us?

"I don't know how to explain it. I have to figure out what it is for myself first." He looked at her. "Are *you* okay?"

"My mom's voice," Yas said quietly. "The way she sounded. So panicked. Can't help but worry."

"Any idea what it could be?"

"None. But the fact that she wouldn't tell me over the phone means it's something pretty serious."

Did it have to do with her father? she wondered. He was driving up. Did something happen on the drive? She flinched at the last words she'd hurled at him. She'd accused him of abandoning their family. She hadn't spoken to him since. Ignoring his nightly calls.

Please be all right, she pleaded.

Walking through her front door, Yas felt a wave of relief. Her father was there. He looked unharmed. But Bea, Ayo, Gil—they were city council folk. What were they doing here? Unease crept over Yas.

"Did Raf already leave?" her mother asked, hurrying toward the window.

"We were hoping to speak with him," Gil explained.

"What happened?" she asked.

"The Naismiths happened." Her mother's eyes were puffy and red. "Turns out they like it here," she said. "They want to invest. Bring back manufacturing. It could bring back hundreds of jobs."

"Isn't that what everyone wants?" Yas said slowly. She took in the group's ashen expressions.

"They have one condition," Bea said. "Laid it out to us at an emergency council meeting a bit ago—in exchange, they want the Golub tree."

"The tree?" Yas repeated. "What do they want with the tree?"

"They want to harvest it."

"As in *cut it down*?"

"It appears the tree is rife with resources," said Bea. "According to them, the medicinal properties in the bark can heal rare disorders. The roots can be ground into potent anxiety medication."

Yas felt like her brain was short-circuiting. "Our waters . . . are they *from* the tree?"

"Hard to say which way the properties flow," Gil said. "From the waters to the tree or the other way around."

"But the shells we collected by the beach closest to Willow Forest were always strongest, weren't they?" Yas asked her mother. "Which means the roots were feeding healing minerals . . . or properties . . . *into* the water."

Her mother nodded, clearly awestruck herself.

So the power in the stars we create . . . it's real? Or at least it had been.

And they wanted to chop down the source. Yas thought of the tour she'd given Warren—the way he'd needled his way into the forest on Raf's good graces—she'd participated in this. She'd led the wolf to the sheep.

"Tell them no," Yas said. "The tree is the only way for anyone from Golub to make it here. And it's their *only* way home."

"It's not so simple," said Bea.

"Bea!" Yas's voice rose. "The tree isn't Moonlight's to give."

"It's on county land," Gil said. "Which means that requests like these automatically go to a public vote."

Yas's knees felt weak. She sank into the sofa. They knew how a vote would go. "Why isn't Ernie here?"

"We're not sure where he stands," Ayo said.

"He's the mayor." She stared at them. "And he's *Ernie*. Of course he'll say no. He'll put an end to all of this."

"Ernie can't make an executive decision about this anyway," her father said.

"But people listen to him," Yas said. "His word would have some impact."

"Remains to be seen how much power words can have in

the face of large sums of money," said Gil. "The Naismiths want the news under wraps until tomorrow. They plan to announce it at the festival. Stun folks with an obscene amount of money they can't say no to and collect their votes immediately."

"Can you reach out to Raf?" her mother asked. "See if Tolki is available to join us as well? They need to be informed about what's to come. We didn't want to intrude at this hour unannounced."

She looked out the window. The Weepers in the distance. As each gray day bled into the other, she thought things couldn't possibly get worse, but that was how life worked, wasn't it? It always had a way of proving you wrong.

Tolki, Raf, and everyone else in the forest needed to know what was happening.

But it was the locals who were doing this.

It was the locals who needed to get their act together. She had to talk to Ernie. He didn't have the power to strike down the offer—but he was the mayor. He held sway. If anyone could help stop this before it began, it would be him.

twenty-seven
RAF

Raf sat on the front stoop of Uncle's house. He'd parked himself there after he'd returned. He'd knocked on the door. Rang the doorbell. No one answered. Uncle went to bed each night at nine o'clock without fail. He rose at five. Today of all days, he wasn't home.

Convenient, Raf thought bitterly.

The sky filled with flecks of color. Raf rubbed his eyes. He hadn't slept. He hadn't eaten. Looking at his wrist, there it was—same as ever. Golden and perfectly stenciled on his inner wrist. At first he thought he'd hallucinated it—his mind refusing to accept the truth. But Yas had seen it too.

What was going on? Only one person could tell him the truth.

"What are you doing out here at this hour?" His mother hurried down the gravel walkway toward him.

"I need to talk to Uncle."

"Are there issues with the kindling for our gathering tonight? Raf . . . what's the matter?"

Worry lined her face. Raf thought of Uncle. He didn't know the extent of it yet, but he knew that Uncle had kept some things from them. It was time Raf stopped doing the same. She needed the truth.

"I went to Surrey yesterday."

"The university? I thought you both were at Edgewood?"

"We were." Was she upset? She didn't seem upset. "I wanted to see the campus."

"Do you want to attend?"

Raf almost laughed. She'd asked him this as though it were a possibility. As though what he wanted played any factor in this.

"Raf." She kneeled until they were face-to-face. "What are you not telling me?"

"I did want to go to Surrey," he told her. "You know Professor Singh. He visits each year."

"Of course. He always gives you his textbooks, doesn't he?"

"He'd gotten me curious about studying at the university."

"He teaches architecture, right?" She nodded. "You love designing things, so this makes sense. You and your father even expanded our closet when Louk was born. It was your idea to put in removable shelves."

"I applied to college this past fall," Raf said. "I don't know why I did it. Just got in my head that I could design homes for real. As a job. I figured it wouldn't hurt to apply. I ended up getting offers to all the places I'd applied to."

"Do you *want* to go?"

"No. I mean yes," he said. "But it doesn't matter."

"Why doesn't it matter?"

"You mean besides the fact that I have to run the diner?" This was not how he'd expected this conversation would go. "Surrey is fifty miles away. It's outside the safety zone."

"You could have commuted. We could have figured out a way. Why didn't you talk to me about this?"

Raf's mouth went dry like sandpaper. Why *hadn't* he ever discussed this with his mother? Uncle had made it seem as though it was absolutely out of the question—and Raf had accepted it as uncontroverted truth. *Had* there been a way to have both?

"Dena's little one starts school in the fall. She could take on more at the diner. We could have figured out a way."

We could have figured out a way. The very thing he'd agonized over for years, resolved so simply? He'd wanted to keep burdens from being added to his mother's shoulders. He didn't want to bother her. He didn't want to see her eyes fill with hurt. But she wouldn't have been hurt, Raf realized. She would have lightened his load.

"You've taken on so much at such a young age." She squeezed his shoulder. "But that doesn't mean your dreams—what *you* want—don't matter."

"I also *wanted* to stay," he told her. "To help with the diner. To help you with the boys. I didn't want to leave you on your own."

"You've done all of this for years, without a word of complaint," she said. "But you need to pursue your dreams. You deserve your happiness—otherwise, what is all this sacrifice we've undertaken even for?"

"There's something else." If he could tell his mother about Surrey, she deserved to know the rest of it. "While I was out yesterday, I lost track of time."

At this his mother leaned back.

"How long?"

"Nearly all day."

Her face paled. "Raf. What are you saying?"

She wrenched his arm toward her. Her eyes landed on the intact leaf. She exhaled with relief, but then confusion spread across her face.

"There's more, Mom," he said. "Uncle's been lying about other matters. His daughter, and Kot. Who knows what else." Before Raf could continue, footsteps crunched against gravel. Uncle walked in from the main path. His shirt was untucked, his pant legs dusty. He looked at Raf and his mother.

"What are you both doing out here?"

"I need to talk to you." Raf rose.

"Not right now," Uncle told him. "There are some pressing matters that require my attention. Can it wait?"

"You lied." Raf blocked his path.

Uncle's expression shifted. It wasn't a look of confusion—it was a look of resignation.

"You *did* lie." Raf felt sick. "About the leaf. About how it works."

Uncle didn't reply.

"Admit it!" Raf's voice rose. "Say *something*!"

Dena hurried out of her home, her hair tangled, her son gripping her hand. "What is the matter?"

Raf couldn't focus on anyone else. Until now, part of him had been hoping Uncle would wave a hand and explain it all away. But he had nothing to say. He looked at them slack-jawed.

He *had* lied, Raf realized. It had all been a lie. Or at least some of it had been. One year earlier, his wrist *had* burned upon seeing Yas and Moses. The seas *did* turn gray. What was true and what wasn't? Raf felt light-headed. Nothing made sense anymore.

"Raf." A hand touched his elbow. Nara stood by his side. Many others were out of their homes now. Some from nearby hamlets. They looked on worriedly.

"My leaf," Raf choked out. "I left the perimeter yesterday. I stayed out all day."

The crowd audibly gasped. Some turned, taking steps back to distance themselves.

"You don't need to run." Raf held up his wrist. "My leaf is still there."

"That's . . . That cannot be possible," Dena whispered.

"I've been with him the past half hour," Raf's mother said. Her eyes fixed on Uncle. "My leaf is intact as well."

"It seems you got lucky, Raf," Uncle said slowly. He straightened. "Sometimes it can happen—a glitch in the system. We can count this as a blessing."

"I didn't get lucky." Uncle wasn't going to gaslight him. Tell him that the sky was red when it was blue. "The leaf did *nothing*—it didn't even flicker."

Yas and I nearly kissed. The leaf did nothing.

"There's something *else* we all need to talk about," Nara said urgently. "I was planning to bring it up with Uncle first thing in the morning. Since we're all here—"

Her voice cut off. She stared at something beyond his shoulder. Following her gaze, Raf saw: Walking toward them, through the main pathway in the light of the gathering dawn, was Kot.

His blond hair was shorter. Sheared to the scalp. He wore jeans and a gray shirt. His frame thinner. His jaw angular.

237

"Nara," Dena said slowly. "If Kot is returning from the main road and not the tree, he did not make it to the other side. He's been gone for weeks. He *must* have lost his leaf."

But he hadn't. Raf knew from the way Uncle barely moved that this wasn't the case. It had never been so.

Nara raced toward him and threw her arms around him. Her body shook with sobs.

Terrified voices rose over one another. People began backing away, and others broke into a run. Though had it been true, it would have been too late. Lost leaves were contagious and Kot was here. In the woods. Close enough to infect them all.

"Check her leaf," Raf said, his eyes dry and clear. "Check yours. For that matter, check Kot's."

Uncle didn't move. No one did.

"Then I will," he said.

"Don't be foolish!" his neighbor cried out.

"Raf! Please!" Dena shouted.

Raf marched toward the siblings. "Let's see your wrist, Nara."

Nara held out her arm.

"It's there," Raf called out.

"Mine's there too." Kot raised his arm. His hands trembled slightly.

"Where have you *been*?" Nara turned to him. "I have been sick with worry. You didn't return from the tree."

"I never went *through* the tree," Kot said. "I was taken on a bus—a day's journey away."

"How did you end up on a bus?" Nara asked.

"Ask him." Kot pointed to Uncle.

Hushed silence fell over the forest.

"Tolki, what's going on?" Raf's mother asked.

Uncle shakily settled down on the stoop in front of his house.

"I can explain," he said. "It's—"

"There's no perimeter," interrupted Kot. "Our leaves don't fade if we leave the vicinity for one hour or ten or twelve."

"That cannot be right," someone said.

"I was growing tired of how we were being treated. The way the locals treat us," Kot said. "I wanted to figure out if Nara and I could make it somewhere else—Uncle kept talking me out of it. I tried to *compromise*. I said Nara and I could shift one town over. Ridgeview. Safe within the perimeter. But then his story shifted. He said there was no way to truly be sure about our safety even one town over. The only place we could absolutely be certain was within this forest.

"I *tried*, I really tried to make it work here. I took the job at the diner. I wanted to make the best of things. Until I couldn't anymore. I felt . . . stifled. I began wondering: We learn so many different things about our history at school, so why did no one talk about fading leaves on the other side? How could they not have shared such an important fact?"

"Because it wasn't true," Raf said.

"That's right, brother." Kot smiled sadly at Raf. "I did an experiment one day. I left town. Left the safety zone. I wandered to Star Side, over two hours from here. I sat on a bench and watched the leaf, waiting. Nothing happened."

"It didn't flare?" Dena asked.

"It flares for me," said Bura. "I go at least every few months to Star Side for meat."

"The leaf *did* send out flares, but the more I focused—I started noticing it's always buzzing, even when we're in the

239

forest. Think about it—doesn't it do that for *all* of you? There's an energy within it. Always there. It acted up most when I focused on it. Worried about it. When I was almost *waiting* for it to do that. When I started training my mind to focus on other things, the buzzing, the warming, the pain—it stopped."

"I notice it flares *all* the time," someone said. "I thought it was just me."

A few others murmured in agreement. Raf looked down at his wrist. It flickered. It was true—it always buzzed to some degree, but could it be so simple? And insidious?

"It's how our leaf is. Uncle wielded it against us. He played mind games to make us believe things that were false. Once I was able to prove to myself it wasn't true, I confronted Uncle. Asked why he'd fed us this story. I told him the choice to stay or leave was ours to make. He insisted I was wrong. Told me just because the leaf hadn't *yet* faded didn't mean it wouldn't. Said the entire community was at risk. I spent that entire day filled with worry. Staring at my leaf. Wondering if he was right. Had I really endangered everyone?" Kot's voice cracked. "Late at night, he told me we needed to speak. He'd made calls and there was a place he could set us up. Three hours north. A place where the locals were kind and friendly. I had to get on the bus arriving within the next ten minutes. I couldn't even say goodbye to Nara. He told me I was like a ticking bomb. That each second here was borrowed time. When the leaf inevitably vanished, all would be compromised." Kot looked at Nara. "I'm so sorry. He said he'd send you in a few days. Once we could confirm the leaf was intact. He *swore* he would . . ." Kot's eyes glistened.

"Where were you?" Nara asked.

"A small town on the edge of the continent," he said. "I had no phone. No money. Nothing. Someone picked me up at a bus stop—Uncle had arranged a cabin for me deep in the northern woods—the driver dropped me there with canned foods and promised me Nara would soon join. I waited three days. My leaf remained intact. No one came. I finally made my way to the closest store—a two-hour walk away—and called the diner, but the line was dead. That's when I realized that Nara wasn't coming. Uncle had banished me. I've been making my way back ever since."

Raf felt dizzy. Tolki Uncle. The person who had cleared this space and settled their community. Who they turned to for guidance and advice. For comfort. All these years, they'd lived under these exacting rules.

And Kot had *tried* to reach out. He'd called the one number he'd memorized while working behind the scenes at the diner. Raf counted back to when their phone line stopped working. Had Uncle cut the line?

"Please." Uncle's voice wavered. He spread out his arms as though to prevent a fall. "I know how all of this sounds. But you must understand. Everything I have done. It was to keep you all safe."

"Why was your daughter here the other day?" Raf asked. "Why was she *really* here?"

"Sh-she comes sometimes," he said. "She wants to heal our breach. We have been apart for so long. It was difficult to turn her away—I am her father—but I needed to set an example." He sighed deeply. "It was a painful sacrifice, but I could not have separate rules for myself. Everything I have done—it's all been for this community. For all of you."

"You keep saying that, but you drove Kot away!" Dena shouted. "You took him to the middle of nowhere and abandoned him! How is that helping our community?"

"Kot had made up his mind," Uncle said. "He was leaving us. I helped him do it safely. But I was *not* going to have Nara go off with him to a dangerous unknown. I have a responsibility. We are *all* we have. In a world that sees us as undesirable and suspicious, we need each other more than ever before. We are so few in number. What happens if *everyone* disperses? What becomes of us?"

"That should be our choice to make," Raf said.

"You made me think I was crazy." Nara's voice trembled with rage. "I knew something was wrong. You lied to my face. You could have taken me to him! Brought him back whenever you wanted! You could have spared me so much pain!"

Raf looked at the crowd. The terror that had filled their eyes when Kot had first appeared was gone. They were furious now.

"Sorry to interrupt," a voice said.

Warren? His hands were at his sides. His expression cloudy. Nara wiped away her tears with the back of her hand. She nodded.

"There's a lot we need to talk about," Nara said. "But there's something urgent Warren and I must tell you. I am afraid it cannot wait."

twenty-eight
YAS

Yas stood on Ernie's porch and banged her fist against his front door. She'd raced to his doorstep soon after learning the truth. He hadn't answered then, but it was morning. He had to be home now.

"I know you're in there!" Yas shouted. "Open up!"

No reply. No sound of footsteps on the wooden floor behind that door. She edged over to the window and peered through the space between the sheer curtains—but save Ernie's cat, who opened one eye and glared at her from atop the sofa, there was no sign of life inside.

Where was he?

Yas hurried down his street and turned left toward Main Street. Her heart pounded. In the distance she saw twinkle lights strung up along the lampposts. Vendor booths installed—in a few hours, people would set out their artwork and ceramics and pottery. The brand-new Ferris wheel loomed steady and tall, as though it'd always been there. In a few hours, the Naismiths would ask the townspeople how much their souls were worth. She had to find Ernie. While there was time.

There he was! Ernie stood in front of the diner looking at

the CLOSED sign and darkened interior. Quickly, she jogged toward him.

"Ernie."

"Hey, Yas." He turned to her. "Can't remember a time when the diner's been closed during regular business hours."

"We need to talk," she said.

"Is Raf all right?"

"He won't be," she replied. "Not if the Naismiths have their way."

Ernie's eyes shifted downward.

"Ernie," she said. "You can't let this happen."

"I only found out last night." He stuck his hands in his pockets. "Still processing it all. I didn't expect they'd actually do it—invest in our town." He sighed. "There's always a price, isn't there?"

"We're not paying the price. The Golub are. Cutting off their pathway home? Removing any way for someone to enter? The land might not legally be theirs, but it's not ours to give to the Naismiths either."

"Matters involving county land must be put to a two-thirds majority vote," Ernie said. "I hate it as much as you do."

"You know how people will vote." Her voice cracked. "Ernie—you used to say we were special to have that Golub tree. That the Golub were our friends. Our neighbors."

"I still feel that way." Ernie studied the asphalt.

"You're the mayor for a reason, aren't you? Talk to people. Go door to door and knock! Get them to change their minds. Even if you can't make the final call, there's plenty you can do. There has to be some other way."

"I understand what you're saying. I do." Ernie's expression was drawn. "The reality is, there's not much I can argue. We're barely holding on, Yas. I made an executive decision and spent our emergency funds for this festival. It ate up all our reserves. We're flat broke. It was a huge gamble, and the council was furious with me. Now Crissy says that the gamble is about to pay off. I've been working around the clock, trying to find other investors to take their place, but no one's biting. This is a no-win situation."

Yas's stomach hurt. Ernie, a regular at the diner. Ernie, who had ripped down flyers against the Golub alongside her. He was sad for the Golub. He'd tried to help. But it hadn't worked, so he was washing his hands of it?

Her eyes brimmed with tears. "What's the use of saving this town if there's nothing left of who we were? If there's nothing left to save?"

"I'm sorry, Yas. Really and truly I am."

So that was it. Her heart felt heavy. She had to tell Raf.

Her feet felt like they were made of lead as she crossed the street. How was she going to say the words? See his expression fall? The Golub had helped with the cleanup for the festival. They'd painted the bandstand. Planted bushes and flowers. They'd participated in the event that would upend their lives.

As she neared Raf's home, she heard conversations in the distance. Turning the bend, a large gathering of people stood near the tree. It was too early for the Hamra gathering. No swirl of blue and red flames spiraled from the fire pit. Instead, standing at the center, as though holding court, was Warren. Nara by his side.

It seemed her mother was right—premonitions were real after all. She'd known. In the deepest part of who she was, she'd sensed something off with Warren the moment she'd laid eyes on him. She'd been told to pretend. To be nice. To swallow her feelings and do what was needed for the sake of the town. *No more.*

"How dare you!" She marched toward them. "How dare you show your face here?"

"Yas," Raf called out. "Wait."

"You used me." She glared at Warren. "You used Nara. You were sniffing for information. You were trying to see how you could take the Golub down."

"You're right." Warren's expression was somber. "I was."

"Do you want to tell them what you've been up to? Or should I?"

"He already did," said Nara.

Yas looked at the crowd—their solemn expressions.

"He told you?" she asked incredulously.

"He let me know last night," Nara said. "I was trying to figure out the best way to tell everyone, but then this morning . . . so much else happened."

Yas followed her gaze. She took a step back.

"Kot? You're . . . you're back?" He raised a hand in greeting. She looked at Raf.

"Long story," Raf said.

"Warren's parents will ask for the fate of our tree to be put to a vote by the townspeople," Dena said. "Tonight."

"We can't let them destroy the tree," Uncle said. He seemed a ghost of his former self. "It's our only way—"

"Home?" Kot glared at him. "Is that what you were going to say? We're not *going* home! It's never going to happen. I'm tired of living for a promise that will never be kept."

"But we still cannot let them chop it down," Uncle said, his voice shaking. "I know there is much for you all to be furious with me about, but if things are deteriorating as bad as they are—even if we never get to go home . . ." His voice broke. "More may need to arrive. How will they if the tree is gone?"

"He's right," Raf said. "There's a lot that doesn't make sense, but the tree is true. They can't take it."

"It's not ours, is it?" Dena said. "We have no say."

"We'll fight this," said Yas. "They plan to announce it at the festival. I was thinking we could come up with some kind of game plan." She looked at Warren. "What is he still doing here?"

"He wants to help," Raf said.

"Sure he does." She crossed her arms. "That's why he didn't say anything earlier. That's why he was snooping around and acting like he was your friend, Nara. He's a spy. He's probably here to report everything we talk about."

"I'm not a spy. I mean I was," he corrected himself. "At first . . . but"—he looked at Nara—"I had a change of heart."

"And we're supposed to believe you because . . ."

"Because I want to help," he said. "You don't have to believe me, but it's the truth."

Yas sighed. They didn't have time to go back and forth on this. If Nara trusted him despite everything, she needed to let that be enough.

"Not *everyone* would vote in their favor," Yas said. "The Weepers won't."

"The Weepers are twenty strong," Raf said. "We'll need more numbers than that."

Her mother would vote against it, of course. So would

Marie. It required a two-thirds majority. Were there enough people for *that*?

"I thought if we tried hard enough, prayed hard enough, their hearts could soften toward us." Uncle shuddered. "In all these years, with all the scenarios I feared, I somehow lacked the imagination to worry about this."

"Who else knows about this?" Yas asked him.

"Just the council," said Warren. "Taking everyone by surprise is their best bet. Lawyers are already drafting language."

"When Ernie delivers his remarks at the midpoint of the festivities," Nara said, "he will bring the Naismiths to the stand. To give a speech about their special announcement."

"They can't make the speech," Yas said.

"Or," Raf said slowly, "we say what we need to say *first*. They want to shock them with the enormous sums of cash so no one would take a breath to think about it—but what if we tell them our side first? Whoever frames the narrative defines the narrative. Maybe then there's some chance?"

Their best shot was barely a shot at all, Yas thought. She said nothing. It was hope—who was she to take it away?

twenty-nine
RAF

"Ready?" Yas asked Raf.

Music blared steps from where they stood by the bandstand. They'd positioned themselves by the stairs leading to the stage. Waiting for the moment when Jeff called for the intermission and brought Ernie up to the microphone for his welcome message. Instead, Raf would take the stage. He would say the words that needed to be spoken.

"Ready as I'll ever be," Raf said.

"I'm sorry you have to do this," she said.

"I just hope it works." It was past eight o' clock. They'd spent the better part of the day talking. Planning. What he'd say. How.

How was this all on Raf? In any other situation, it would have been Uncle. But all these years, Tolki lied to them all. Told them they had to choose—between their loved ones or a life of their own choosing. He made it so it was impossible for those who wished to choose both. And for this lie, Nara, Kot, and Raf himself, they'd all suffered. For what? And worst of all were the things Raf *didn't* know. What was true? What wasn't? The day he saw Yas and Moses, the sensation practically *seared* through his bones. It had been real.

Focus, he told himself. There would be time to unpack all of that later. Right now, he had one important task before him. And his whole community was relying on him. Every Golub was there. Their expressions pinched. Somber. "If they intend to destroy the tree—they will do it looking us square in the eye," Dena had said.

Raf folded and refolded the paper on which he'd written his words. This had to work. But . . . what happened if it didn't? Even if their leaves didn't fade—even if they could leave and keep their birthmarks intact—the tree mattered.

Raf glanced to the side. Ernie stood a few feet away. He had his own piece of paper clutched tight. His face was coated in a sheen of sweat. Though he looked on the verge of vomiting, he was still going to do it. He was still going to introduce Peter and Siobhan Naismith. Nearly every morning, Ernie grabbed a cup of coffee at their diner. But what did all that solidarity amount to? When it came to the rich and powerful, he was following their marching orders.

Warren stood with his parents in the front row before the bandstand. Their eyes met and he nodded imperceptibly at Raf.

At last, the music stopped. Jeff swung the guitar around his back and walked to the mic. "We're the Backyard Bandits, and that's the end of the first half of our show," he announced. "We'll be back in a few, but before we do, it's my pleasure to introduce you to our one and only mayor. Ernie, please join us up here and share a few welcoming words!"

Now.

The audience clapped. Raf made his move. He took the steps two at a time. He marched toward the stage.

"Hey, Raf," Jeff said with surprise. "What's up?"

"Sorry, Jeff," Raf said. "There's something I have to do."

He turned to the crowd. The floodlights shining on top of him obscured his vision. Jake and Crissy were out there. But also Dena. And Bura. His mother and brothers.

"I need to talk to all of you," Raf said. The faces before him grew more focused. Clearer. Instead of reading the paper, Raf spoke from his heart.

"I remember when we first arrived, how afraid I had been. We'd left everything and everyone we knew to flee our dangerous circumstances in our beloved homeland. I grew up here. I graduated high school from Moonlight High. I went to school with many of your kids. This is my home. And the Golub tree within Willow Forest is how we arrived. Without it, we may not have survived. That tree is the key to our safety during the difficult times we are facing in Golub. A path out for anyone else who can reach it and make it through. The Naismiths aren't here because they like our town. They're here for our tree." He swallowed. "And tonight they're going to ask to buy your conscience. They want you to stand back as they cut it down. I'm asking you to please consider what you'd be agreeing to if you said yes. What the cost of that would truly be. We are begging you to please say no. This is literally a matter of life or death."

He drew a breath. The crowd was silent. Their expressions unreadable.

"Ernie." Crissy was the first to speak. "Is that true?"

Ernie approached the microphone. He looked sadly at Raf. "I'm afraid so."

"So they *do* want to invest in the town?" Skylar asked.

"Did you not hear what Raf said?" Yas practically flew up the stairs, her face flushed. "They want it so they can kick out the Golub. Our neighbors. They want to help us if we agree to take the one thing that the Golub can't live without—their tree."

"Well, kids, thanks for stealing our thunder," Siobhan said coolly. She turned to the crowd, raising her voice. "Peter and I were certainly looking forward to sharing the good news ourselves. The details are far more complex. Nevertheless—the bones of what he said are correct. We wish to make an offer to buy Moonlight Bay."

"What does that mean?" Jake asked suspiciously. "Buying our town?"

"It means," Peter said, "we infuse our support into the shops and the schools and infrastructure. We'll fix the potholed road running toward the highway. We'll renovate the factory—see if we can't get some manufacturing going again."

"At our expense," Raf said. "We *can't* lose the tree."

"How does this work?" Jake frowned. "Ernie?"

"Well . . ." Ernie tugged at his collar. "I guess— The thing is—"

"It's simple. We want to give you money," Siobhan interrupted. "Lots of it. You've all been through a lot. We can help."

"It— it's not quite *that* simple," Ernie fidgeted. "This is not a decision to be made lightly. For what it's worth, I think this is a big mistake."

"Too bad it's not up to you," Siobhan replied. "This isn't a dictatorship, is it?"

"It'll be an easy enough vote," Peter said.

"Easy?" Yas's eyes glistened with tears. "There's nothing easy about this!"

"The country is large and wide," Siobhan replied. "To be honest, the tree was holding you back, don't you think? We'll see to it you are provided a place to establish roots elsewhere."

"Ernie." Uncle's voice wavered. "Crissy. Jake. Please."

There was a protracted silence, and then—

"How much money are we talking?" Jake asked.

"Jake!" Yas burst out.

"We are open to discussion on that point," Siobhan said. "But the sooner you decide, the better the terms will be."

"Siobhan is right. The answer to this is simple," Crissy said.

Jake nodded. "Where's the contract?"

His words felt like shrapnel. They didn't care to hear the sum—they'd have agreed to chop it down without any financial motivation. Raf glanced at the others. This would not be a difficult decision for this town. Not even close.

Suddenly, a shout pierced the air.

"Watch out!"

The Weepers. There were thirty of them in all. They approached from the shoreline—with their dark clothing they practically blended into the night. They walked slowly but with purpose. They carried canvases. Letters spelling out a word: REMEMBER. Looped around each frame was a swirl of flame glowing orange against the setting sun.

thirty
YAS

The Weepers grew closer as the crowd drew back. The fire flickered wildly with the wind. Kendall clucked his tongue. The Weepers behind him raised their signs. Or rather, *paintings*. Of the once-pink-and-lavender sea. Sammy. Tears sprang to Yas's eyes. So many portraits of Sammy. By a sandcastle. On the swings. His twinkling eyes shining back at them. *Was this what Mateo was doing in secret?*

If the Weepers wanted to stun everyone, they succeeded. Everyone stood frozen.

"Kendall?" Ernie said. His voice two octaves higher. "What are you doing?"

"I warned you!" Kendall shouted. With synchronized movements, the group took another step toward the bandstand. His eyes burned fiery beneath the warm glow. "We don't do this—we don't move on—we don't pretend. I may not have had a vote in this festival, but I *will* be heard."

"You wouldn't listen then," Olive said. "You'll listen now."

Yas took in their determined faces. Their steely resolve. With horror, she realized—*They're going to burn this park to the ground.*

thirty-one
RAF

Raf stared at the fire. It swirled higher and higher into the sky. The Weepers' faces were flushed from the heat of the burning flames. As one, they marched forward. Yas's eyes darted to the trees. Her worries mirrored his own. He had no idea what the Weepers intended to do, but even if they weren't *planning* to burn the park to the ground, one errant ember—a fumble— and the grass would light. A tree could catch. And it would spell the end. For the park. Willow Forest. The Golub tree.

Warren's parents raced up the steps. Peter grabbed the microphone.

"Don't do anything rash," he said. "You just missed the announcement moments earlier—we're here bearing good news! We know how hard this past year has been. That's why we want to help. We're prepared to inject millions into Moon- light! To fix up your schools, your roads—the factory too." He smiled at the crowd. "And we can offer everyone a quarter million dollars each as a gesture of gratitude."

The crowd drew a collective gasp.

"Are you . . . are you serious?" Skylar asked. She held her squirming toddler on her hip.

"As serious as can be." Warren's mother nodded.

"Your bribery will undoubtedly work on them. Not us," Kendall replied, unfazed. "These waters are what matter. Fixing up roads and stores—so what? That's putting bandages over sores. We must *heal* the water before—"

"Will you shut up already?" Jake shouted.

Raf eyed the flames rising higher and higher. Smoke filled the park. He coughed as his eyes watered.

"Jake," Ernie cried. "Please don't—"

"No, I'm sick of it!" Jake's face was flushed red. His eyes bulged. "Your moping and whining is *why* we can't move on. Standing there all day long is messing with your minds—crying, crying, crying. What good has it done? No way. You're not ruining it for the rest of us!"

"I got this!" a voice shouted. Crissy. She and another local raced forward carrying fire extinguishers. Mateo jerked back as a jet stream unleashed against him, pushing him backward. The Weepers crumpled to the ground.

In a matter of moments, the fire was extinguished. The canvases lay lifeless on the ground as Kendall, Mateo, and the others rose. They were soaked from head to toe. But there was no space for Raf to feel any relief.

"Now that that's over with . . ." Jake breathed heavily. He turned to the Naismiths. "Where do I sign?"

"It's not only up to you!" Yas shouted.

"That's right!" Bea nodded. "A vote means all of us have a say."

"So let's do it!" Crissy crossed her arms. "We know how it will go. Let's get it over with."

"Now, wait one second." Bea's eyes narrowed.

The crowd murmured. People exchanged worried glances.

Siobhan took the microphone from her husband. "It's clear you have issues to sort out." Her lips pressed into a thin line. "You have until tomorrow. Have your little vote and sign the paperwork. Our lawyers are on standby."

Raf looked at Jake and Crissy. The others in the periphery. A vote? By people who would've run them out of town free of charge?

First, there was Uncle's betrayal. Then, Kot's revelation. Now this? They wanted to cut down the one path in and out? Tear away the one avenue of safety for anyone brave enough to venture to find their way? There was so much he needed to unpack about their leaf and the lies Uncle had spun, but Raf knew one thing for certain: The Golub tree was real. No matter what, they couldn't lose it.

thirty-two
YAS

You up? Yas texted Raf.

It was three o'clock in the morning. The moon cast a glow over the dark sea. He was probably sleeping. How much more could his body and mind take? For Yas, it was hard to imagine ever sleeping again. She'd paced all night in her bedroom, scrolling her laptop, scouring the town's bylaws. Trying to find a way—any way—to stop what was coming. The walls felt like they were closing in on her.

I need air.

Stepping onto the back porch, she inhaled deeply, letting the sea air fill her lungs fully before releasing. Breathe in for ten and out for ten—but breathing exercises could not ease the doom blooming in the pit of her stomach. Raf's and his people's future was perilous. The soul of her town was on the line. Everything felt broken.

She took the steps down to the shore. The sea churned in the distance. She looked at the mural, spotlit beneath the light of the moon. She'd been trying to say goodbye to her town with that mural. She'd wanted to remind them who they'd been. But what was the point? After what she saw at the festival, she knew: They weren't that town anymore. They would never be again.

"You're up early." Patty approached her in sweatpants and a zipped-up jacket.

"What are you doing up at this hour?" Yas asked.

"Insomnia, sadly," Patty replied. "At my age, I'm afraid it's become somewhat of a constant companion. Something contemplative, though, about being up when most of the world is tucked away at least." She looked at Yas sympathetically. "I heard about yesterday evening."

"I'm *disgusted*."

"Money is a powerful motivator. It can make you forget who you are or what matters."

Money had been driving Yas all summer. She had been saving as much as she could. From cleaning up the gallery. From selling Mateo's work. Money was why her mother needed to close up shop. Why her father moved to Yaksta. But how much money could justify this?

"Doing deals with the devil, it's just going to make our problems worse," Yas said. "They'll regret it eventually. It won't make them happy. Even if they think it will. Deep down they know that. They've got to know that."

"Maybe they need to be reminded," Patty said.

"I tried talking to Ernie. I *begged* him to use his influence. Hold an emergency town hall. Go door to door. Do whatever he needs to do. He's acting like he can't change anyone's mind."

"It wasn't Ernie I was thinking of."

Yas looked quizzically at her. Patty smiled.

"Me?" Yas said, her eyebrows rising. "Why would anyone listen to me?"

"Maybe because you're the one who's trying to better this town." Patty nodded to the mural in the distance. "Everyone's so busy forgetting, or trying to, anyway. You've been facing the pain every day with that mural—you've been remembering."

"The Weepers are remembering too," Yas said. "Didn't do much good."

"Their way is different from yours, though, isn't it? Even when it's hurt you—you created. That mural is a contribution to this town. A net good. You also helped Mateo's gallery get back up on its feet. Maybe you're the only one who can remind this town of who they were and who they could be."

It felt impossible to imagine that this town could ever redeem itself. Yas thought of Raf's crestfallen expression when Jake sneered at them. The townspeople discussed the Golub as though they were chess pieces to move around and not residents of their town for nearly two decades. They'd turned their hearts into stone toward them.

But whether she liked it or not, Yas was a local too. Didn't that mean she had an obligation? A duty to do something. If she didn't, who would?

"By the way," Patty said, "I'm heading home next week. Wanted to set aside a time to discuss a commission from you. Your mural of the town is enchanting. You know Moonlight Bay has my heart—it would be lovely to have something similar for my home."

"Thanks, Patty," Yas said. "I'd love to create something for you."

"I could do seventeen hundred. That's how much Mateo's work would run me."

Yas moved to speak, but no words came.

She finally said, "You want to *pay* me to create a painting for you. As much you paid *Mateo*?"

"I told you, I can't draw worth a lick, but I know good art when I see it." She smiled. "I'd like to say I own a Yas original. Get a chance to brag I knew you when. Think on it?"

Yas's phone buzzed. Pulling it out, she saw that Raf had replied.

I'm up. Not doing great.

Meet me at our spot?

She thanked Patty and hurried toward Willow Forest. She'd talk to Raf. She'd be the listening ear he needed. Then she'd figure out what to do to stop the poison that had seeped into her town from spreading and consuming them all.

thirty-three
RAF

Yas listened silently as Raf told her everything. About Kot. Tolki Uncle. They sat side by side, their legs matted with sand from the wet earth beneath them.

"So he lied?" she asked him. "About all of it?"

"That's the hard part." He thought of his leaf. "I don't know what's true and what isn't. He was the keeper of knowledge. Almost everything I know about where I'm from, it's all from him."

"And he was the reason you believed college couldn't happen."

"He was part of the reason," he said. "The diner *did* need me. Who knows what happens with it now. If they cut that tree down." Raf shivered. "I don't know what happens next. I can't process it."

"Nothing's happened yet. We'll figure it out. We'll find a way."

"I don't want to be around any of these people anymore. But the tree . . ."

"We won't stop fighting until the Naismiths back off and get the hell out of town. What's Golub for 'not taking no for an answer'?"

"Jaland abor dia."

"*That*, all right?" She squeezed his arm. "Exactly that."

He glanced at the mural shining beneath the moonlight. "You're almost done."

"Almost."

"Seeing the sandcastles, and the dolphins, and the movie theater—it got me choked up a little. Weird, right?" He forced a laugh. A funny look passed across her face. "Yas. What's the matter?"

"Did you . . . did you notice anything in particular about the mural?"

He'd said the wrong thing, hadn't he? He turned his attention back to the distant wall and squinted.

"What'd I miss, Yas . . . Yas?"

She looked at her lap. Her thumbs circling each other.

"What is it?" he asked her.

"I've asked you so many Golub words over the years." She looked up at him. Her eyes glistened. "But what's the Golub word for 'love'?"

"Love," he repeated. "Th-there's more than one word for love. There's friendship love—silan. Gratitude love—baya. Nostalgic love—ruman. There's . . . there are forty words for love."

"What if, hypothetically, you feel all those ways about someone?"

"Hypothetically?"

"No." She held his gaze. "Actually not hypothetically at all."

Looking into her eyes, Raf found himself unable to speak.

"I . . . I started working on that mural randomly. I didn't even plan it out properly. What did it matter? Not like anyone's given a crap about that mural since the storm came through. And what did I end up creating? The dolphins we swam with," she said. "The sandcastles we made together. Everything on there . . . Do you see it, Raf?"

There was Main Street—the movie theater. Tilted Tales, where they sat for hours on end reading comics. The entire street was there, but it was both of these locations that shone with a sheen of glitter. He took it all in.

"It's us," he said slowly. "You painted *our* places. Our favorite memories."

"I love you, Raf." Her voice quivered. "Silan—the friendship one. Baya, the gratitude one. Ruman. Nostalgia for what we were. All of it. I love you in all the ways I know."

Raf felt unable to move. To breathe. It was as though they were back again at Surrey. In the back of his truck. That moment before the phone call had torn them apart.

"I don't even know how to trace back to when it happened. Maybe it's been that way from the start but I didn't have the words for it. Until now. And . . . I'm sorry if I made things awkward." Her voice trembled. "You don't have to say anything. But I couldn't live with myself if I didn't tell you. I needed you to know."

I love you.

Yas loved him. Three words he'd longed to hear. Those three words he'd gone in search of just one year earlier. He tried speaking, but pain suddenly shot through his wrist. Raf gasped. The white-hot pain radiated through him. Just as it had one year earlier.

So was it true, then? His heart raced. Uncle had lied about the nature of their leaf—but had *this* part been real? Once again, here he was, ready to confess his feelings, and once again, he found himself in so much pain, he could barely speak.

"I—" He gasped through the pain. "I can't," he said hoarsely.

"Right." She flushed. "I— I shouldn't have said anything. I've messed everything up, haven't I?"

"It's not . . . it's not that." He shuddered. "Everything that night, a year ago, it *might* have been my fault." Raf choked the words out through the pain. "The ocean rising the way it did. The sea turning gray. Sammy." His voice broke.

"What?" She shifted closer. "Raf. No—that's not true. Why would any of that be because of you?"

Raf tried to listen as she spoke about the nanny who'd not been paying attention. Sammy sneaking out in search of Moses. His arm hurt so much, it felt difficult to fixate on anything else.

"I wish I could have found Sammy in time too," Yas told him. "Just because you didn't catch him before he went in doesn't mean you're to blame. That's the same as the Golub getting blamed because Nara and Kot happened to arrive the same day. This isn't your fault. And the ocean had been shifting to dark for moments at a time before it dimmed permanently, don't you remember?"

"That's not why I blame myself," he managed to say. "It's because . . . of what I was about to tell you that night." His eyes shifted to the sea. Was it churning higher now? Was it going to happen again?

"What were you going to say?"

"I can't." He shook his head. "What if it happens again? What if those waves come closer? What if . . . ?"

"What if it doesn't?" She nodded to the water. "Your leaf is hurting, but the waves are calm."

Raf looked at Yas. This person he'd loved for so long. Who he carefully maneuvered around all year, lest a hand touch.

A shoulder graze. Uncle had lied. About the way their leaves worked. About where Kot had been. About the safety perimeter. But what if the leaf *was* warning him right now? He thought of what Kot had said he'd done to calm his flickering birthmark when he left the perimeter. He said he'd focused his attention on something else. Raf took a deep breath. He looked at Yas. He felt the sweetness of her breath so close to his face. He took in her worried eyes. He focused completely on her.

"Yas. I . . ." His breath hitched. "I love you, Yas."

Tears glittered in Yas's eyes.

The ocean remained gray. The waves crashed to shore with the same intensity as they had moments earlier. His leaf wasn't hurting. It was still there. He'd said the words. Nothing happened.

Yas edged closer until there was barely any space between them. Her fuzzy sweater tickled his arm.

"Let's see what happens when I do this," she said. She kissed his forehead.

"And this." His temples.

She traced his jaw and cupped his face, cradling it with her hands. They looked into each other's eyes and drew closer. Gingerly, she kissed him. Her lips soft against his mouth. Raf shivered. He tasted her strawberry lip gloss. Raf ran a hand through her hair and then drew his arms around her and pulled her to his lap. He kissed her back. Gently and then with more urgency. As though making up for lost time.

What *was* time? Time stilled. Did it even exist anymore?

There was more to come. Darkness to right. But in this moment, Raf's heart was full. His leaf still.

thrity-four
YAS

Yas walked down Main Street. But it felt like she was float-ing. The ground more cloudlike than pavement. Just a few moments ago she'd been with Raf at the edge of his forest overlooking the sea. She'd felt a swell of terror rise up before the words left her mouth. Once she said them out loud, they would never be the same again.

Then—they'd kissed. He'd drawn her into his arms. His warm breath against hers. His hair brushing her forehead. His stubble tickling her face. She traced her hand against his jaw and tasted the sea salt on his lips.

And they would never be the same again.

She hadn't wanted to leave—she could have stayed that way forever. But there was no time for such luxuries. She had work to do. She needed to gather the council people. Make a list of all who would definitely vote against this obscenity and make sure they actually came out to vote. She mentally tallied all the locals she could convince. She'd knock on their doors herself. She wouldn't leave their front porches until they saw reason. Nothing was set in stone yet—until it was, she'd do everything she could.

Turning the corner, she slowed. Ernie hurried down the

street, clad in a matching striped pajama set. His hair was rumpled like he'd jumped out of bed and gone straight for a jog.

"Ernie?" she called out.

He didn't seem to hear her. He flew toward the rickety town hall building, yanked the door open, and slipped inside.

Trailing behind, Yas opened the door. She froze. She hadn't been here since last year. The same floor-to-ceiling windows lined the back wall overlooking the sea, but an unfamiliar musty scent from months of disuse filled her senses. The back door was propped open, and fans circled overhead, buzzing noisily. Yas looked at the clock. Was this some sort of fever dream? It was four thirty in the morning. The sky was still dark. Twenty-five or so people were assembled, seated in folding chairs. Jake. Crissy. Their spouses.

"This is not how we do things!" Ernie cried out. "This is not who we are!"

"Who told him?" Jake barked. "We invited those we *thought* we could trust."

A child began to cry. Skylar sat toward the front of the room. Ozzy wore a pale-blue onesie and squirmed in her arms.

Yas scanned the crowd. *They're voting.* They'd gathered to vote in secret.

"I'm the *mayor*." Ernie panted. "I need to be here."

"You don't, actually." Crissy held up the bylaws. She raised her voice above the crying toddler. "This is a vote for the people, by the people. Your thoughts count like anyone else's. So long as we have one council member present to observe— me—and a quorum of twenty, a two-thirds vote is valid."

Yas pulled out her phone. Get to city hall. Now. She texted her parents and Raf. She messaged Kendall, Laura, Olive. Mateo.

She reached out to everyone and anyone who could stop this from happening.

In the meantime, she'd stall.

"Most of the town is *sleeping*!" Yas stormed to the front of the room. "If you cared what everyone here wanted—for and *by* the people—you wouldn't be meeting in secret like this."

"Now, honestly." Jake scoffed.

"And the Golub aren't even here! You're not going to give them a chance to defend themselves?"

"Golub don't get a vote. And we're doing this *for* Moonlight Bay," Crissy said. "Everyone asleep or awake wants the same thing. The *Golub* don't get to hold this town hostage by saying they disagree."

Oscar nodded. "I'd say a multimillion-dollar cash infusion will be an unequivocal win for our town."

"And what about this town's soul?" Yas retorted.

"Soul?" Crissy snorted. "Towns don't have souls."

"Enough drama," Jake said. "Let's get this over with. We can do a simple show of hands. It should suffice."

A hand vote? Yas watched Skylar hush Ozzy. It would be tallied and wrapped up within moments! "The Naismiths," she said quickly. "Shouldn't they be here to witness it all too? Didn't they say they had lawyers in town?"

"The bylaws don't require them," Jake retorted.

"Wouldn't they want to be here anyway?" Yas pressed on. This was the only angle, wasn't it? The only hope to get them to stop this runaway train before others could arrive to help. "If this gets disputed—which it will—*I* will dispute it. It'll get messy."

Oscar grumbled. "Hate to say it, but she's right about that."

Yas felt shaky. She'd bought time. Even if only for a short while.

"Great," Ernie said, relieved. "I'll send out an email. We'll have an emergency meeting this afternoon—that way, everyone has time to think on it some more and—"

"The Naismiths are coming." Crissy held up her phone. "Just sent them a message. Thanks, Yas. Good suggestion."

The front door burst open. Yas's parents entered. Kendall and others hurried inside behind them. Yas breathed a sigh of relief.

"Just great." Jake's expression darkened as Tolki Uncle, Raf, and others from the Golub community arrived.

"This is vile!" Yas's mother fumed. "Voting in secret? We have a right to speak our piece. My vote is absolutely not. I can't even believe I have to say this. The Golub can't access their home any other way. There's no price you can put on that."

"But there *is* a price." Jake folded his arms.

"Leena is right," Mateo said. "We can't do this."

"*Now* you speak?" Jake rolled his eyes.

"When something's worth speaking about, I will," Mateo growled. "This isn't right. You know it."

"You disagree with me? You and your fellow Weepers are welcome to head out of town with the leaf people. I've had it with *all* of you," Jake retorted. "Once the tree's gone, no reason for them to stay anyhow. Don't worry—if they want to go back to Golub, we'll give them the chance before it's taken down."

"Sorry we're late." The Naismiths appeared. Siobhan smiled. "I take it the vote is happening sooner than expected?"

"That's the plan," Crissy told them.

"Makes sense. Why wait?" Peter said.

"Don't get too excited," Kendall retorted. "We don't move on like this. Pretending the past never happened. The life we had before—"

"Will you quit it?" Crissy's face flushed. "All we have is *now*. The sooner you get it, the sooner any of us have a chance. We're doing this for *all* of us!"

"You'd really vote for this?" Yas glared at the Naismiths and turned back to the locals. "You're fine accepting that this town—that we—are completely bigoted?"

"Bigoted?" Jake's voice rose. "What exactly have we done? Brought over baskets of food and helped them build their homes when they arrived?"

"We welcomed them," Skylar said, setting Ozzy down. "We donated blankets and pillows. We tolerated them for two decades."

"Tolerated us?" Raf repeated.

Raf and Uncle and Dena stood with their backs pressed against the wall, their expressions desolate.

"Do you hear yourselves? The *Golub* are the reason this town had anything worth anything in the first place," Yas said. "Don't you even know why the Naismiths want to chop the tree down? Is your greed so big, you didn't stop to wonder what they'd like to do with it?" Her voice wavered. "They want the bark for its healing properties. They want the roots to make medication for anxiety. Does that ring a bell? What does our water do? All the billions the Hollers made. All the people they employed. The prosperity we enjoyed. *All of us.* It came from that water. It came from the Golub tree. *We* should be thanking *them*."

"That's— That's not true," Skylar said. "Don't try to justify things by conjuring up fanciful rationales."

"It *is* true," Yas said. "But even if the water isn't from the tree—it is still unconscionable what you're willing to do."

"And it *is* true," Warren said. All eyes turned to him.

"Warren," his mother said sharply.

"The roots did meld its properties into the water. There's great power in it. And there's a lot of money to be made as well," Warren said quietly.

Everyone gawked at Warren. Silence permeated the room.

"Listen," Jake growled. "I don't know about any of that. All I know is the moment those gray-eyed teens arrived, everything ended. Sammy dies the *same* night and we're supposed to accept it's a coincidence?"

"And did any Golub apologize? Any of them come by to see how we're doing?" interrupted Oscar. "Not a one of you. We lost *Sammy*. But *we're* the unreasonable ones?"

Sammy.

People's angry voices rose over one another—but inside of Yas, an uneasy stillness grew. She scanned the room. Ozzy had been an anguished hum of frustration since she'd stepped into this building. The toddler was eerily quiet now. Where was he?

"What's the matter?" Raf hurried at her side.

"I don't see Ozzy. Do you?" she whispered.

"No . . ." His voice trailed off. She saw where he was looking. The propped-open back door. Her heart dropped.

They hurried to the door. Stepped onto the beach—

"There he is," Raf gasped.

Ozzy. The tiny child's frame was illuminated beneath the moonlight. He was heading toward the sea.

Raf and Yas both broke into a run.

"Ozzy!" she heard Skylar cry out behind her.

With chubby baby legs, the boy toddled into the water. He was only calf-deep, but the current could be strong. If he went any farther, given his size, he risked getting swept away. Swept away like Sammy had. Was *this* what had happened that night? Yas's chest tightened as she picked up her pace. Raf raced alongside her.

"Ozzy, come back!" Raf shouted. But the toddler seemed impervious to anyone's pleas.

Tears stung her eyes. Had Sammy done this too? A quick dip in the ocean? Or had it been a search for his brother? Did an errant wave take him in while he was simply standing safely by the shore? There was no way to know, was there? That was what hurt the most. There would never be an answer. That there could never be any fixing a tragedy like losing Sammy. Sometimes there were no answers, as badly as people may have wanted them.

She reached the water and splashed in. He was inches from her—she lurched forward and swept him into her arms. Her knees grew weak. Feeling the heft of him in her arms, her eyes stung with tears. Ozzy was okay. He was safe.

It was only when Skylar took the baby from Yas that Yas winced. She was in ordinary house slippers, and now that the adrenaline was leaving her body, she felt the pain of the shell shards pricking her heels.

"Blue!" the boy shrieked.

Yas followed the toddler's pointing finger. The ocean around them rippled with their movement. The water was not pink. Nor lavender. It did not glimmer. Pooling in swirls around her ankles were ribbons of aqua and teal. Threads of silver and gold.

"Raf?" she whispered. "You see it, don't you?"

"I . . . Y-yes, I do."

From the shoreline, Ernie stared with his jaw parted at the ripples of color. Not bothering to roll up his pajama bottoms, he walked into the water, the sea sloshing around his feet. Spirals of daffodil yellow puddled around his ankles.

"What . . . what is happening?" he whispered.

Others stepped into the water. They winced at the shards pricking their feet.

The shards. Yas kneeled in the water. She pulled out a jagged, cracked shell fragment from the ocean floor and cradled it in her palm—the salt water dripping from it trailed rivulets of color down her hands, which glimmered beneath the still-dark sky.

"It's the shells." Yas leaned down and scooped out more. She raised her hand and opened her palm—the crowd gasped as gold and red trailed down her arm.

"The color is . . ." Oscar's voice trailed off. "It's *leaking* out of the broken shells?"

"I don't understand." Crissy's voice trembled.

"That's not how the sea works," Jake said.

"Is this the first time this is happening?" asked Skylar.

"Hard to say. No one splashes around in the water at night. Not after last year," Ernie replied. "Don't think anyone stopped to see."

Yas looked at Ernie. "We see it now, though. Don't we?"

For a long while, no one said a word. Then, in a shaky voice, Skylar spoke. "We were so busy fighting, I lost track of my own child. I can't . . . I can't even imagine what would have happened if Yas and Raf hadn't noticed him missing."

"Sammy . . ." Bea's voice cracked. "He would've been six by now."

"Not a day goes by when I don't think about him," Olive said.

"Me too," said Ernie. "He was such a sweet boy."

"It wasn't fair."

Tears glistened in everyone's eyes.

"It was a tragedy, and there's no fixing it," Yas said. "But we can't pretend it didn't happen. Our old life *is* gone. The pink-and-lavender sea is gone." She choked up at this. The plentiful shells of the past were gone too, weren't they? She missed those shells. She missed that sea. So much. "But there's this?"

She looked at the colors beneath her feet; they were fading as the sky above brightened with the rising sun.

"You think it's that easy?" Jake snorted. "Color we're seeing could be a fluke. *Money* is real. You want us to pretend that's not the cold, hard reality of the situation? We're supposed to sing 'Kumbaya' and go back to the way it used to be?"

"I don't want to go back to the way things used to be," Raf said. "I want a home that can't be ripped away from me on a whim. I want to live where I don't have to worry that someone's mood might upend my life." He took Yas's hand and looked at Uncle. "I want to live the life I want."

"There's no going back to what Moonlight was—those days are gone," said Yas. "But maybe this new version doesn't have to be worse. It could even be better. Maybe we can work on figuring it out together. Maybe that's what the Naismiths are here for. A test. If we have any chance of surviving and growing from the heartache we've had to endure this past year, it's now. For the future of Moonlight—we have a chance."

"Jake." Siobhan's eyes flashed. "This is getting out of hand."

Yas eyed the crowd—people murmured to one another. Would even this moment not be enough? Would nothing crack through their hearts?

"Jake," Yas began. "Please—"

"No, no." Ernie waved a hand. "Siobhan is correct. A promise is a promise. Let's take the matter to a vote. I'll tell you my vote is a solid no." He smiled at Yas and then at the gathered crowd. "What's the point of saving this town if there's nothing worth saving?"

Yas clenched Raf's hand tightly as Ernie began the vote. One by one, the locals began to decide. To accept. Or reject.

Jake's vote was unsurprising. Crissy's as well. But Skylar, despite her husband's protests, slowly shook her head. As did Mateo and Marie, who emphatically declined. Her parents. Others in town, going down the line, said no. There *were* those who voted to accept the terms. It was to be expected, but it felt crushing all the same—but as the count continued, the important thing grew clearer and clearer: The vote wouldn't pass. The tree was safe.

She glanced at them. At Raf.

"Something feels different, doesn't it?" she asked.

"The air," he said. "It's lighter."

It wasn't much, but enough to feel—pressure releasing from her skin, the subtlest bit. Like after so long, she could finally breathe.

After the After

thirty-five
RAF

Raf finished watering the flowers by the edge of his home. Rolling up the water hose, he gingerly rested it against his house. Willow Forest was quiet today—windows of nearby homes were slid open and curtains billowed from the circulating fans inside on a humid afternoon.

Raf took in the Golub tree in the distance. The sun's light hit it directly from above, coating the tree in a warm glow. Even now, one month since the town hall meeting, he felt weak-kneed with relief. It was there. Jutting past the surrounding tree canopy. Its branches were still frost coated. Its trunk was still cool to the touch. But the tree itself was safe. *They* were safe. And the Naismiths were gone. They'd left soon after the votes were cast. Holler Mansion once again sat empty.

Early on, nearly everyone within the forest and beyond seemed immobilized by the discovery. Wrapping their minds around all that had unfolded. But now, slowly, things were beginning to shift.

Just last week, Ernie had come by. He was inquiring with lawyers about how to deed Willow Forest's six acres formally to the Golub. So such a thing could never happen again. There was no way to know if anything would come of it—there were many legal hurdles to overcome, and a vote would be necessary as well. Raf couldn't see around this corner to know what was coming, but as his father once said, while darkness could lurk—so could the light. And when the darkness *had* come for them, they'd found a way, hadn't they? His community had made it through.

But his community was also grieving. At the hurt that had accumulated over the last year. At all that Uncle Tolki had done.

"Ready to go?" Raf's mother asked him when he stepped back inside.

"I'm not holding my breath," Raf said. He pulled open the fridge and grabbed a bottle of water. "Professor Singh already found his assistant. Classes start next week. I'm not sure how this will even go."

"He got you a meeting with the dean of the architecture college, though, didn't he?" his mother asked.

"I don't think—"

"And if it's a no for now—it can work out next semester."

"Yeah." Raf smiled at her. "Maybe."

It felt surreal to talk about this openly with her. Without the constant weight of guilt pressing down on him.

"And if you go away to school, I'll be the oldest!" Mac grinned.

"Nah," Raf said. "I'm still the oldest. Even if I'm not around. Besides, being the oldest comes with a lot of baggage."

"Raf's right." His mother squeezed his arm. "And he's been hard at work paving the path for you both."

"Do you really think Dena will be okay leading the diner if things work out for me? She wasn't just saying so because she didn't want to hold me back?"

"Did you see her expression?" his mother asked. "She *shouted* yes. Fio begins school next week—she can do this."

"And you?" Raf asked. "Looking after the kids? It's not easy."

"I'm going into first grade." Mac frowned. "I'm not a baby or anything."

"Dar will help," his mother said. "Let me parent the kids, including you."

"What about our community?" Raf worried the edge of his shirt. "If Surrey's a yes . . . I don't know how I can leave everyone behind at a time like this. There's so much to deal with between Moonlight Bay matters and Tolki Uncle."

Uncle wasn't their leader anymore, but unraveling his lies would take time. Tolki barely left his home these days. He'd stopped joining them for community meals, and when he did emerge, his expression was haggard—it was clear he was unwell. Raf helped locate Shar. Just yesterday he'd made contact. It turned out she lived in Yaksta—all this time, she'd been a three-hour drive away from them. He explained to her the broad strokes of what had happened. She'd promised to come tomorrow to speak with him. Perhaps, she said, she would take him back home with her, at least for a while.

"The matters the locals are dealing with are matters *they* need to unpack themselves," his mother told him. "As far as I'm concerned, their opinions of us are not my concern. We have enough on our plates. As for Tolki, leave it with us, this once? You've worried about everyone for long enough. How about you worry about you for a change? Dena is already rescheduling the Hamra gathering."

"Maybe she'll take his place."

"Maybe."

Raf smiled a little. There was a lot to figure out—the work was not close to over. There was so much to undo—but it wasn't all on him to fix. Raf was leaning on others. They were helping him carry the load.

thirty-six
YAS

Yas peered out the window in the kitchen and bit back a smile. It was the middle of the afternoon—there was not even a remote chance of seeing any bioluminescence with the sun as bright as it was, but people still lingered in clumps along the shoreline.

The reporters arrived within days of the discovery to document the shift. Tourists, eager to be among the first to bear witness, quickly followed. They swam among rivers of color under a dark sky. For the first time in over a year, the Iguana Motor Lodge had turned off its glowing red VACANCY sign yesterday. Every room occupied.

The hum of her favorite truck, belonging to her favorite person, sounded on the street outside.

"That's Raf!" Yas peeked out the window to confirm. She walked up to her mother and gave her a quick kiss on the cheek.

"Have fun," her mother said. "Take detailed notes, and don't forget to ask if we can request a specific spot—a table right by the entrance would be ideal."

"For the twentieth time, I won't forget," Yas teased.

Her mother had taken Yas up on an idea she had shortly after the discovery of the broken shards. They would stop combing for whole shells. Instead, they began to scoop out the broken ones. Melding them to create stars, yes, but also crescents, as well as shapes with no names. They were still in the early days, but feedback from customers was proving promising. Now, with this sudden surplus of raw materials, they could make plans for designing souvenirs again, for selling at the artist market. For their future. Yas was even starting to think about getting her own necklace made to process all that had transpired this past summer.

"Yas," her mother tried again, "it's not too late. You can still tell Hisae you're in."

"I think she posted that she just locked in a new roommate, but I'm good, Mom. This is what I want. Business is going to start picking up here. I can feel it. Besides, I got three more people who promised to show up and vote in our favor to parcel off Willow Forest to the Golub. Plus, Patty—she's commissioned *another* painting from me."

"Isn't that the third one?"

"It's for her daughter," Yas said. "She even talked me up to her local doctor's office. They want me to send some sketches for a possible series for their waiting room. She's kind of becoming my patron?"

"I always knew I liked Patty."

"Marie said I can showcase my work in the gallery whenever I'm ready."

"Is Mateo painting again?"

"Not yet. But Marie said he seems better lately. Maybe someday?"

"Well, selfishly, I'm glad you're staying on. Just know if you ever want to change your mind—you can."

"I know."

Her father was still in Yaksta. Yas and her mother planned to drive there tomorrow and spend the weekend with him. Maybe, she hoped, things could change enough in Moonlight that he could find work here again. They could all be in the same town again or, better yet, united again as a family. She hoped her parents could map out what their future looked like—but she also knew that this was between them.

Moonlight? It was hers. She wanted to fight for what she knew it could be. To get through the messy but important work of healing. It was her town that had broken so deeply; she wanted to be there to do the work of cleaning it up.

Yas wanted to stay.

"Hey." Raf smiled when Yas hopped into the passenger seat.

"Are you nervous?" she asked him.

"No expectations," he said. "But yeah . . ." He grinned sheepishly. "A little."

"The good news is, even if it's not this fall, Surrey's happening! I hate to say it, but I do think I told you so."

"You don't hate to say it all!" He leaned over and kissed her.

Raf and Yas. Yas and Raf. Was anything more perfect than this?

Raf looked at Holler Mansion next door.

"Can't believe they left that fast."

"Hope they stay gone."

Nara and Warren still kept in touch. He was backpacking overseas. Settling his mind. He'd invited Nara along, but she had other things to sort out. Like where she and Kot were going. Because they were done with Moonlight Bay. Yas and

Raf had been at their house just the other day, helping them tape up their few belongings as they mapped out their next steps. With all the pain Uncle brought them and the year they'd endured with the people of Moonlight, they had no interest in reconciliations, and who could blame them? They promised that wherever they ended up, they'd stay in touch.

"How are things going in Willow Forest?" Yas asked Raf. "Are the Jugnus settled over in Ridgeview yet?"

Raf nodded. "Two other families are talking about joining them. But most want to stay put. At least for now."

"I still can't believe Uncle would do such a thing."

"Me neither. I know it was out of a twisted definition of love—to protect us—but it *wasn't* love, having things his way no matter the cost. I don't know if anything can fix it."

"At least now you can make decisions based on truth."

The one and only traffic light in town turned red as they approached it. Yas pulled out her phone. She hadn't checked Moses's feed in a few weeks, and now, for a split second, she thought she'd clicked the wrong site. But there it was. After a year, a new photo. A kayak resting by a lake. No caption. Yas stared at it. With a small smile, she clicked unfollow. Moses was trying to move on. It was time she did the same.

Raf's hand touched her shoulder.

"You okay?" he asked.

She leaned over and kissed him. His breath was sweet and warm. He pulled her tighter to him. A car honked, and they sprang apart. A green light. They looked at each other and burst into laughter.

She took in the ocean flowing parallel to the road. The

water was gray as ever—but she knew better now what lay within its depths.

Yas read the sign they were approaching. Workers were in the process of hammering it in.

COMING SOON!
GLASS-BOTTOM KAYAK TOURS!
SWIM WITH THE COLORS!

Ernie moved fast. Already, he'd presented the council with ten different plans to revitalize tourism. The night tours were just the beginning. Specialty shoe stores for treading the prickly beachy bottom. He'd applied for a grant from a nearby university to have marine biologists study the water more deeply. To see what else they'd missed all this time.

How long would *these* waters stay? she wondered.

There was no telling. But they were here right now. And right now, this was enough.

She looked at the heavy clouds in the sky. They were still there—dark and charcoal—but they were starting to shift, thinning out bit by bit. New light shone through each day.

Acknowledgments

I am so grateful to everyone who helped to bring this book into being:

Zareen Jaffery, thank you for the long conversations to unpack ideas and analyze the characters. For loving these characters as much as I do. For your patience as I wrangled this story during a global pandemic. I'm not sure I can properly articulate how much your support, encouragement, guidance, and wisdom meant to me in this journey. I could not imagine telling this story without your partnership.

Thank you to Namrata Tripathi, Joanna Cárdenas, and the entire Kokila team for your early reads and feedback. Thank you as well to Cindy Howle, Kristie Radwilowicz, Theresa Evangelista, Jasmin Rubero, Ariela Rudy Zaltzman, Jacqueline Hornberger, and everyone at Penguin for everything. Grateful to be part of the Penguin family.

Thank you, Enid Din, for the brilliant cover and for capturing the heart of the story so brilliantly.

Thank you, Taylor Martindale Kean, for finding a home for *Forty Words for Love*.

Thank you to my agent, Faye Bender, for reading early drafts and for your advice, support, and feedback along the way.

Thank you, Tracy Lopez, Ayesha Mattu, Becky Albertalli, Samira Ahmed, S. K. Ali, and Sabaa Tahir, for giving me invaluable feedback along the way and for your friendships. Grateful to all of you.

Anna Marie McLemore, thank you for holding my hand as I embarked on a new area of writing within the world of magical realism. Your stories inspire me so deeply, and your generosity and insights have meant everything.

Ami and Abu, thank you for always being proud of me. Thank you to my spouse, without whom writing a book during a pandemic would have been literally impossible.

And last but never least, to my three boys—these stories are for you. You are my light. My heart. You are the reason I write.